S0-AXV-071

"A TOUCHING AND TRAGIC STORY OF THE BONDS BETWEEN TWO GROWN AND VERY DIFFERENT BROTHERS ... Brown has taken a complex set of relationships and lays them open with skill and intensity."
—*Toledo Blade*

"Many of the ingredients here are the same ones used by Bret Easton Ellis and Jay McInerney—alcoholism, sex, drug dealing, and alienation—with a countrified location and a touch of black humor. In his first novel the author shows a knack for characterization."
—*Library Journal*

"BROWN KNOWS THE NARRATIVE VALUE OF SUSPENSE ... HE GRADUALLY TIGHTENS THE PLOT SO WE ARE COMPELLED TO WALK CLOSELY AND ATTENTIVELY WITH DEAN THROUGH THE DARKEST CORRIDORS OF HIS LIFE."
—*Columbus Dispatch*

"A GENUINELY EXPLOSIVE FIRST NOVEL about a troubled Kentucky family ... as an examination of the devastating effects of alcohol upon a family, and as an exploration of the unsuitability of going home again, this is a creditable first effort."
—*Kirkus Reviews*

MICHAEL DAVID BROWN attended the Berklee College of Music, Harvard University, and graduated with a degree in music from Capital University in Columbus, Ohio. He has been a jazz musician in Boston and is currently working toward an MFA in creative writing at Ohio University in Athens, Ohio. He is at work on his second novel.

UNDER HEAT

MICHAEL DAVID BROWN

A PLUME BOOK

NEW AMERICAN LIBRARY

A DIVISION OF PENGUIN BOOKS USA INC., NEW YORK
PUBLISHED IN CANADA BY
PENGUIN BOOKS CANADA LIMITED, MARKHAM, ONTARIO

NAL BOOKS ARE AVAILABLE AT QUANTITY DISCOUNTS WHEN USED
TO PROMOTE PRODUCTS OR SERVICES. FOR INFORMATION PLEASE
WRITE TO PREMIUM MARKETING DIVISION, NEW AMERICAN LIBRARY,
1633 BROADWAY, NEW YORK, NEW YORK 10019.

PLUME TRADEMARK REG. U.S. PAT. OFF. AND FOREIGN COUNTRIES
REGISTERED TRADEMARK—MARCA REGISTRADA
HECHO EN DRESDEN, TN, U.S.A.

SIGNET, SIGNET CLASSIC, MENTOR, ONYX, PLUME, MERIDIAN
and NAL BOOKS are published *in the United States* by New American Library,
a division of Penguin Books USA Inc.,
1633 Broadway, New York, New York 10019,
in Canada by Penguin Books Canada Limited,
2801 John Street, Markham, Ontario L3R 1B4

Library of Congress Cataloging-in-Pubication Data

Brown, Michael David.
    Under heat / Michael David Brown.
        p.   cm.
    ISBN 0-453-00602-7
            0-452-26372-7 (pbk.)
    I. Title.
PS3552.R6947U54   1989
813'.54—dc19   88-19491
                                                                CIP

First Plume Printing, January, 1990

1   2   3   4   5   6   7   8   9

PRINTED IN THE UNITED STATES OF AMERICA

For Mama Jane and Brother Bob.
And to the memory of my dad, Jimmy.

*Necessity has a way of obliterating from our con-
duct various delicate scruples regarding honor and
pride.*

—*William Faulkner*
Absalom, Absalom!

PART ONE

I.

I DON'T KNOW it yet but I'm getting yelled at for walking
under the wing. It's one of your no-frills airlines, where
you pay in the air, and when you land they wheel the
obsolete stepladders up to the nose and tail, make you
walk the tarmac over to the terminal, through the weather.
She's assisting passengers descending the nose, the cabin
attendant is.

Hiding my face from the wind, I step into the side of
her shoe. I look up. She's holding onto her embossed
airway cap; her rain coat cracks behind her like a fire. A
fresh evening storm is blowing in; the wind smells like a
pot of geraniums, but the noise of it makes me have to
ask her what she's yelling about. She bends her knee,
raises the foot behind her and dusts the shoe with a long,
manicured finger.

"Clumsy of me," I shout. I try for a nice rearrange-
ment of my face.

"Weren't you even listening to the flight attendant?"
she hollers. "Sherry just announced on board to please
walk *around* the wing!" Taking a little unction out of my
face, she lightens up some. "Sherry just announced that,
sir." Alternately she smiles for some of the descending
nose passengers, touches their elbows, hurries them away
towards the terminal.

I'm in no hurry, to say the truth. I look back at the
tail, then up the ladder. I see the other flight attendant's
back, Sherry's up there. I tell this stewardess to tell

Sherry that there's no excuse for what I did and I know it; and if it will make Sherry feel better, I'll go back up the ramp and start over and get it right.

She says good-bye to the last of her passengers, then turns to me. "Wise ass," she says.

Seven hundred dollars cash and a return ticket are riding in the secret pocket of my jacket. Under the jacket my T-shirt reads:

NEW ORLEANS
SURROUNDED BY WATER
SERVICED BY FAIRIES
PROTECTED BY DYKES

Where I'm coming from, you might say. Without much trouble I spot my older brother Milo standing inside the observation window. He's wearing a bandage above the right eye, a wound received from his wife Velda. Velda is Milo's third wife.

I got a letter from our mother Jane a few days ago. I'm carrying it. Here it is:

Dear Dean,

Milo and Velda had a big fight in the wee hours of Saturday morning. She had borrowed my car to take a friend of hers to Cincinnati to get an abortion and had called Milo and said she would be late getting home. After work Milo went to the Hideaway and someone told him Velda had been going to some other guy's apartment when Milo had to work nights, so when Velda pulled in at 3 A.M. Sat. morning, Milo hit her with what he'd heard, which he believed to be true, since she stayed out all night every night he worked. So Velda proceeded to slice up the water bed, threw Milo's contact lenses someplace or other, broke his glasses while they were still on his face and told him he had no balls, whereupon Milo hit her in the mouth, and of course her braces cut her lips. She called her mother to come get her and help pack up her things but instead Milo left and came home to my house. I guess mama told Milo to never darken their door again.

Here we go! You never know what Milo will do, but you know what he did last time. I can't do anything with him, so I think it would help if you came up right away.

Love,
Mom

Milo's gone into his ugly period. You know it not just by having the knowledge he's in between wives again; you see it. Checking him out from a distance I see a black T-shirt, a seam opened up between the top of its arm and collar piping. A flap results. His scapula sticks out. Silk-screened on the back is a bristly tarantula in white, its legs curling all the way around to hug his ribs. A piece of nicely toned belly shows between the bottom of his shirt and top of his jeans. The jeans, which are faded out but also have that yellow sheen from continuous wear, are trying to strangle his long, wiry legs. My brother Milo is trying this time for New Wave ugly. The hair, never what you would have called neat to begin with, is dark black, spiky. Under it all, you realize he's not bad looking—in the way of, say, a Springsteen, if that does anything for you. Milo is a laid-off fireman slash philosopher in the town where we were boys; father of two, compulsive track gambler, a lot of things. He's smoking, drinking from a styrofoam cup, staring unselfconsciously at the sweaty airport people crashing in on one another. He doesn't notice me until I'm up to arm's length. "Hear you got your bed stabbed," I say.

Milo gulps the rest of his cup. Wild Turkey, I would imagine from the scent, unless he switched. Turkey 101. He steps his cigarette out with a surplus jungle boot. "Bet you were surprised."

"I thought, actually, you might have a new wife by now."

He brings out a new pack of Gitanes and zips the cellophane string around it with his teeth, saying, "I don't think that's very funny." He offers me one and I take it. Then he spreads open my jacket, takes a look at the message on my shirt. "I knew it," he says, flashing up a Cricket, putting it to his exotic smoke, then to mine.

"Well, I'm blowing the gaff."

He says, "I knew it a long time ago."

"So did I." I spin him around and poke him between the shoulders. "What about this?"

Here's where I get the first straight view, right in through his eyes and for just the space of time his head's turned back on me. There's a look about the eyes like a swarm of bluebottle flies walking on your window. Because I've seen them myself, from inside, from his perspective. See, it's the family parasite: other stuff, but whiskey, mainly. Some of us can get shut of it for a while, but here it is, the monster in close-up, and like the big wind out there, it tends to augur—the picture in his eyes, not the one on his back.

"Spider," says Milo, pulling loose, leading the way to Baggage Claim, not even aware of it, naturally.

Last time I was around Milo he was in mourning over his second wife, Juliet. He'd lost her through bathtub drowning. This was the incident Mom referred to in my letter, when Milo had gone mad for a while and tried to punish the doctor responsible for Juliet's barbiturate habit.

And that's how we've learned (Mom and I) to see it coming. "It's a terrific spider," I say, "in the literal sense."

"It's a helpless, put-upon thing, your spider." He sounds jolly enough, though. "They give it a terrifying PR is all." He steps up the pace. "I identify strongly."

"Oh. I thought it was just part of the punk drag in general."

"No!" skidding to a halt. "And don't be using none of your damn homo epithets on me!"

We continue through the mezzanine considerably faster, until he slows up the pace to have the last pull from his cigarette and drop it less than half-used on the floor. He cracks his knuckles in thought. "No, look at the poor guy as a humble, self-sacrificing citizen." He means our spider again. He tells me not to forget the story—an entomological reality, in fact—of the guy who watched a spider spin and build and each time his entire creation was lost. Collapsed on him. "The spider failed, you might say."

"I remember," I tell him.

"But did that stop him? No. He went on respinning and respinning, didn't he? Till it took hold, right? The guy will do that, you know. He's responsible for some heavy philosophy there. They've done experiments where they'll pick a spider's work apart enough times that the poor little guy just has to lie down and die. Check it out. Only still trying. He don't give it up, he dies trying."

You get started on these things with Milo. It's hard pulling out of a topic before he's all finished with it. "That what you're suggesting you're dealing with?" I ask. "Allegorically? Dying trying?"

"Allegorically . . . that's a good one. No," Milo says. "Maybe."

In the fifties, out back in our shed, we had a loft to do as we liked in. We had all the steamy summer nights for much smoking, beating off, conjuring of hocus-pocus; the usuals. But I just remembered the spiders. The plumpest barn spiders we could capture were carefully imprisoned and subjected to The Mighty Needle and Candle Torture. Always a nauseating business for me, but then the hours we gave it brought up our profoundest thoughts about death.

"Hold it." I push us towards a snack counter. "I have to eat something. I haven't eaten all day."

"Don't spoil your supper. Mom's getting up some sort of gala for you tonight."

"Yeah? Well, I told her I was eating meat again," I say. "I expect nothing short of a slab of meat, in one form or another."

"Rib eyes." Milo pops his eyes, tongues his lips. "You guessed it."

I buy a microwave sandwich. But before I can get it to the thing to warm it, Milo's gone. I take out after him, chewing on cold mystery meat, working in a tube of mustard—greenish, oozy.

People are looking. Tarantulas are not as outré as all that nowadays, but this here is the underpart of the nation, and people are looking, and not like they're interested. "It's interesting," I say.

"What is?"

"We both have these shirts to tell about."

"Yeah, really, very interesting."

"This spider stuff, I assume it has something to do with you and Velda then." I take more sandwich into my mouth.

"I believe," Milo declares, "that anything, to the lowest creature, has a right to get himself a web he can live with. A den, a nest, a castle, what-have-you."

"You been hatching public proclamations—"

"So a woman. Could be any woman, some unknown woman, she comes along, catches him doing his level best, the best he knows how, way off in some out-of-the-way corner, and swats the juice out of him."

"That so."

"The end."

"I wouldn't know, exactly."

"Splat!" goes Milo. "Always under some goddamn lady's flyflap."

We walk on a ways in silence. Once we've mounted the escalator, he whispers, "You think maybe I'm gay too?" He looks at me twice, the second time seriously. I ought to be flattered by the notion, he thinks. The complicity.

"No," I tell him. "Not if you have to ask. I'd have to say there's a problem with girls there, but I wouldn't say it's that."

II.

"Y ES SIR, 'FREEDOM, real freedom, starts with the decision, it does not wait for the act.' "

Milo is quoting me a truth from Faulkner. We're driving through the rain to the mud country where home is, in the Appalachian hills. We're sitting up in the cab of Milo's Chevy pickup, thumping rhythmically over the measured-off seams in the old state road where the pitch sticks up. It's a bitch of an August thunderstorm outside and we have about fifty miles to go. I don't recall that one. *"Light in August?"* I ask.

While steering, Milo pounds back a hit of bourbon from a new half pint. *"Soldier's Pay,"* he says.

We had us a great-uncle by the name of Bado. Between the wars Bado abandoned home, wife, and children to go into the oil speculation in Mississippi, and for some years was set up at Oxford, where he became well acquainted, he claimed, with the local literary enigma down there. Brought him whiskey, is about what it was, and helped him use it. Eventually, when Bado felt he was close enough to dying, he returned to the lap of his family and, in the interim before the end, like many an old boy of his nature, just waited around the house recounting. With always a brandy snifter in hand, Bado regaled his young nephews with tales of this Faulkner. "Bill. You may've heard of him; they give him the Nobel." Our favorite tale was an actual reported fact, for Bado bore the newsprint to prove it. This took place shortly after that very occasion in Stockholm, when Faulkner returned to find his yard swarmed with reporters and photographers. "Now this was a mighty private, guarded man, boys," Bado told us. "He could be mighty angry, or then again . . ." and here Bado's lip canted roguishly, "mighty mischievous." As it happened, Bill would not allow the press in and neither would the press go home. When Bado dropped over to deliver congratulations he found the novelist upstairs drinking whiskey, fretting over and cussing the situation out in his yard. They had a few more, Bado and Bill, and studied on it. Finally it was nature that presented one of them with the idea. As the Oxford news printed it: "Mr. Faulkner, accompanied by an unidentified portly gentleman, stepped out on the upper veranda and urinated over the rail." Milo and I read the guy's books, after that, till we could actually comprehend some of it.

"*Soldier's Pay*, that's the worst one," I say. "If you asked me about Faulkner anymore, I'd tell you he was nothing but an old dipso gas bag."

"Who asked you?"

"I recall him saying somewhere that all a writer needs is pencil, paper, a little tobacco, and a little whiskey. If you ask me, he choked on all four."

"Nobody asked you. Besides, we were talking about freedom," Milo says. "Freedom is my new tack, and I intend to stay the hell away from acts of retribution this time. So I want to enlighten you on something, little brother: you needn't have come home on that account."

"Furious outrage. Depravity," I say. "That's all he could write. Eyes the color of new ax blades. Everyone riding up the baked dirt path on gaunt mules. Things always happening in furious retrograde, ratiocination, shit like that."

"So much for Book World," says Milo. "Now listen up, I have something—"

"Now if you want to talk Twain—"

"Quiet!" He leans forward suddenly, perking up his ears. "Listen . . ."

"What?" I ask, listening.

"Did you hear that?"

We're whispering. "What?"

"That's because you weren't listening! Now shut up and listen!"

While I wait for him to go ahead he tips the bottle up until it touches his nose and lets it empty on its own. He squints against the burn, blinking his eyes down the road, drops the little empty to the floor and squeezes the wheel in both hands. A pocket of air rises and escapes through his lips. "I'm worried about our mother," he says.

Now I'm starting to get the feel of going home again. I repeat Milo's unfathomable sentence to myself.

"That's right," he says, "and I thought you ought to be here to see what's going on for yourself."

"What's going on?"

"That's why I gave Mom that bit about Velda and me, knowing full well she'd hand it to you verbatim and you'd be here just like that. It worked without a snag. Am I clever or what?"

"You're a fucking liar. Tell me what I'm here, under false pretenses, to see for myself."

"That our mother's finally losing her marbles, buddy— correction, has lost." Milo swings us wide of a semi. We catch the blinding slap of its wheelwater on the windshield. He kicks us into overdrive.

"We're hydroplaning!"

"Relax," he answers over the white noise of our wheels slashing through sheets of road puddle. "Don't get your bowels in an uproar. I guess I was completely jettisoned when my wife took her weight-lifting set out of the back." He cuts us back to the right-hand lane.

Glancing over my shoulder I see the semi's fancy chrome

grillwork bearing down on our heels. "What are you doing!" The trucker is exhorting us with his baritone horn, giving us the dimmer treatment, making Milo's lunatic face flicker on and off in the reflection of our rearview.

Milo swings us over to the jump lane. The truck barrels past. We catch the Doppler effect of its laid-on horn: a moan, then a sigh.

The sweat cools on my scalp. "That was very nice," I say, my heart and balls slipping back into place. "You want to tell me what you're trying to prove before I jettison *myself!*"

Now the rain is coming on horizontally.

"I know what I'm doing," says Milo.

We're still riding on the gravel apron, lightning providing only spot visibility. "Why don't we stop, give this a chance to blow over?"

"I know what I'm doing."

Presently we churn into a gravel lot where I can just make out through the storm pink, blue, and green neon framing a low cinder block hillbilly bar.

"Now listen up and I'll explain." He's sitting at one of the tables for two in the Scenic Inn and wanting me to share it with him. The room is dark, damp, smells predominantly of mildewed rug. Ours is the furthest corner from the bar, lamplit by an old fifties juke. My eye cuts to the overhead color set. Underneath it the proprietor and his clientele—three hulking back-country types leaning their full-blown beefiness up to the bar—were, till as recent as our walking in, attending to the Cincinnati–Pittsburgh game. Now they're not.

I'm scared of these kinds. I tell him I'd just as soon go out and wait as get hit.

"Okay, so it ain't one of your swishy Bourbon Street joints. So what," he says. "Sit down."

"I'm not drinking."

"I am." He is for good reason, too, if you care to look at it that way. Not doing it for the effect, but against it. Maintenance stuff, and we both know it. I'm not so far removed from this myself I can't remember what has to be done. I sit.

The bartender has a towel tucked in the front of his pants. He wraps his fist up in it, starts working the knuckles. "What," he states.

"Who's winning?" Milo takes his time fishing into his jeans pocket for money.

"Pittsburgh, 3–0. Waddaya want."

"Sure is a nice rain we're having." Milo tips back his chair, taps a finger over the table, over the bills he spreads. His head, barely touching the jukebox, gingerly supports him. "Wouldn't you say?"

I cover my eyes ruefully with both hands.

Knuckles' quiet lasts forever.

Milo says, "I'll have a Turkey, the higher octane of the two, straight up, a cold draft beside it, and my brother here'll have a cup of tea, or whatever you have for people that don't drink anymore."

"A cup of tea . . ." May as well have said a saucer of prunes. The loin cloth slips from the guy's waist and becomes a wad. He is clearly deciding: Thumbs up or down on these two?

"Whatever." Milo isn't looking at him anymore. He rights himself to the table, leans in, and continues with me. "Now, like I was saying . . ."

"Coke," I tell the man, leaving out the customary wedge of lemon. I don't see so much as feel Knuckles go away.

" . . . she's trying to make it look real innocent, but she's pulling some very crazy things. *Very* crazy things."

"First," I interrupt, "two questions. This water bed fairy tale, did any of it even take place? Number two:

why didn't you just phone me yourself and tell me Mom's in trouble—if she even is—instead of all the duplicity?"

"Forget about that," Milo says.

I get up and walk out.

I wait some time in the parking lot, in the rain, my shirt off, count maybe twenty of the big rigs rumbling by, gloved, I observe to myself poetically, in roadwater cocoons, before Milo comes up behind and says, "My wife and I are separated, in actual fact, and I am beautifully free and unscathed. Number two: Mom would only keep her nose clean if she knew you were here to examine her goings on. Plus, I cannot just call you; you don't have a phone. You are too goddamn sensitive is your problem. Now get in."

III.

THE RAIN HAS slacked off to where you can make out the illuminated billboards advertising our hometown Baptist church, extending warm welcomes from the Chamber of Commerce, the Elks, Rotary. Milo says, "Now here's the one that cinches it. Last week, middle of the night, see, Mom's cruising around in her car. Alec Cranitz, some old bub down on East Hunter, hears this bumpity-bumpity-bump outside on the railroad tracks."

"What was an old bub doing up in the middle of the night?"

"Shut up, goddamit!"

"Sorry."

"So old Alec, see, he goes out to investigate, and lo and behold, guess who he finds out there with her oil pan snagged on a rail spike?"

"Yeah?" I say, awaiting the rest.

"Well?"

"Well, so what? She was hung up at a crossing. That can happen to—"

"Driving up the tracks!" Milo shouts. "I don't mean crossing them, buddy. She was headed up the tracks. Due north. The way the trains go."

"Come on."

"Our mother was headed for the abyss, kiddo. The big one. I mean, we get at least two freights a day through here."

"She was drunk," I remind him. "Was she drunk?"

"Does a fat dog fart?"

"Well that explains that. She didn't know what she was doing. You know as well as I do—"

"I know *better* than you do. She was driving home from Evie's. That's about as straight a line as they make. She's done it right for the better part of sixty-six years and could do it in her sleep, I don't have any doubt. Now don't you suppose, if she can climb in her car and get it started, even after one of Evie's soirees, don't you suppose she can find her way home?"

"Guess I'd have to grant you that, all right," I say. "So what you're saying—"

"Is our Mom's fixing to buy herself the farm. Just like Dad. That's my definite impression. Yes."

"Holy shit!"

IV.

T HERE'S THE PLACE. In daylight and without all this rain, once you got on top of the first real hill like this, you'd look down and find it: Ambrose, bunched up down there in the crotch looking small. You would have to look hard to find anything but pretense to its ever being food for the gods. The small farmer stays to his outlying hills and seems to make it on the once-a-week bygone formula: loading up and going back out; once a year he will fill the fairgrounds. The Goodyear runs to about half-capacity since the year after it moved in, but the clay sewer pipe plant does a flourishing industry. Which stands to reason. "After all," its owner, an Ambrose millionaire, has been quoted as saying, "long as you need to flush a toilet you'll need to pipe the stuff away." The bigger merchants would tend to live on the hill, in relative luxury, and be Catholic. They generally don't go in for reading books but are just as much behind the proliferation of recreational drugs and divorce as the rest of the upper-middle. The town is not big enough to have a daily paper but it does, carrying mostly ads and wire copy; its Letters to the Editor invariably are Thankyou's to everyone who helped make our pot luck, etc. Reason I lean on this, the paper, is, it used to be under the command of my father. It won awards for excellence—until the chief died. Then the *Ambrose Daily* made a dandy mat for catching dog water.

Ambrose on the whole is like a place cleaned out of

good men by war. Those it has pick their watering hole
for life, drink in it and make trouble for each other.

There are exceptions of course, but the young ladies
will try to stay pretty until they've had a baby or two.
After that their Appalachian skin starts to show up—a
pale, semen green, given to sag. They begin to look
tired; one becomes conscious of the liver-colored half-
moons under their eyes. They are fond of Dr. Pepper
(alcoholism actually seems rare among them), alcoholic
boys with all-enclosed vans, and of babies, of having
them, for something to do.

Milo has married three exceptions. (On the other hand,
most would agree he might have gone too far in his bid
for an exception with this last one, Velda.) Pat was the
first. She was country, but had that streak of Indian in
her, which kept her hard and lean and dark. She had
light hair and high cheekbones and was the only wife to
have children with Milo, two little girls they gave French
names to, Daphne and Claudette. Daph and Claude are
still here—not in town, exactly, but nearby, living with
their mother and stepdad, Wagoner, a fellow I've never
met. Wagoner owns a stud farm, a big one, standard-
breds and thoroughbreds both, and Pat, something of an
equine genius, has been everything to his horses: swipe,
blacksmith, trainer, jockey. Winters, when Wagoner takes
his show to the races in Florida, he takes Pat along,
realizing it's she more than his pedigrees that brings in
the purse money. In fact it's Pat who built up his winning
momentum to where he finally got to the Preakness.

During the winter, when Pat and Milo were still attached, Milo kept the girls. The arrangement seemed
workable (better than my own, which at the time was a
period of dark drinking plus a tenuous first step with my
glands). My brother would write: "I've got the kids reading *Lear*. We'll run around the house rhyming and curs-
ing like crusty bards . . ." or "Daph seems to be turning

out genius-level work in the watercolor area. We're thinking about the Sorbonne!" Daph and Claude would have
been around five and six.

In the spring and summer the kids would help Pat in
the stables. She taught them to whip Wagoner's trotters
and pacers into submission. I was told they could half-
mile the sulkies with aplomb.

Pat and Milo had themselves two rugged, leather-skinned
little intellectuals.

But then, according to Milo's vivid recollection of it,
the last April that Pat came home to him, deep in her
Indian tan, hair bleached and bound to the skull in a
headband, body sending out that mild whiff of masculine
perspiration, she stepped up in her roughed out riding
boots and confessed to have been putting in some sack
time with her boss, the other Ambrose millionaire. Wagoner. She was going to marry the guy, she said, instead
of just shovelling his horseshit.

You won't see them anymore, not even Milo's girls,
though they summer in a nice place not ten miles out
on Nickle Plate, some idyllic acreage surrounded by big
pines, spirited Dobermans and electronic devices—pre-
cautions against such as Milo's stealing in and snatching
his children away, trying to carry them over state lines
again.

Since then, since he abused his privileges, I don't ask
after Milo's kids. He'd jump down my throat, not being
able to give an answer. It's a sore subject.

V.

HE DROPS ME in the alley back of Mom's and spins off in the mud, leaving me to feel my way on in the dark drench. Aiming for the bug light on her porch I shoulder my luggage and advance through clumps of backyard garden, scramble over a few wet shrubberies.

On the porch I hang back of the screen door a while watching Mom and her favorite friend Evie drink whiskey in the kitchen. Mom is shooting a glare across the table that means business, accusing Evie of becoming too drunk to comprehend. "You can't anymore listen to good sense than have it come out your mouth!" she swears, draining her drink. This kind of comportment between them is not unusual.

Evie is showing me her broad back. I see her ruffle and improve her posture. "PAH!" she goes at Mom, like a cannon.

I open the door and my mother's whole soul changes. She calls out, "There's my boy!" pushing off from the table to stand herself up. It pains her a little, but then she manages a twinkle and comes at me with wings spread and summoning fingers.

It appears she is receding into age. Each time I return anymore I see her shorter and bearing more lines. She gets me in a tight wrap and nails the claws to my back. The way the whiskey smells coming off her goes right back to my boyhood—not unpleasant, but fusty as the inside of a grandfather clock. Unclutching me Mom says,

21

"You're all wet! Lay that knapsack down, will you, and have a drink with the old troops." She sweeps up her glass and goes into the ice compartment. "No, no, I forget you're not drinking. You don't mind if I have a little one, do you? Evie and I are a little bit drunk, I'm afraid. You don't mind, do you?"

Willie Nelson is rendering "Stardust" on the old Zenith.

"Hi, Evie."

"Velda broke in and stole your mother's jewelry," Evie says, moiling her lips together as if mushing a new coat of lipstick. Evie is in that state of glow I've known her all my life to get to. The involuntary lip spasms are what give it away.

"Nonsense!" Mom says, "We don't know she did it, so you just don't say anything." She is bending into the freezer, rattling through the ice.

"Well, I'm just saying." Evie stretches across the table poking a glass along in front of her finger. "Fix me one too, Janie."

"'Three–four,'" sings Mom.

Evie goes, "Get the goddamn wisenheimer off the stage, will you?"

"Sit," Mom tells me. "Have you seen your brother?"

"I have."

"I'd be embarrassed being seen with that bum," says Evie.

"What do you think?" Mom asks.

"I think . . . he's trying."

"For what?" she says. "If looking the way he looks amounts to trying then I don't know what he bothers for." She drops cubes into her and Evie's glasses, pours over the Canadian, turns to the sink. "Water?" She runs a trickle over hers.

"Dean?" Evie says, "What I'd like to know is how can you live in New Orleans and not drink. Stein and me went down once and there was nothing to do but." Stein is Evie's mister. Evie comes from pure Scots people. Her face is red and big, mostly jaw, and there are short waves of untidy orange on top—looking as if she combed them back with her fingers—with slick, flat fins against the sides. Her voice is something like a wheezing bagpipe; it gets to you, the way a person clipping their nails in the same room will.

I answer, "Sweat a lot, I guess. I don't know."

"He doesn't like to talk about it, so just lay off him!" says Mom, dropping onto a chair beside me. "There, that's better." She sighs and begins swirling the big cubes around with her pinky to get a good chill to her drink. They each sip and set their glasses on bamboo place mats.

This table of hers is no ordinary kitchen piece but an oaken monster that fills up an unfavorable proportion of floor space. It has legs like fat snakes twining to the ground. It is a major token of my dad, too, whose library upstairs it once furnished. Mom uses it to push off again. "There went my Willie," she says, taking cautious little steps over to the hi-fi. She lifts the cabinet lid and drops the tone arm over the first cut again.

Willie goes into "Georgia on My Mind."

"Not that again, Jane. I'm sick of it. Jesus Christ, she's wearing it smooth!"

"I don't care, I love my Willie Nelson. Dean gave it to me, didn't you?"

I regret that I did.

"Why can't you play that Sammy Davis *I* gave you? Don't you love him, Dean? Isn't he the cutest little fart?"

"No, Dean doesn't like him!" says Mom. "Don't be silly."

"The two of you are ganging up on me already," Evie complains, "and you can just quit."

Mom drinks and ignores. "Now then, what can I get you? How are you?"

"He's hungry." Somehow Milo has come in unnoticed. His head is in the refrigerator. He's been rooting around in there. "I'm fixing us some supper now." He comes out of the fridge holding a stack of rib eyes individually wrapped in meat paper, a lettuce head, a Baggie full of shelled peas from Mom's garden.

"You know what you look like, Milo?" says Evie, "Like you were shot at and missed and shit at and hit." She draws herself up and laughs. "You know what? Just looking at you I could gag on a spoon!"

"Bite your tongue, Evie," he says.

"She's right," says Mom, "you look like the wrath of God in that hair. It's not natural. It looks like oil."

"Uh, if I'm not mistaken your hair is purple."

"That's different entirely. A lady my age has to have a rinse on her hair because otherwise our heads would be yellow. Who wants to be an old parchment head? And it is not either purple."

Like a brother I suggest that my brother, with his spikes and all, is after attention.

Hearing me, Milo lays the food aside. He steps over to my face. He takes hold of my cheek, right under the eye, and tenderly screws the flesh. Several things about this all at once: first, the stronghold of his own face is all unfastened, as before, only the eyes are missing now by an inch, and there's the shake in his drinking hand coming through to my cheek. There's the fact that my brother has never laid hand on my face in our grown-up lives. He breathes the whiskey smell on me. "Let's face it, pal, it's the eighties," he says. "You may continue cleaving to the past, but let me tell you what the eighties are all about—"

"If you want to stand away and tell me then all right."

Still twisting my face, he says, "It's a chance for all of us that were never in to be in."

In time we show our separate ways of disapproval. Evie, schmoozing her lips in the foulest way, says, "I don't get what you're trying to say, but you *were* pretty before you did *that*. That's a compliment for you if you were listening."

"Not by eighties standards," Milo says. "Now I'm pretty by eighties standards. You'll see. You might get the backwash of the last twenty years, but that's what you get; that's what counts these days; you'll just have to live with it."

He goes over to the big Canadian bottle, measures out a liquid ounce, upsets multivitamins into his palm, throws the whole unsteady mess, two-fisted, to the back of his throat. The hands come under control some but the face reads that he's still under siege; he cannot take it anymore.

For some reason my heart is going out.

"Call me a fool," says Milo, "but I'm *de rigueur*."

Evie goes at him once more: "You're really deep. Oh, you're so heavy!"

He turns his back to us three as if for peace. We view the spider, the black ducktail down his neck. He says that that was an unfortunate turn of phrase, for a fat lady.

This gala will have to go ahead without Dean. It has become necessary to climb the stairs. To kick the wet things off. To step into a hot bath.

After a good soak I put on dry things from my pack.

Across the hallway I go, to the room of my dead father's bookcases. Like always. There they stand in dust and disrepair, their once milky paint turned yellow as old teeth. I will select certain of my father's inventory and find a note made on newsprint that he himself tucked in there. This was Dad, constrained to tuck notes into the books he battered himself with. So much—the books, the memoranda—that, moving beyond most things he went

into oblivion. He should have had regular conversations
with somebody, for a reason to quit surrounding himself.

Milo will never disturb this place, just to prove the
awful hatred he thinks he had with his father.

I reach for the leather volume with the note I want,
that I'm familiar with. Because of my own suspicions I
need to read it again, lengthy and crude as it is, in his
miniscule hand with soft edit pencil (his principal tool at
the *Daily*). The other pages are missing, but it's of no
consequence. Milo was no more than ten, I'd say. The
old man was puzzled. Get this:

*. . . make of his accusations? Case in point: I had
had a few drinks last night. It was a long day and I
had needed to—because of this executive session business at the school. I was angry in the first place that I
had to cover the board meeting myself, and then
Martha, as soon as she saw me come in, pulling that
executive session. We all know there's news in this
thing! And we know I'll get it! But naturally I felt a
good deal of resentment over Martha's wasting—
deliberately!—my time. But I have been good lately. I
stopped at three, I'm sure it was no more—and those
short ones, Jones was pouring—and came home. I
came directly upstairs to type my notes, paltry as they
were, and had just lighted my pipe when Milo came
in. He hadn't knocked. Dad, he said, I've just decided I'm going to tell you. I've been afraid to (his
exact words) but it's gone too far now and I have to.
He stayed by the door, apart from me, this was
evident. I asked what this was all about. I was rather
in a hurry, I'm afraid, to finish my work and get on
to some reading before bed. He told me that it was
about this problem of mine, said I wasn't fooling
anyone, said the situation around here was deplorable
(again his exact words. I remember thinking a better*

word might have been insupportable), and that he
*was the only one brave enough, etc. Again, I'm afraid
I lost my temper. But, all things considered, and
combined . . .*

*The puzzling thing—I cannot tell whether he came
to me with charity and forgiveness in him, despite his
statement of "the only one brave enough," etc. or
whether it was, more accurately,* fear *that he was
expressing, and therefore* hate.

*I have thoughts, I confess, of hurting him without
meaning to. Lord Almighty, do not allow it. I would
stick my hand in hell for him! But it worries me, what
I've seen of his intelligence: he thieves. He has started
smoking lately. That's not so bad, but it's self-abuse,
and in all probability he will take on some uglier
alternatives: he will practice masturbation once he has
it figured out; or, if it doesn't embarrass him or make
him sick, he will lie. He will make up reasons for all
this, too, like Hard Life. Already he makes too much
myth out of everything, trying desperately to be iden-
tified as the victim, even martyr. It moves him so. It
lifts the little fucker! I cannot be made to . . .*

In Louisiana I have a Cajun friend who helped rid me
of whiskey, which he himself had used considerable help
doing, he said, having been as partial to the stuff as I.
You want to shake it off, I can tell, he told me. You
come in the morning, I'll show you.

I found the place, an old slave quarters on Elysian. He
began by pouring down me some dozen cups of chickory,
then waited with amazing patience for my stomach to
give it back up. We waited longer. Finally I started to
shake in every limb and hallucinate the insects and crustaceans. The center part of my vision looked like a bowl
of crawfish bisque.

His name is Beauraine.

Now behold all that and listen to it, he impelled me. All this is what your devils of yesterday and the day before was keeping away from you.

I could deny it except that these things were cavorting upon my eye surfaces. For ten years I had been keeping them company—eighteen if you want to count the drugs—and they had never been revealed like this.

My time was up.

He sent me to his bed. I was lying down with vomit and those creatures and for so long I pitched about with them. I covered miles. I came to with sheet burn. There was a terrible abandon to sobbing then, but so out of self-respect was I that my crying went out mainly for this man's spoiled bedclothes.

The men of this family have been undone by alcohol. The long line of us have done our devotion. Some have prospered and made fortunes in this county, but too much devotion seizes others of us, coaxes a way out of failure and suffering that's against the law of nature. But suicide, when it works, is beyond the law—above it, some would say.

It has taken us down.

VI.

HERE AND THERE the screen walls of the back porch are pearled with dew. Half-awake, I'm stepping out on the foggy lawn. It is 7 A.M., all haze and bird noise. Mom brings out coffee and a laundry basket and sits with me at the picnic table. We celebrate with a succession of cigarettes.

"What are you thinking?"

"That I'm down in the country for a couple weeks and don't have to go to work."

Out on the street in front some factory traffic buckets over potholes. Birds are clucking overhead. There's more food than any bird needs and no one to keep them from it except our old Siamese Just Bill. Just about in the middle is a low birdbath between two silver spruces; way over on the right is the vegetable garden; behind that a ring of peony with space in the middle to hide in; after that the white shed; and beyond everything rises a hill gray with treetops. There's an owl someplace. There are jays, starlings, a thousand sparrows. It is foggy and peaceful. Somewhere down the street you can hear a neighbor open up her silverware drawer. A widow neighbor left a white blanket hanging over her clothesline in the rain; it is wet through with nothing to move it, not even a little breeze. A robin bounces over her yard, stops, bounces left, pivots right, listens, drops its nose to the ground and brings it up empty. Birds in the trees, on the power lines. The sun is a white dime coming over the gray hill, so pale

29

you can look at it. It could be the moon. Just Bill comes ripping out of a corn row in the garden chasing a rabbit. It's getting brighter, the dime. Now you can feel it when you look. Green starts to happen. Now it's no longer a dime and the fog is burning away. The blanket will be dry by noon.

"I had a good sleep, but I had this dream."

She has done my washing already and is folding and stacking everything on the table. Wearing a look of pleasure she smoothes out a pair of my underpants. There is no memory or remorse in her over last night. Not that there should be. But how can she do this? Drink like a gentleman when she is of this family? "What was it?" She places the folded garment on the stack.

"I dreamed that Milo was walking around with spiders inside him. You could see them in his rib cage trying to break out. But he kept going and didn't know it."

"I sometimes think Milo is my late husband in disguise. History repeating itself. There he is," Mom says.

"Where?"

She whispers, "Look out there in the peony. He's got his tent set up in it. It's where he's been sleeping ever since Velda pushed him out."

Milo shows up a bluish ghost in the fog. He stretches in naked profile, the nakedest part swollen with morning, ranging out in front of him like a jackknife blade.

"I don't suppose the rain bothered him any," says Mom.

He starts letting go over the peony.

"Don't pee there!" she yells, making him ease his head over.

He finishes off then comes across the yard wiping out his eyes with the heel of a hand, rubbing toes along the cold grass, complaining: "Jesus, my head!" hard-on shrinking fast into its dark brown beard. Then he stops to raise Cain with the sky. "Would these birds be quiet up there!"

But the face comes back down wearing a grin that goes on as long as it takes him to get here. Stringy muscles, upturned wedge of teeth, inky hair, whiskered skin the bluish appearance of curling smoke.

"He's not even sober yet," says Mom, watching.

He comes closer and I can make out, there on the very tip of him, which looks like a big removable pencil eraser, the single drop it carries.

"Morning, all you lovely people," bending over me to grab one of my cigarettes, "If it ain't a family picnic." His droplet narrowly misses my lap. He fixes the cigarette in his grin.

There's an anchovy smell to his body which I tell him about.

"And for heaven's sake put something on! Here!" Mom flings my shorts at his feet.

"Well who pooped in *your* cornflakes?"

"Don't step on those, they're mine." What did I say that for? But they're my favorite, my briefest ones. Cherry red with an Italian tag. I just asked for it.

"Oh–my–God! Panties!" Pinching them up: "All right, Mother," he begins, "I've got news. I'm just going to give it to you. Your second son here is queer as a football bat. Look at this and say it isn't so." Holding them out, like a rag, on a finger.

"Don't you think I know it's so?" says our mother. "Good Lord," says she, "I knew that before *he* did."

The two brothers ask as one, "You did?"

"Of course. There are few things a mother doesn't know. You weren't fooling me. But I'll tell you something—I hope you're being careful, they're getting this disease, the gays are, I read about it all the time and I worry about you."

Says Milo, "Sodom's Revenge."

"Cram it, Milo!"

"It's not funny, they're dying, these boys. Dean, tell me this, do you have one partner, or many?"

"Not many. I'm very careful."

"My brother in lingerie!"

"Good," she says. "Because I don't need to see you go before I do. And that won't be long from now."

"Did you hear that?" Milo asks me, but, thinking better of it, says, "Buddy, you're lucky we don't have a redneck for a mother, or you'd just be out of the inheritance." He runs my Armanis up his legs, gives them a snap at the hip, exhales a fart.

VII.

I RUN INTO Velda at the Kroger store. I'm shopping in produce when she wheels her basket up alongside, wearing a midriff T-shirt and bathing suit bottom. Her stomach is tanned and greasy with lotion. She smiles, careful not to show her braces. "Dean. What are you doing here?"

"Getting stuff for a picnic." Milo's idea. He had it thinking it might be nice if we tried doing something as a family and we bought it out of plain astonishment. But I don't tell any of this to Velda.

"No, I mean doing back in Ambrose," she wants to know.

"Vacation." I see no reason for the whole truth on this one either. Not that I don't care for it, but I don't care for the question, or for the one asking.

"I guess you heard what happened between me and your dumb-ass brother."

But I roll ahead, eyes on my list. I select a nice melon, a celery bunch, start thumbing for ripe avocados. The Kroger is new here and I am a little delighted with all the size and stock. Velda comes along in my direction, her cart full of instant cake mix, Dr. Pepper, sticky buns. Her teeth will rot under those braces before they've had a chance to do their work.

"All right, look," she says, "I know what you-all think I am. So, okay, you can take Milo's side of it. You will anyhow." She has dropped back.

I push on toward condiments.

Now Velda is setting up a fit from behind. "That's the way I'd expect of you-all, anyway! I've got a little surprise for that man, you can tell him!"

I turn and yell for her to stop broadcasting it.

The lady shoppers stop likewise and turn their interest down our aisle.

"It's no secret!" Velda goes on. "It sure wasn't no surprise to anyone that's the least furmiliar with that mean crazy asshole!" She catches up, showing me a menacing galvanized overbite.

"Milo's new wave now," I say. "What can you expect?"

"He's in big trouble, and you can tell him that."

"All right, what is it?"

"All right then, there's this little matter of pregnancy that he screwed up royal. Mine!"

"Oh?" I can feel lawyer coming off her. Given half a chance she'd furnish the details, which I haven't the time or any use for. "That's awful, Velda. Did my brother know he was about to have a baby? Or was he?"

"I was fixing to tell him but he never gave me a chance. He goes off swearing I been with all these guys and don't even give me a chance, but starts slapping me around all over the place. I've got medical papers. I've got a lawyer. You tell him I've got a lawyer, Dean. He'll be interested in that. You can tell Milo I'm going to have his ass, not that it's worth anything."

"Money, you mean."

"Yeah. Money."

"That's what I thought. Listen, Velda." I touch her shopping cart, lean in close, take her into my confidence. "I was going to ask you to be generous with him, Velda. See, Milo's not doing real good right now. You'll do it, won't you?" I ask. "I hear you're getting awfully well-known for your generosity," I say.

*   *   *

Probably getting around some, as I have done, has taught me. I was one of those with no honorable reason to stick, not that he could mention, because of queerness or what have you, that got himself across the street and around the block as early as possible. Trying to forever lose track of the place he comes from. But the hillbilly of me will not release; it comes on at each frontier: Once, in New York, I bought a pair of shoes. I asked innocently enough whether I couldn't have a sack for my shoe box, as I had pretty much walking to do. I awoke some humor in the sullen cashier, enough for him to call his buddy over and make him witness this guy from the Midwest or South or something. Did he hear me use *sack* and *please* both in the same drawled out sentence?

Hauling my sacks across the lot to Mom's Fiat I can feel it coming on, that old part that refuses to cut loose. I am back here and I am close to shame for the hillbilly trash I have to be intimate with.

When Milo married his latest one, Velda, there was a fine party set up at our mother's. A certain ticklish lull in things moved Velda to speak to the hostess: "When you croak, Janie, can I have this old couch?" She was making herself comfortable all over Mom's handsome Victorian passed down from the old Yankee history.

A few of us begged her pardon.

Velda had missed her chance at spreading familiarity around so kept on: "Could I have this, too? I just love this." Now she was favoring the cloisonné cannister that I had bought and stuffed with reefer and risked my life in carrying up here from Mexico in '73. That one item was dear to me. It was Velda's great recklessness to have me in earshot. I took the thing back and weighed her in utter disesteem for about half a second.

"Get out!" I said. I said, "Get the fuck away from my people! My family has come through years and years, and we are at home! You," I said, "are not *enough* here!"

The only reason I hadn't laid violence on her was her and my brother's troth, which had just become a plighted goddamn reality!

Not to be outdone, Milo invited me into the yard and showed his disparagement over me until our good clothes were destroyed.

All that and the bitch was never shamed.

As a type she is ignorant of her own gall; she will come back at you with a look of new innocence each time. Velda suggests the tawdriness of those leading ladies in the made-for-TVs—the ones that will deliver lines of embarrassing passion over videotape, because all they did to get the work was have lust and show producers that moist female advantage. Because they are blank regret, unlike the real ladies who toil, whose real genuine actual hearts have cried, trying to learn the acting profession.

But there's no making glamorous comparisons either, when public toilets in several places in this county give utterance to Velda's fame on their walls. She is even mentioned, in filth, I am told, at Boy Scout camp. She is counted among the chosen handful to have been scrubbed away and scrawled back anew.

Velda is imbued with filth!

VIII.

JANE, MY MOTHER, has a suitor named Ken, a strapping old boy of sixty-one, wealthy in county land, who wears sherbet-colored slacks and is pretty content with the way he is doing life. Also, Ken owns a full fleet of motor vehicles, including the custom Ford camper that Jane and he will take to some private orchard ground he owns when the weather is up. They will drink, fish, and pretend fight through a weekend, for they are both keen for salacious argument. Or they'll maybe sing old songs together. Slowed down now, both of them, with minor arthritis, they take occasional tokes on some okay weed that Ken grows on a back hillside. It provides the medicine without their booze getting mixed up with pharmaceuticals.

Ken and Jane can be prone to calamity. For instance, he once backed his camper over Mom's foot while they were loading up from our back porch. Pinned there and helpless with the hurt, she made a dent in the roof with the Sony. When the tire rolled off, and Jane caught her breath, she cried, in a confusion of words, "Get off my sonofabitch foot, you!" Obeying, Ken shifted into a forward roll, snapping what survived of her tarsal bones.

Anymore, Jane will move with something of a limp.

We try it. It's not perfect, but then we are not all practiced in the picnic environment. There's Ken, Mom, Milo, me. We have the bread she baked for yesterday,

my homecoming. Here is her potato salad, with the vine-
gar, the mustard, the hard eggs, the skins on. Here is the
ham and the Jell-O. They have Miller by the case and a
jug of Canadian. I am drinking ice tea, without sugar.

After cocktails, Ken and I hike into some pines on this
side of the lake for Man Talk. Our feet make soft falls
over the mat of brown leaf drop. The water's surface
twinkles like wrinkled chrome. We stop at the edge and
squint.

"You wouldn't want to fish it now."

"No."

"Too hot. There's no feeding in this."

"Right."

"They're all played out, laying down lazy on the
bottom."

"I know."

"They're treating you pretty good down where you
live," Ken tells me in that staunch hard-line Republican,
licking his set of fake teeth.

"Pretty good."

"You're doing all right for yourself."

"Pretty much."

He sniffs, content, itches the silver brush of his hair,
hikes the dynamic colored trousers up past his beltline.

We turn and go back.

IX.

MY BROTHER AND I are on our way home. We
have sunset in the windshield, the air is cooling
and picking up, disturbing just right through our open
truck windows. We said good-bye to the two oldsters,
left them high in spirit, wending towards the lake and
their fly-casting element. Just to see what happiness looks
like I incline my outside mirror so as to check my face in
it, when Milo has something to show me.

He pulls over by our river, the Hocking, a low-running,
skinny neck of water down to its shallow muddiest by this
time of summer. I jump out and follow him down the
shady bank, needing to lace a path around the grapevine,
the moldy elm roots and red fungus. That loamy smell on
everything.

I know this place. In this place many of us boys played
with real danger, with high adventure such as the Mississippi. Then, a little later on, some of us toyed with
co-nakedness, used this place for the shy adventures of
early sex.

We're standing on a shelf of rock bottom. In shallow
times like now the surface is dry, smooth, extending off
the riverbank like a toenail; and even when the reach is
up there's no real depth to it until somewhere around the
middle, out where the course takes a wide turn for the
waterworks. Then you drop off into sudden deep. And
there's the dangerous part: then starts up a whorl of
water you want to be ready for.

But here's something new. Swinging over the drop-off on a guy wire, this bravely painted sign. The words are barely readable for the sundown, but once I've got the big red and black words into focus I have to laugh: CAUTION, I read. DEATH HOLE. I'll be damned.

"Stop laughing!"

I spin around and spot Milo on the bank looking back. His balance has left him. He has his back up to a tree for purchase. Somehow, looking out at the DEATH HOLE sign, Milo has grown serious. His glutted eyes open in their redness as if something unwholesome had informed them. "You hear me? Don't!"

"Why? What does it say that for? It never did that to us."

First he smashes the empty in his hand and pops open one of the extras he brought. He lights up a smoke. Then he says, "Because a kid walked out there. Just walked out and the hole sucked him in. I had to pull him up."

"Was he . . . ?"

"Yeah. I didn't know they'd hung a sign. Maybe they thought it was going to start collecting people."

"Why you?"

"Except for Juliet and our old man, it's the closest I've been to witnessing pure unnecessary death before . . . This one was right like this in my arms."

"Are you going to tell me about it?"

"They wouldn't dip a toe in to help me, either, the fuckers!" He has found a tree stump to dispose himself on, or in, because the crown of it is scooped out like a bowl. He fits himself in and I take a seat on the moss while he drains the last of the can and starts.

He was on duty at the fire station. It was a spring Sunday this year. Milo was out back in the bright afternoon practicing some karate steps you wouldn't believe. His partner of the day, Smitty, a divorced jock from

Michigan, a guy Milo says he can seriously relate to, was out there. Smitty was still going at the old Seagrave pumper's chrome with his buffing cloth when the short-wave invoked Maydays in a powerful series. The code of distress spread in turn to other men in the municipal line of duty—deputies, rangers, the county paramedic team. Minutes later the Sunday air of all Ambrose was corrupted by multiple sirens.

They attained the bridge. A wail of uniforms on parade, they created a turmoil of shimmying steel.

Not much further on and they were there. Nothing to know it by but the scourged looking man on the riverbank they were told to watch for.

"What's happening, Mister?" Milo and Smitty were the first ones down.

He was streaming sweat but otherwise handsomely dressed in the cut of outdoorwear you find in the Bean catalog. He himself resembled one of the Bean characters, what with his tall, graying, distinguished looks. His mouth stammered oaths at all the flanking vehicles with their alarm beacons going. He was fitful under the sun.

Milo did not recognize him.

"Oh Jesus!" the fellow said. "Jesus no! Don't let this be . . ."

"We got a call there was a drowning."

"I don't believe this . . ." The weeping man brought his hands together as in prayer, raised them to his face, continued beseeching.

"Would you want to get ahold of yourself and explain?"

The eyesight voided, the red and raw sinuses clamped over.

"Or is this a joke or what?" asked Smitty.

"I'll be all right, I'll be all right."

A moment passed. Gently, Milo opened a space out of the man's fingers, enough for him to look out and recall the catastrophe through. "Out there . . ."

They looked.

"I warned the boy not to go out there . . ."

"A kid you say."

"I don't see nothing," Smitty said.

"He's dead," the man told them.

Two deputies, both fat ones, were climbing down.

"It's a kid!" yelled Milo.

The one named Sigler stepped up working for breath. He knew the guy. "What have we got, Mr. Miller?"

Once he saw the pistol and clothing of sheriff's deputies criminal negligence took over Miller's thoughts. "I want you to know that I am in no way responsible for this." He was a different man. "They boy entered that water on his own. Entirely against my warning."

"Hold on," answered the other deputy, named Imboden. "Just who do we have out there, Mr. Miller?"

"Nobody, now! A corpse!" Miller gave the name of his nephew, a nine-year-old visiting from St. Louis, where he, Miller, had recently moved from. They had been out here on foot exploring the countryside for fossils when the boy strayed off. Miller saw the last of his nephew wading out over that high bottom.

"Goes out 'ere quite a ways," Deputy Sigler put in.

The kid was excited. Not up to his knees yet. Amazed! He dared it further and further: "Look at me!" he hollered back at the uncle, "Just like Jesus, just like Jesus!" Miller was ordering the kid out right up to when he lost him. A goner. "A corpse!" Miller said again, more thin-skinned and fidgety about it, Milo observed, than anything else.

"Your undertow out there," Sigler said, "it's quite a bit of suck for a young boy to get involved in."

"So, what you're saying, Mr. Miller," said Imboden, "the boy's out there in the draw."

"Yes."

"That he's, in your opinion, dead already."

"That's what I said," Miller said.

"Then it don't look like we're in any hurry," said Imboden. "Better wait for Thompson. He's the man with the diving suit. I want the coroner too. We'll leave these paramedics standing by. Mr. Miller, it don't look to me as if you tried saving the victim."

"Saving!" Miller nailed the pair of officers with scrutiny. He discerned the blubbery displacement of their uniform shirts, the hat straps pinching up a tender bulb under the lips, the way these deputies girdled themselves in their bullet-belts. This was a cartoon! Uncle Miller gained some confidence by it. "I can't even swim! That's not a crime, is it? What do you expect? I jump in there and kill myself?"

"All right, Mr. Miller, I just meant—"

"And then it's the both of us. That what you want? Get that guy out of here! I'm not answering any questions!"

Brown, the *Daily News* reporter, was pushing in, trying to put his 35mm to the tall, obstreperous Miller. By then it was a disorder of volunteers milling around as if they were out here to do something and were doing it. You had the clean garbed team of paramedics, the highway trooper, the state forest mounty sitting his pretty brown and white mare, you had the Citizen's Auxiliary.

The uncle was making no more show of grief. Instead, with the fiery color coming back in his face, he said maligning things of the dead little boy. Miller said that the nephew was an adopted curse to his sister since the beginning. Obstinate, rambunctious little devil with no respect for authority. The day he arrived in Miller's home Miller had to punish him for lighting matches in the basement. "I told him this would happen, but he had to keep going, didn't he? He had to prove it, didn't he? He invited this if you ask me. He was asking for it. That's right. Simple as that!"

"What!" Milo had been listening. "We're wasting time.

Fuck Thompson and his frog suit. Just show us the spot and let's get moving!"

"Shut up, Milo!" One of the porky deputies stuck Milo with his finger. "Mr. Miller, try and settle down. Why don't you come up in the cruiser and we'll radio for Thompson."

But Milo was resolute, unbowed. He stripped and got a line around his waist and had Smitty pay him out while he went down in the place that took the kid. They shared in bringing the boy, full of water and dead sixty minutes, up from the silt and mud. He was blue. Milo carried the body in and lay it down and the medics tried CPR on him. It was a valiant attempt, said the headline. But undocumented with photographs. The newspaperman had had to vomit.

The uncle would not go near the body. Milo had to seek him out. "Must be real rough on you. Must be an awful thing to bear. I'm the one that pulled your nephew out. Name is Milo. Why don't you let me give you a ride?"

"Thanks. And thanks for doing it. The boy and all."

The mosquitos are agressive, obnoxious. Night is upon us now to where there's only a slip of light the color of saxophone over west. Milo rattling in his beer sack and the two of us slapping our necks for bug relief is all you hear, besides the frogs, a few weird birds, then the river.

Around Milo's feet lies the garbage of his empties; it's looking good to me, for some reason, his beverage, though I rarely ever drank a can of beer. "The beer's starting to look good, Milo. Will you finish up the story if you're going to and let's get out of here, before I do anything harmful to myself? Besides, I'm getting stung like crazy."

"Don't start correcting me."

"Who's correcting?"

"If you want one of these, have it, but don't start correcting me."

"No thanks. Every now and then it looks appealing. But I don't need it. I don't have to anymore."

"I don't have to anymore!" Milo mocks the words through his nose; they go skimming across the river and bounce off the other bank.

"No. I don't. I used to, but I reached a moment of truth with the stuff. It was very prickly, letting it go. I try to keep the memory of that fresh so I don't lose track of the . . ."

"Epiphany?"

"Yeah, that's close enough, I guess. But I remember what it's like, what you're doing. Where you maybe don't *want* to, but you *have* to."

"*Like* to," Milo says. "*Choose* to."

"You don't have any choice."

"Listen, that kind of shit ain't going over here, pal. And don't go pulling Dad's alcoholism into this, either, to back you up, because I don't get that kind of wasted. I don't get that kind of sad."

"Yet."

"All right, *you* choose. Either you're interested and want to shut up and let me finish, or you want to guess at the best part of this."

"Go ahead. It's what we're suffering out here in this swamp to find out, isn't it? So what's the payoff? Give us the best part. Just make it quick."

"I was going to give it to you when you started correcting me. Now I cannot think of any use for that kind of interference."

"You're deluded. The booze is putting this persecution thing on you, but it's a hoax. I can see it now, from a sober perspective."

"That does it!" I can hear Milo rustle about, preparing to go. "Guess away!"

"All right. Here. Here's my guess." This stops him. "My guess is, you drove this Miller straight home and kissed him good night. Furthermore, I guess the two of you meet privately now, say once a week, for a few dozen rounds of drinks and some stimulating talk about molesting children. The best of confederates—"

If I could say any more it would be, One day, Milo, you will be peeling an orange, and when the skin doesn't strip away just as you intended, you will kill somebody. Because of fruit, the streets won't be safe.

I would say that because he might. However, Milo is suddenly on me, fingers digging into my throat and his knee right close to where my legs meet. He is hurling a set of homosexual adjectives at me.

He stops himself just short of real pain. Then comes the contents of his can over my face. A good portion goes up my nose: warm, burning with the active fizz.

After that he climbs off and disappears.

For a while there is a silence, and I take account of my neck, burnt raw by the sweaty finger marks, plus the grit, the bites, the yeasty viscid beer.

The voice comes from where Milo is making a puddle: "That there was to teach you a new perspective."

That there was, I guess, some comeuppance for Milo's little brother.

Good thing the lights are out and I don't have to look. Better to just hear him falter and snake around, get recuperated in his log. Better not to see him reach in his bag for more chemical clarity.

Looks like we're staying a while. "All right, you've humbled me, Milo. You, and the dark out here, and something about this prime-time mystery of yours, the suspense of which is killing me. Let's see if we can't get it over with. Tell us about giving the guy his, Milo. Come on."

"Where was I?" comes the slobbering voice. "I can't see worth a shit."

"It's all right, night fell. You were giving the villain uncle a ride, remember?" It occurs to me I might walk up there to the truck and maybe he would follow. It occurs to me I might want to try it before he falls out of his bowl and I have to carry him.

"Life can be very strange . . ." Sounds like Milo is slipping into his contemplative aspect. "Look what they'll throw you. You take yourself a clean, perfect Sunday such as that . . . you're light and absolute. You're just about ready to trust in anything, and look what they throw you. A sunken kid. And his uncle. Dry, rude. A miscreant. That's where I was. Yeah, I sought to have me some evil fun with the survivor, see. For being a survivor. You know? You know what I hate most? This guy Miller thought the whole thing was over and done with *and the sonofabitch wanted to write me a check!*"

No doubt lots of winged creatures were disturbed by that in their roosting. Frogs obviously were squelched and heard to slip under cover.

"So it was time I took this Miller down some," Milo continues, "just for the worthless shitsucker he was. For that alone, mind you, but add to that this guy's notion of recompensing me for cleaning up the river! Something about the way he was dressed, besides . . . but worse, him wearing his checkbook. It made me have to . . ."

"Have to what?"

"What do you think?"

"How should I know?"

"Along those exact lines, Dean, buddy. Those lines exactly. See, I didn't have it yet either. But so far the man was making it easy—climbing in, letting me drive around and think about it. 'I want to pay you something for your trouble,' he says. I gave him a long look, took the whole man in; he had this safari outfit on: ironed, creased, pockets all over everywhere. Maybe he was dirtied a little with the sweat rings but he was keeping up pretty good with his roll-on. There was a facial scar, something from a golf accident perhaps. Sleazy little silver mustache. Overall, he looked like one of those military despots down in Latin America. And he goes and pulls a checkbook on me for smugness: 'Here,' he says, 'let me pay you something for your trouble.' But Milo here was keeping his own counsel. 'Not me,' I told him. 'I fetched up your nephew, yes, but put that away. I'm not kidding.' The man was making my intestines react. I tell you, I had thoughts of running him through my safety glass . . .

"What's wrong here!" Milo took a turn.

"What?" I say.

"Huh?" Milo is temporarily disoriented. "Why," he says, "do I feel like I'm in a closet?"

"Must be . . ." But I let it hang. I'm not about to pose that probability again.

After a while Milo kicks back in, as if there'd been no closet: "Now here's when I heard the voice," he says, "not to be kinky and unnatural. It said to me, Do not, for example, drive upstream and push the bastard in so you can watch him flounder. Don't be stupid, it said, be propi . . . propish . . . be just. Think. Go for your maximum rehabilitation, this voice was telling me, but no death, no brain damage. Leave the memory functions alone, it said."

"A voice told you that."

"Call it what you will. It said, Do not haul his sleazy ass into that nearby wood and cream it to a tree. Nothing like that."

"Admit it," I say, "you plain couldn't do it. You're a good hater, Milo, but you couldn't keep it fresh forever and it slipped away. The idea of murder, it was too much for you. Hell, I can't even see my hand in front of my face and I can see right through you."

"You keep looking for your hand, queen, and leave me the hell out of it. Now I was umpire of this one and it was, it was . . . sensible, that's all it was. It's the memory, see. It's the memory in trouble. That's where you exact the best justice, the longest. Take our Dad. Dad's mind was in it deep."

"I thought we were leaving Dad out of this."

"Look what it did to him. Made him do it in with a bottle of cocksucking vodka and a sweeper hose. You think that was it, what hurt him? The bottle and the sweeper hose? Hey, the clincher, buddy, was his memory in constant deep, is what it was."

I neglected to mention: this is the one that keeps Milo down. Makes Milo want to go into it, whenever he gets the magnitude in him. The big one, Dad's crossing over to the other side when my brother and I were thirteen and twelve. Fastened Mom's sweeper thing to the exhaust on our family station wagon. It was no accident, Milo is trying to say.

"I understand," I say, "but you're losing the thread. Don't drop the thread now. Why are you crying, Milo?"

"I don't know. I don't, Dean. Maybe it's this lousy swill sitting on my belly. I don't know. Good Christ, don't ever let me lick the foam off another warm one. This is the last there is. It's nasty. It is. But it's going to get me there yet.

"What's that?" Milo fires up a match. Then he touches off the whole book. He slices the big torch through the air in front of his face. "What *was* that!"

"Look at you," I say. "The shit's got you between the eyes. It's got you down to sobbing and hallucination now. Someday, Milo, it's going to soak you to where you'll quit doing this to yourself."

The fire burns down to his fingertips. He drops it

without pain. "Lord, I'm almost at the end. Let me go on."

"Well, just go on then."

"Let me. For my brother here believes I'm making all the mistakes he's finished making. Thinks I've lost it."

"You have."

"Thinks I hate through the head and love through the balls, just because it's what *he's* used to doing. Thinks he's outgrown our Dad and all of it. But I ain't lost it yet."

"I love you, Milo, but you have. You've had it. Every day you've had it."

"I love *you*. I *love* you, Dean. Thing is . . . thing is, I haven't had my vitamins today. Maybe I need to take out and dust off my tongue a little, too, but otherwise I'm right here. I can see my way through this clean. Let me talk. I've got what's-his-name, Miller, over in the seat trying to write. I'm racing us through the curves, like this. Why? Because the fucking lawyer's got it all down, all but my last name, and he's still trying to write after I told him to quit."

"Lawyer?"

"Shut up! Will you shut up? Throw me one of them smokes. Miller says, 'Now what's that last name, Milo?' And I says, 'Look, mister,' I says, 'you don't know it but I just gave you the last chance you're getting and you threw it back. I was looking for some tenderness, mister. Right, tenderness. Something from here!' Now he gives me his attention on this because, see, I'm changing channels on him. He's still holding the checkbook on his knee, holding his nice fountain pen. I took it off him and threw it out my window: *whooooos*! The fountain pen: *whoooooosh*! He comes up looking like what-the-fuck. 'Let's just forget about your dollars,' I tell him, 'okay? For the fucking trouble your nephew caused,' I says, 'Okay?'

"So by now he's getting hip to our surroundings. He says, 'Hey, where are we?' He says, 'Say, this isn't the way back to Ambrose.' 'Sit still,' I says, 'Never mind about that. I want to talk about your nephew. Let's get back to that,' I says. 'Your nephew just died in a pretty ugly way back there and you were the agent of it.' 'Babababababababa,' the dude goes. 'Did you even look? That was two chances ago,' I tell him, 'but you missed again. You could've looked. It was supposed to cause a permanent change in you! It was supposed to make remorse part of your everyday memory. Because, you know what your problem is? It'll tell you: your heart. You have the worst kind. Goddamit, you need a better one!' "

"Hold it a minute," I interrupt. "Just what are you getting all up and righteous about? I mean, Miller didn't *push* the kid in, did he? The kid didn't just *jump* in that hole."

"He calls me boy. He says, 'You know what your problem is, boy? You're in the wrong line of work. Can't take it, boy. Too soft. Too soft!' 'Wrong,' I says, 'mine is I have this memory, see. I have been cursed with the memory that won't cut anything loose, and the minutiae of what you did back there are burning into it already. Here,' I says, 'I'll give you a for-instance. A person such as your nephew there runs out of air, their blood turns blue. That's a familiar one now. I had my old man turn blue. I had my second wife turn blue on me, mister. Eyes down in the soup just like your kiddy there, except, turn them over and they're staring full at you, full of great big surprise. It's hard to watch, like you're looking in on something personal. Private.

" 'See, as it happens,' I tell him, 'I made me this family of daughters. This was during Vietnam, where most of my buddies had to go but I didn't. I drew the high number, I went to college. But they're in the custody of my first wife now, my girls are. Her and her rich stud farmer husband . . .' Toss me the matches, will you?"

I hand him my lighter and implore him, "Could you get back on the track?"

"So I says to him, 'I have to sneak looks if I want to see my own children. Because the law has made me a shame and a disgrace to my very own two daughters, Daph and Claude. They're the most beautiful little things. I made them. I love them. The point is,' I says to him, 'do you know why I love them? Because they might turn blue, Miller. Do you know what I'm saying? People I love, they have a habit of turning blue!

" 'Now, look at it this way. You could be driving up my babies' lane someday, Miller, and run my kids over; and I wouldn't want to hear that you did that. I'll be equally damned if I'd ever want to hear you say it served my kids right for crossing the road while you were using it. I would never *ever* want to hear you say, What the fuck, those kids were not going to live forever!' "

Milo is crying again, the kind of cry that squeezes your lungs empty, making the noises of chills and fornication. He keeps the nose drip from getting away.

" 'Hey, Miller! Maybe you'd like to hear a funny scatological joke, Miller. Now this concerns my second ex, the one that ODed in the tub. All right, she had her, what you call, modern-day depression to deal with. Maybe she was dead into chewing on her Valium for remedy. Maybe, all right, she had a little bit of the lesbian to her besides, but she had brains, like me, and you can love that. What's the difference? She exed herself out . . . in the bathtub.' "

"Scatological," I remind.

"But the scatological part: 'when I lifted her up out of there, see, she messed all down her legs and my legs both. Your nephew, he blew his business in his pants. There it is if you want to know. Now who ever said if there was but one thing left to say it had to be said with any dignity? You get it, Miller? That's the joke. Kind of exceeds the language thing, wouldn't you say? See, it's right here in my memory. Whoops, no, here it is on my hands. Still fresh. Here, wanna smell?'

"Miller says no he didn't. He says, 'Was there supposed to be something funny there?' I says, 'If you think monkeys are funny.' "

Milo finds a neat place here to break off and light his cigarette. He goes on:

"All right, now we're just about there. I'm driving us out on Big Pine now. Nothing out here but a couple hunting cabins and lily ponds and that old coal mine. Here's a place—I don't have to tell you, I know this county inside out—and here's a place you could commit any sort of violent crime there is and get away with it, because there's nobody around. Nobody. And now's when I pulled over and told him to get out. I told him, I says, 'I sure hope you had your supper, because you're walking.' Did I mention is was good and dark by now, Dean? I can still see it perfectly, him sitting there handing me all kinds of *are you fucking* . . . So I told him he could take his shoes and socks off too, before he got out and walked back to town. Of course, being the clever attorney he comes out with all his flashiest legalese, and I says, 'Why, sue me then. You can think about the charges along with what else we've been talking about while you're walking. And if you don't think I'm being soft enough,' I says, 'then I'll give you a choice: you can either walk down that road there or you can bleed your way home in my vehicle.' "

I look over, listen. "That's it?"

"That's it. Think it was good enough?"

"I think it was just right."

"Some sporty vignette, huh?"

"Just right. Can we go now?"

"Somewhere down the road I did throw out his shoes and socks for him."

"That was more than decent."

Talking to Milo has been just like having one long, long-distance phone conversation in the woods, in the dark. You have the night sounds, the smells of root and mud. The moon is whole. It looks greasy. Going to be a hot one tomorrow. There's an owl someplace, and another owl somewhere else. The river is close by, sluicing by with the sign hanging over it, the moon hanging over that. My brother hits the ground with his whole drunk body. "Dean?" I hear.

"What is it," I say.

He says, "I'm high now."

PART TWO

PART TWO

I.

AFTER WAKING UP around noon to a strangle of floral sheets about my knees and a shortness of breath, I made the discovery that Mom's cat Just Bill was couched in feckless comfort over my abdomen, wearing the cunning smile that accompanies dreaming. Speaking of dreams, I was into a good one before having to come out of it and fight the hot, recumbent animal off me and get down here to where I can use the toilet.

In certain ways this vacation has me on a calm footing; it has its better moments, like the weather, which is mid-August and superb. Take my sleeping in like this, a thing I haven't had much of since the work week became ritual. But lately I'm having the blissful sleep of the fourteen-year-old me. Ample sleep seems to be making my bowels come back. I get to enjoy the smell and thunder of myself first thing in the day. The punctual cleansing you hear about.

Better still is this new power of dream recall. What happened in this one was I was pregnant. Feeling down around my tummy, what should have been a flat, somewhat washboardlike affair, turned out to be a great dome bulging into my lap. I gathered it up making a loud to-do: "Quick! I'm about to give birth to some damn thing! It's right here kicking me!" The *Twilight Zone* music came on. Wind and sight flew out of me. I went to faint . . . and then to find out it's only this sonofabitch cat.

* * *

I've been walking the downstairs looking around. The house of my birth, where I grew up learning my personality. Yet there's nothing much of the soddened part, which is my Dad, to dwell on—Jane, my mother, had a healthy way of moving back to square one: of storing the memory but sundering the old man's things.

What's here is the rugs, the woodwork, the marble, lamps, curtains, pillows, candles, clocks, the old paintings that have shadows in them, the frames.

Elegant stuff at a minimum.

I'm glad to see Mom doesn't keep the house of a retired lady and widow. Doesn't put herself in the chair to make afghans and look at TV, her slippered foot patting over the rag rug as if waiting for the stroke or heart attack.

There are all imaginable houseplants. The plants were telling me something, what with their branches and leaves bending. It's not like Jane to neglect her plants. So I went around giving their pots a drink sweetened with plant food and did a little light misting and pruning, turned their shady sides to the window. Even gave talking to them a chance, which is what Mom does, with flowers, cats, all the little people. But I sounded like a robot, like somebody's phone-answering machine.

In the kitchen was Mom's note, taped to her Mr. Coffee: COFFEE MADE. GONE TO DOCTOR. I put the doctor thing behind me and began scrambling some eggs.

Here are the eggs piled high on my plate, covered with some hollandaise I found refrigerating in a jar, toast on the burnt side, raspberries under honey, melon wedge, coffee, and juice. A Julia Child kind of breakfast. The whole thing out on the porch on a tray, along with one of the three to four packs of Camel Lights I have working and *The Ambrose Daily* from yesterday evening.

I read here on page one where Jerry Falwell was

speaking to the "I Love America" rally up at Cincinnati. Jerry expected a massive turnout, it says, but a big storm blew in, driving back the greater segment of his flock and knocking over his $75,000 TV camera. The Reverend was all set up to show the viewers a multitude like they get at these big rock festivals, but only the die-hards of his Majority and a few protesters turned out. The protest, says the news wire, was over Jerry's new crusade against the AIDS carrier. "We, as Christians, ought to save the homosexual from himself by looking upon him as Moral Pervert. If America only knew," says Jerry, "the filthy and bloody, perverted acts that go on—not just the oral sex, but filthy and bloody . . ."

But forget that for now. An awful noise is being made somewhere in our yard.

A boy in his late teens with next to nothing on is out there cutting our grass. I watch him shave a halo around the birdbath and make an aisle straight for me. Here he is, pushing his flagrant appliance alongside my porch. If not for this screen I could knock him down for being such a nuisance.

But on second thought why not gaze a bit at the healthy lad.

Most if not all is deeply red, burnished, with the deeper brick color to his cheeks. The eyes hiding under the visor of his baseball cap, which is molded in that cocky tubular way, for optimum brow- and eye-shade; a skinny Walkman headset clamped over the hat, fixed into the ears, while the little tape box rides the trim waist of the boy's athletic shorts.

Except for the shorts—immodest ones at that—the pair of grassed up Nikes and hat, the rest is out there in plain view: a sinewy arrangement of leg, hip, shoulder, torso, rib section. Close in sleekness and bearing to the yearlings I used to watch my ex-sister-in-law Pat coax into being thoroughbred racehorses. All physical features italicized in sweat, toiling out there in the sun.

* * *

Mom just popped in, then popped out again. While she was here I pointed out the golden thing she was retaining for groundskeeping.

"What *about* him?" she said.

"Just curious."

"Well, he's one of those trouble boys they farm out to the country in the summer. He's from Boston. Father Labounty's got him. He asked if we couldn't give the boy some work to do for his spending money."

Sandy Labounty is the priest at our Episcopal church. A saint almost, and friend of the family. An ex-drunk, like me.

She added of the savory teen, "Kinda handsome, isn't he?"

"Hadn't noticed."

Jane handed me a ten to pay him with.

"Are you serious?" I said. "This ain't shit for a job that size."

"We're not supposed to pay him a decent wage. He'll spend it on dope, which Sandy says he's just liable to do."

Jane saw that I was wearing my favorite underpants only, underneath my newspaper. She asked, before leaving, "Doesn't anyone wear clothing anymore?"

That's okay. When the boy came to get his reward I was finished reading. I stood up with the money. Asked whether he would care to double it.

You would?

Best keep up our life insurance.

WE'RE IN MAUREEN'S Toyota wagon—me, Maureen, her son Ryan, a kid of two and a half who's stomping heels all over the backseat as if needing a place to tinkle. We're headed west on 664 towards the lake, all dressed down for a swim.

No doubt Maureen chose the one-piece suit to go over her extra figure, which began two and a half years ago when she becamed stalled in the critical phase of having Ryan. It took the surgeons over a day of stretching Maureen with their dilation tool and finally going in with the incision, and it about killed her. Funny how, narrowly coming back from this kind of thing, a mother often will cherish the little being she's made all the more.

Maureen grew up on a farm out here on a road someplace, with five or six brothers and everything else. We went all the way to graduation in the same high school, Maureen and I, although we didn't realize it until later, when we met. The reason being that the kids of my crowd—who woke up in our big neighborhood homes and walked the hill to school, who were turning to drugs and trying to show facial hair, who were growing ebullient in the anti-Vietnam thing—we didn't traffic with Country: a sort known to use the school busses that pulled in behind the track and football field. For a few years Maureen was married to one of us: Monroe, a grievous abuser of accelerating substances, and violent. Monroe did an eventual number on Maureen's head, then lit out for Miami, toward almost certain prosecution in the serious drug trade. But Maureen bounced back and married a decent jock type, a county surveyor, like Thoreau, and he's still good to her. Even gave her a new house back on some lonesome real estate. Now Maureen's back to being a country girl.

She has a tape going that might better appeal to the individuals in the beer commercials that haven't had enough good nooky since turning ugly and starting to drive semi-truck than it does me. She unplugs her cigarette lighter, shakes it at the sky. She says, "Watch. Soon as we're out here the sun'll go back. It always does that on me." She touches off her mentholated 100 and breathes in the cool.

The weather's peaking to three digits. Things before us ripple in heat mirage. I've got sweat in my ears; there are drops of it swimming inside my sunglass rims. Mix in the flying dust of all these coal trucks and it's the kind of oppressive that makes you sleepy and pretty dull conversation. This because Maureen's AC is busted, as happens with most extras once you pass warranty.

But Ambrose has her lake. Once you drive beyond these trailer parks and highway overpass and get to the end of this long hill it's two miles of manmade fishing hole in the shape of a boomerang: There's a crescent of sand and weeds down at the end they call a beach, with a graded hillock next-door and stratum of gravel for parking.

We find a space near the refreshment stand. While I haul the two chaises out the rear, Maureen manages her big canvas bag and little boy and all his water things—bucket, shovel, and blowup horsey—and heads over to the counter for eats.

In the water are 150 children in buoyant motion. A few notable adults up here on the sand, too, such as on the yellow towel I just passed, stretching out his stomach: the kind water wouldn't roll off of. Maureen and I settle our chairs into the oozy slip where lake meet sand, footrests at ease, and fan our toes in the mild water, which passes a certain odor of pee-pee and Band-Aids. So far the sun is still with us and we're basted for a #6 tan.

"Are you still off the drinking, Dean?"

"Um hmm."

"You do look about fifty times better."

"Thanks."

We already talked about what I do in Louisiana, which is just a job and nothing much else, and what Maureen does, which is being a secretary to the commissioners upstairs at the county courthouse. And now we're having a quiet minute taking the sun. For no good reason I close my eyes and think of the heat in Mexico—the wetter yellow of the Baja sunlight, the green it makes in the blue shoals off Hermosillo; the fish blazing under your snorkle mask like one of those extravagant video games without all the noise; the caramel smell of the hills; the redder dust . . .

But she wants me for something else.

"Now someone ought to get your brother to try it," Maureen says.

"What."

"I saw him last Thursday, and you know it was like the scare of God was put in him. Have you seen?"

"Some. He's sleeping under the stars, in Janie's back yard."

"All wired up and gritty. He looks the way Kurt used to get." That's Monroe, the husband who opened up Maureen's eye and left a scar under it and changed her smile. "Not that it's any of my affairs," says Maureen, "but I said, 'That man is in for the same kind of trouble. He's scary.' "

"So much of that might be true," I say. "He's got himself dispossessed again recently."

"I don't know, he looks more than depressed to me."

"No, kicked out. Velda turned him out of their trailer, for being a little vicious, I guess."

"Probably the sweetest thing she ever done for him," Maureen says, "knowing her. Of course I had figured something had come between those two, since I was all the time seeing Velda at the courthouse anymore. You know, she'll go right by and not even speak, not that I give a flying you-know-what. So don't speak to me, bitch, see if I care. I hope Milo's not depressed over that woman. I mean it. Really. He can't be that hard up—oooh, look!"

I open my eyes.

Maureen has her Instamatic poised over Ryan as he paddles by our ankles, plastic float humping up behind. She gets a snapshot of him grinning and squirting a mouthful of lake. "Don't you go and swallow that, Ryan Michael! No. PTAAH—filthy!" But Maureen packs her camera away looking almost teary with affection and proud over having this family with all its needing and inconvenience.

Looking over here again, she says, "No kidding, Dean, you *do* look good."

"Think so?"

"So does every other girl here." She has to add, "It's too bad you have to be gay."

I steer us off that subject. "What's that about Velda? What did you say Velda was up to at the courthouse?"

"I'd think filing, wouldn't you?"

"I understand she's getting up something prettier than just a divorce."

"Come to think of it," says Maureen, "it's not Mrs. Dix's office (she's Domestic) you'll see her come from, it's the prosecutor's."

"County prosecutor. That sounds more like it. That's Voit, isn't it?"

"Voit died of his cancer, finally."

Right. Voit had him a slow-burning cancer. "That's a pity."

"Only in his early forties too. The commissioners appointed them this new guy, from St. Louis or somewhere."

There went the fourth one I've seen stroll by. They're young ones, a lot younger and smaller than Maureen, yet they are mothers, bearing between navel and bathing-suit bottom the silvery suture of knife damage. Half child, half mother, with teeth disintegrating. Six pounds of potatoes in a five-pound sack . . . *"What? Did you say St. Louis?"*

"Yeah, his name's—"

"Don't tell me. Miller. Right?"

"Otto Miller. How'd you know that?"

"Otto. Please."

III.

I'M ABOUT TO come! Jesus, the sudden rising! Like the warm complaint of tears rising in the throat. The boy from a few days ago, Simon, has his throat around my whole thing. That's fine, but don't make me come, it's too soon yet! To part with it now would be shameful, pretty much amount to impotence, according to those two in their sex study. I have to look over there and bite down on my upper arm, near to breaking the skin, just to fight back the end. Simon, you deliver a beautiful trace of teeth. But easy does it, Simon, don't chew. Not too much teeth!

It works. Three minutes later I'm still here.

I'm good for another ten, so, resting back on the moss, I have Simon get on my ribs, knees spread to the ground. After some time on him my eye wanders upward, thinking to catch Simon working on his own arm a little. Instead there are the wide brown eyes of trust, patience, casting over the treetops somewhere. Giving over to meditation!

Here are my wet eyes from so much mauling at the back of the throat.

We're using the woods out back of Father Labounty's for this. I thought I knew it by heart here, but Simon couldn't wait to talk about dominant trees, the genus and classifications of things. It turns out Simon knows everything about ecosystems. He went out to the tree we're under and began foraging around the base, sifting through the mulch and twigs. He came up with a handful of dirty fur and mouse skeletons. What do you think about that? Spit up by an owl way up in those branches! We sat down and Simon pulled something from his pocket and handed it to me. Of all the ill-sorted things, it was a page of male smut from one of those triple-X faggot publications. Two males, about Simon's age, photographed in the setting of nature, somewhat as here, doing about the same as now.

One of them *was* Simon! "Sorry, I'm not very impressed with this," I had to tell him.

"It pays pretty good," he said, seeing I was frowning at his picture. "Well, some boys just like to rub their dicks together," Simon said.

"Come on my face," I tell him.

"What?!"

Simon's narrow hips, white where there isn't any tan, the abundant cadence—in-out–in—do it! Of course! Yes! Not being swallowed up by each other we'll check the spread of anything unwholesome, even deadly. Long as we don't ingest. "Come on my face. Do it!"

"Okay." Simon rears back where I can examine him and get ready.

What's this? He heaves forward lapping it not too gently alongside my face. Both sides!

The hips. The incredible bottom brushing over my chest . . .

That did it! That last thing took me over the line into climaxing all over Simon's back. I thought there'd be no stopping.

But then it did: *Don't* come on my face!

IV.

I WAS ABOUT to say, I haven't seen my brother in two days, but then I remembered this morning, before I was finished sleeping:

I was drinking again from a jug of Daniel's (my old favorite) when these giants the size of clouds came hulking over the horizon. It was one of those where your legs and your guts give out just as the giants are coming to snuff you. And then something was nudging me awake. It wasn't Just Bill.

In ten minutes I found myself facing Milo over our big wooden kitchen table. We had our hands playing with whatever there was while the birds were out there. So was the customary dew, I guess, lying around harsh and unbeauteous. Just like the face I was interrupted midsleep to climb down here and deal with. It was a vacancy, lines of distress running up and down like fingers, and the redness of bathing in sorrow.

And all he wanted was money!

"What for?"

"For my children's education."

"Be serious, goddamit, it's hardly even dawn yet."

"I am serious. For that and the vain hope of reconciling with my wife, which I believe is actually in the cards now."

"Your wife and that attorney have been seen together. I hear they're in sympathy against you."

"I'm not talking about that wife. That, what you hear,

is so much shit tossed between fools. I'm talking about my kids' mother."

"Yeah, well they're pulling a criminal case together."

"Who is?"

"Your current wife, Velda, and that lawyer you told me about. The one with the dead little nephew and the wild hair you placed up his ass."

"Shit tossed between fools. Tell me something I don't know, why don't you, like, how much money have you got."

Stravinsky was coming in over the college FM. It took me a while to figure out where the interference was coming from. It was some cracker pilot cruising his Cessna over the room; his motor was rubbing the bassoons and basses in Igor's ballet and the weird rumble in the air for a second made me think it was the giants, the ones of my dream, again. "For your hooch and drugs, right? For a lawyer? Maybe you need a color TV for your tent? Or I bet you have you a new, tent-sized wife out there already, right?"

"That's right. With sex down to here. Some young thing that does it too much. Gets you tired and ashamed of moaning after all the beauty. Now that you know, what can you front me? Mind you, to keep what you've got you've got to give it away. That's scripture."

It's pathetic. It is at least from your middle-class-morality point of view, the way my brother and I both fail in the relationship department. You hear about these bourgeois liberals in Boston and California adapting healthy relationships from their support groups and a reading list. And then you have the rest of us . . . "I'm not about to subsidize your next family."

"*Original* family."

"Forget it. Why don't you look into getting your job back? I don't see that you've got anything to laugh about." He was laughing. I told him I was going back to bed.

"Let's never mind that—I forget your sense of humor. Now I'm going to run it by you one last time. As much as I'm at liberty to reveal. This is merely an investment in my and my childrens' future, and if you choose to make it part of yours then that too. You don't have to. I'm not begging, understand, because I'll do this with or without you. I'm *allowing* you in, out of brotherly compassion, nothing more. Common consideration. This here's a low-risk, high-gain, legitimate—some would even say ethical—investment. You wouldn't want to know more for the sake of your big mouth. Whether you know it or not. Now how much have you got?"

I told him.

"Good, then I'll take five hundred."

"You're crazy!"

"I'm serious, and I'm not giving you too many more chances to do something right for a change. When did it ever cease to be in your own best interest to double your assets without lifting a finger?"

"Well . . ." I eyed him, a little more awake. "I might go in for the high-gain part," I said.

"Now you're talking. That's because you can vouch for my on-the-whole spotless winning record. Now I'd be prepared to pay say 10 to 15 percent over the dollar—"

"I thought you said double."

"Let's not be pigs about it, okay? I'm talking realistic. At the very least fifteen, all right? Probably more. I don't need to spell it out for you, where I got the free-enterprising knack, either. Because you know all that. You were my little brother. I don't have to."

Our daddy could have been filthy rich, what with his knack for changing modest money into a handsome sum. Mainly on the predictions of horseflesh, although there was also the money market, and the oil and gas. There are family photos of us standing behind a scrim of track dust on summer vacations, the old man's eyes fixed on the tote board and Milo counting out bills. From Kentucky on down the circuit. Rare moments when the pair of them would quit before losing it all back. On my dad's and twelve-year-old brother's system we drove a new Buick home from South Carolina in '62.

"When? I don't want to have to cash in my return ticket just to get by."

"Soon. You won't."

"All right then, but you'll have to wait here."

I went upstairs and came back down. I handed over five of the seven hundred I was worth.

"You love me," said Milo.

I went back to bed.

That was this morning.

V

BASICALLY, AFTER DOING it I feel pretty much my right self again. But once dressed and following the path to Sandy's the flying insects are back to swarming us—one of the truly annoying reverberations of nature. Maybe it's our smacking at them, or this terrible thirst, something, but Simon and I don't have much to say.

We step out of the lush part into a broad clearing of high weeds, sun bearing straight down and the grass odor sweetening over us in hot syrupy waves. A billion more bugs out here choiring like high-voltage wires. If you were unsure of getting relief someplace soon you'd have to give up right here and perish. You could be someplace like the Everglades or subtropics—the *African Queen*. Leeches clipping hold, malaria orbiting your head, you become illogical, delirious . . . But why think so, you're not. Only some sweat and a drowsy mood. In need, you feel, of a cool beverage and something to say.

In the nick of time there's a stream. Simon runs for it peeling off his shirt. Underneath it is the coloring hardly ever seen on a blond, enhanced overall with bones and slippery muscle. Tell you the truth, even having it to myself as I just did, beauty like this is painful to watch; it scares me simple!

Simon and I sit down together on the creek pebbles getting wet. I ask whether he would mind reaching into his Boston past for why he's in so much trouble. Besides slithering around naked, sucking and breeding in front of a camera, it seems he was arrested for selling it on the street. Reaching further back, he tells me of some Ginger person—glamorous drag queen and owner of a fashionable Beacon Hill condo—who found Simon hanging around the cruddy Combat Zone of Boston where she ran her disreputable lounge. Taken in for underage drinking and sent back to Youth Detention in the shabby precinct where he grew up, Simon came across Ginger's calling card. Next day Ginger was there in eyeglasses, handbag, the perfume of a sober lady. Credible stalwart relative of Simon. She took him fiercely by the wrist and conveyed him out to the street.

"Ginger, she was okay. She was good to me." Simon is watching the mud come up between his toes. "Maybe she was a little fucked up, and, like, sad, you know? But she was real kind. You should've seen her place too, antiques and all that shit. She like took me in and she never laid a hand on me neither. She got me working. And hey, I'm not ashamed of it neither."

"It's okay with me."

"There's guys that have a real need. They pay real money for it."

"That's true enough."

"So what. What do *you* do for money? I mean, what I mean is, there probably ain't that much difference, if you think about it."

"Probably not."

"Sometimes they aren't very nice. You know, kinky, all right?"

"What do you mean?"

Simon is looking at the water. The clear water's moving past and he just watches.

"So what happened?"

"So I did it for this guy, this cop, all right? This straight guy. The cocksucker puts his gun on me and makes me go down on him anyway."

"Jesus."

"It happened, all right? The cop says, 'Who cares about little faggots like you, anyway.' "

"Aw, come here."

We're back on the trail, single file, restored completely. "What did you say, Simon?"

"I said I want to do it with you again."

"That's nice . . ."

"Because I sort of get off on older guys."

"It's probably not very magnanimous of me, Simon, but I can't keep you like Ginger did—"

Simon wheels around and pulls up close to my face: "Who said I wanted that! Whatever that word fucking means, I take care of myself. I just like it with you, Dean. I like you because . . . you're nice."

There's this that Turgenev said: "There are touching situations from which one is nevertheless anxious to escape as soon as possible."

"Tell me how it is you know so much science," I say.

From here you see the tower on Sandy's rectory, medieval thing of black stone against the sky on the west ridge of town; Gothic, ivy-infested place that looks more like itself in a bad electrical storm. In any light handsomer than his Episcopal church down on Main.

Sanford Labounty's in there. Never have I loved a man more than Sandy, almost like God Almighty walking the planet again, never hurt a human that I know of except maybe back in Korea where he tried to kill from the tail of a B-29. But the wind and gunfire blew his eardrums, dropped his hearing below half. It cured him of soldiering.

I asked Sandy once what made him choose Christ over being the architect he practiced to become. He thought it was the war. Close enough to mortality that something like pure truth happened. He wouldn't elaborate, except to say, "Dean, God just came down to me like Pepto-Bismol."

I love the man more than my hideous life, but I don't want to see him now, I don't want him to know what Simon and I have been doing. I feel like I've broken every commandment and embarrassed myself by doing it over again without much shame.

He'll see it in the guilt and cynicism running off me.

Though my guess is, Sandy wouldn't mind as long as we weren't harming each other. But Sandy knows a side of me that gives whatever feels good a chance to get abusive. He is a man of industry, compassion, and so forth. But then again, even he has his fifteen Pepsis a day plus all the Chesterfields.

"Quit itching. You look like a monkey. I don't want Sandy—"

"I can't," Simon protests, "there's all kind of leaves and shit under my clothes."

The garden is heavy into bloom, thanks to Simon. His orchids, ripe and exotic, come out to your nostrils from a hundred feet. Sandy is out there and we call from a fair distance. He straightens up from the potting table, takes a studied look at his slate roof, then returns to pencil and protractor and marks a big diagram.

"What's all this, Doctor?"

Here is Sandy, at almost seventy still tall in the black outfit and collar of the Church. We light cigarettes. With a hand over my shoulder Sandy tells me about putting his draft of solar installations before the diocese.

He's measured inside and out, made computations on his home terminal as to compass point exposures, the going cost of solar versus expenses in the long run. Sandy talks about the photovoltaic array, the sun space, and adding south glass for passive gain. That, explains Sandy, coupled with the internal thermal mass, the domestic

water collectors, the sublevel heat sink will virtually elim-
inate utility bills. "Of course, the whole kit and caboodle
is probably wishful thinking. Well, what the hell do you
think, Dean?"

I put aside the reading. This interests me about as
much as a tax form. "You bet. Fascinating stuff. Why so
long getting around to it?"

"Right. Absolutely," says Sandy, "and I have an answer for you, Dean, though you may not realize you
were fishing for one." Sandy pauses a moment to reflect.
His clear old eyes cast about the town. "You take my
flock here. A modest congregation, certainly, yet one
that I feel I have contributed to nurturing, sharpening
over the years, over thirty in fact, into a few sufficiently
stainless Christians. Of course I am thankful, albeit swollen
with pride . . . But only now that His work and I have
presently idled am I giving myself a short vacation in
which to harness some sun—and to perhaps dip into
some of my old pagan masterpieces, such as Joyce,
Proust."

"Like hell!" Simon is kneeling down weeding a cluster
of delphiniums. "Get off it. He won't be around for none
of this solar stuff because he's quitting. He's moving,
aren't you? To Florida."

"Simon," the Father says, "would you kindly go find
us all a Pepsi?"

Instead Simon fetches the hose. He wags mist over
some shrimp pink flowers, clamorous in voice to get
through Sandy's deafness: "I'm only telling him because
you're standing there shitting him! You're supposed to
be a priest! Why don't you tell him the truth?"

"Profundo!" Sandy wears the hailing smile. "Well done.
Did you hear that? I tell you we should all take example
to be as forthright as this young man. Simon is a power
of example to me. By God, he is! All right, without the
prevaricating then, Labounty here has turned into . . .

into an old codger, if you will. He is doing, inevitably, predictably, things an old codger will do. Take this: Thursday, I believe it was, I awoke unable to find my eyeglasses. And where do you suppose they turned up? *In the icebox!* Hell's bells, I'll be hanging my shoes in the pantry before long!"

"Sandy, I've never heard you complain for yourself in my life."

He takes a serious turn. "My stomach's had it. I'm told it's not coming back. I'll be on drugs, probably have surgery. Blow it, I'm too old *not* to complain. I tell you, Dean, I've done the hospices. I've seen the final ones, watched them lie there and . . . Damn it, I'm going to be the meanest old sonofabitch you ever saw! Yes, and I've even considered Florida."

"Good for you," I say. "Move to Florida then. Read Joyce till you're tapioca."

"Fuck yourself!" Simon chokes off the nozzle. He searches deliberately down his pants after organic deposit. "I'm going in there and take a shower."

We watch him go.

"Fine weather we're having," says Sandy.

"He has something of a personal hair up his ass."

"He gets excited," Sandy informs me, "He gets very attached to certain people. Kindness of strangers and all that . . . Why don't you go see him. Give him some faith, Dean. I seem to be all out of faith today."

VI

IT'S SEVEN WHEN I get home. Milo's kids are there, Daphne and Claudette. They're lobbing lawn darts around back.

I watch from the stoop.

The younger one, Claude, just tossed her dart and then pranced after it weightless as a bird.

They're barefoot and their legs under the short jumpers are like clean, white twigs bending stiffly, with grassy bulbs of knee in the middle.

Claude's dart flopped on the grass short of the orange plastic hoop she was aiming for. It's Daphne's turn but her sister's still dancing around the target area; she raises the hoop and drops it over her dart. "I win! I win! I win! I win!"

"No sir, you have to stick. You didn't even stick!" Daph is shaking the metal spike of her dart in a menacing way.

Megaphoning my hands, I intervene: "Cheaters never win!"

Claude gives me the tip of her pink tongue and a vulgar jut with the hip.

Bending way over I catch a hug from the older one. Meanwhile Claudette circles around straight-arming my butt and thigh.

I move on in the direction of their dad.

Milo is out by the shed finishing the wax job on his pickup, and I'm thinking: Isn't it nice to have us back, young and old, in the yard safe and sound and doing these things again?

Behind me the girls streak in and out of Milo's tent. Above me I hear, "You'll be glad to see I've made some improvements." He is atop the cab taking a soft rag with Windex to his alarm beacon. He is better looking somehow, shaved and less dissipated. "My children? My job? I have them back."

"I'm glad of it. Looks like you've worked some sort of miracle. Their mother must be relenting."

"Their mother was never *un*relenting."

"Does this mean you're their father again?"

"I have them for the night. On approval, you might say. Pat is very busy tonight."

"What did you do, rent them?"

He breaks up a virorous rubbing to contemplate his glistening red bubble. "What's that supposed to mean?"

"Just wondering. Wondering what became of my money."

"Money?"

"That you wheedled out of me this very morning to make us a nice premium off of. I'm not dreaming; I've overruled dreaming because I checked upstairs and it's sure enough gone."

"Well, what of it?"

"I was just wondering, seeing these improvements and all, just how it was being managed."

"Dean, buddy, let me tell you something."

"I would appreciate it if you did."

"Having your little bit of cash in my pocket inspires me to great moments of confidence. Now there's most of how this recovery came about, and I have no one but you to thank for it. So let me hasten that I will be forever grateful—"

"Yeah, well I was kind of hoping to be grateful to you. Remember?"

"Then my advice to you is to not be getting your panties all in a wad. Because what is passed from your particular realm of business has passed into mine. Understand?"

"If by that you mean I'm still above bankruptcy—"

"By that I mean that you, Dean, should summon up the proper attitude here: Treat that money like it don't exist. Okay? Then we'll all be better off. Because, matter of fact, Dean, it's out of my hands now too."

"*What!* I thought you said it was in your—"

"Oh, but I'm vigilant, vigilant as hell, don't you worry. Enough for the both of us, I assure you. Only I have mastered the proper attitude and that makes all the difference. Truth is, Dean, there are many other investors, like yourself, involved here, only they have faith where you have none. And you know what the Bible teaches us about—"

"Goddamit, who's got my money!"

Here Milo rotates his head, does a privacy check over both shoulders, sets us a lower tone. "My wife."

"*Velda!*"

"Hush up. No. Pat."

"What the hell's Pat doing with it?"

"I'm not at liberty—"

"*Tell.*"

"All right. I'll tell you some of it. And mind you this is not to reach the ears of Mom or my children or anyone else. You promise?"

"I promise. What."

"Well, to begin with, it might just be that my kids and their mother are getting another chance with me . . ."

"Keep going."

"And you ought to see some proof of it this evening—"

"*Daddy!*" Milo's daughters are pointing towards the side of the house, to the carport and Jane's Fiat. "Uncle

Dean! Daddy! Look!" Giggling but pointing hard. At what is not clear.

Looking closer, we're in time to catch the last of Jane's leg, in powder blue stretchies, a bare ankle, then a canvas shoe, slip inside the trunk. Her hand brings the lid to a close.

On the ground are her five grocery sacks.

"I wasn't going to let it catch. For goodness sake how stupid do you think I am? And thrash around in here like a hen stuck in a barrel?"

"Stand up out of there!" Milo's order.

We're all flanking the bumper, however. Not an opening for her to breach if she wanted to.

"If you're not the stupidest woman! Explain this."

Collecting her thoughts, Jane says, "I was just thinking —as I was watching the grocery boy load up my trunk, I got to wondering . . ."

"So when did they start serving Kentucky distilled in the grocery?"

"A fine one to talk of improbable thirst," I observe. "Hark at you."

"Dad? What's Mimi doing in the trunk?"

". . . whether or not it would hold me. Well, is somebody going to help me out or do I have to sprawl and break my hip?"

"Don't touch her!" says Milo.

Nobody does.

"All right, look." Mother sits up. She spreads her chest and becomes steadfast. "I may not be around here forever. In fact let's say that I suspect I won't be. All of you had just better get used to the idea. And when it comes time that I'm not, I have made arrangments that I am to be taken away and disposed of. I will not give another red cent to an undertaker, as you both know. I will be cremated at the lowest possible expense. Furthermore, after thinking it over, I realize that you, Milo, will probably be the one who has to handle me. Now it won't be very pleasant packing me into the back of your truck, not to mention hygienic, unless you had me wrapped in polyethylene and bound with twine, in which case I should think you would be too sick to drive—"

"You're plain drunk," I say.

"So that leaves my car. Are you going to want to ride me in the backseat? I should think not . . ."

"Stinking drunk!" I say.

"I'm no such thing. I had one at Evie's, but I'm fine, except that anymore life tends to turn my stomach. At any rate, that left only my trunk. All I needed was to see that I could fit, and I can. So that's that. Now."

"Hear that, kids? This is what your grown-up Mimi will do for attention." Milo cracks his knuckles very close to our mother's face; he digs them back into his elbows. He is not looking at his children when he tells them: "Go play. I'm going to be mean to your grandmother."

"No."

"No."

"Very well then, suppose, Mimi, Mother, you tell us just exactly what the fuck you think you're doing!"

"Doing? What I would *like* to be doing is getting supper. I hadn't intended on being in here the duration of the evening. These kids are starved. I bought SpagettiOs for them, meat for us. I have 9 Lives for Bill. He gets 9 Lives exclusively. Will you remember that? Now, if someone will carry in those—"

"Don't touch them!"

"I will not be terrorized!"

When Milo gets seriously angered you will see his upper lip curl. His color climbs. He disperses heat. His eyes go athwart.

We have been observing a silence.

"I don't see what you're so upset about."

"Shut up! From what you're saying I can intuit what you're saying. You're saying you intend to kill yourself. In plain English, suicide! A coward, the same as your husband!"

"That's right," I take over. "Why, what's there to be upset by indeed? A parent of this family getting drunk in the afternoon and diddling with the family vehicle? Nothing to be upset about."

"For the last time, I'm not drunk! And I've told you to not talk disrespectfully of your father."

"I'm confiscating your sweeper hose," Milo says, "I'll tell you right now. At least Dad didn't wave the thing around the backyard like some sort of flag. This was your big mistake, this was. Your husband would have said so. Not only that, he would have made you sleep in there."

Mom starts to cry.

"Do you think," says Milo, "that just when I was getting reinstated as father and fireman and hadn't had a drink all the goddamn weekend, I needed this horseshit to deal with? No. I need a drink."

My nieces are taking part in the blubbering also.

If there's a thing I cannot bear it's to see my mother cry.

Milo takes one arm and I take the other.

NOBODY ATE MUCH except the kids, and they're out in the night. Mom cleared things away and she's been facing the window over the faucets. Still snivelling from before. A sigh blows through her. And then Milo speaks from his tipped back chair, bare feet reaching the tabletop:

"Stare long enough it'll disappear."

His Plectron is back with him—the walky-talky affair with the string of red blipping lights that firemen carry around to relay each other with.

When he gets nothing he says, "No, what it is is you're just afraid to turn around here and look at us."

"You're both staring me in the back and I know it. I can feel it." Mom is sipping whiskey from a teacup. Limoges. You can hear her swallowing. "Exactly the way your father used to," she says, "whenever we quarreled."

Says my brother while pouring another over his same ice, "More dirt on the family skeleton?"

"I hate it. You'd think I wasn't worth an argument. Do I give that impression? That I'm to be stared at instead of talked to? I must."

She is wearing a sleeveless pullover. Her drinking arm is fawny with freckles and waddles a little when raising her cup. My arm still has the teeth marks probably. "It's what it sometimes takes," I say.

"Well it's purgatory and I wish you'd quit. You can see it's not producing anything."

"You could always kill youself," offers Milo.

"Yeah, you could."

"Yes. I could."

"Wouldn't have to deal with any of it that way."

"That suits me."

"Of course we could try and talk you out of it, too." Milo's on maybe his fifth or sixth, holding them pretty nicely so far.

"No. I wish you wouldn't."

"Come on, Dean, she wants us to talk her out of it."

"Don't try to make me look silly, you two. We're beyond that."

"I thought you wanted an argument."

"Not over that. I'll . . . discuss it."

"All right, we'll discuss it," he says. "Let's look the situation over. Now here you are, a grandmother, a mother—hale and firm. Hell, it's past a decade since you've had a cough."

I just remembered her note of the other day. Plus something that Labounty just let me in on. "She was at the doctor's the other day . . ."

"Shut up." He lights up and continues. "All right, you got the big house here on the nice, leafy street. Look at this kitchen. It's got the wooden walls and cabinets, all warm and buttery in the lamplight. You got the dish-towel in your hand. You got me and Dean and such as it is we all got each other. A bottle on the table. Now there's people that don't have a rat's ass, and you're complaining. You ought to be happy."

"Ha!"

"You should look forward to living it out in relative comfort," he says.

She says, her head nodding affirmation false and hard, "I'll tell you something you don't know. When *my* mother finally went she was way past comfort. As was I. Mom started on the downside of comfort about the time she started 'living it out,' as you call it. It was Mother still, but mostly it wasn't. Mother was dead, only aboveground. Who knows comfortable when they're like that? I knew what comfortable was, and that was not comfortable. Are you starting to get the drift of what I'm saying? You don't just drop someone like that behind the couch! Now can you blame me for not wanting to burden *my* children with my dribbly bowels and my feeble intellect?"

"Three hearty cheers for your good intentions," Milo says. "The road to hell is paved with—"

"That I will not discuss."

"Well," I say, "the suicide part excepted, this is the same load of crap I was just getting from Father Labounty."

"You saw him?"

"And he saw you. At the clinic yesterday. Said it was pretty queer."

"I told Sandy that if he's going to retire I wish he'd wait and do my funeral first. What's wrong with that?"

"There–won't–be–any–corpse–there," says Milo.

"I told him he did a lovely job with your father's. Of course they were such good friends. Anyone would want as much for their funeral."

"You're an embarrassment, Ma."

"Anyway, he's the only clergy I know. Although I now have my doubts about him—I trusted him to keep this in."

It's impossible to keep myself from laughing; therefore I don't. "I don't think anyone's taking this quite the way you want, Mother," I say.

Now she's pretending heedlessness, gazing on something out there—a pair of blinking lightning bugs on the other side of the glass, the moon. Who knows?

"Hey, are you still here?"

"You know what Father Labounty told me?" she says. "This was a long time ago. He told me this when your father died. He said the suicide is innocent. He's helpless and hopeless and innocent. He said that suicide had its own patron saint, sort of like a Gabriel fella, that comes down and looks at these empty people and he takes them by the hand and looks straight into innocence itself, with all the trouble and tribulation stripped out. He said it wasn't exactly a church idea, that he got it from some big long poem. But he said it's as much worth believing as all that retribution the Romans believe in. It's funny," she says, stretching now to the enigmatic, "after you spend your whole life wondering what it's like . . ."

"You're empty," says Milo. "Let me fix you one."

"That's what accounts for most of it, I bet," she says.

"Well, maybe it'll rearrange your thinking, once it gets to you. You'll come to see a lot of things for what they really are. Besides, with Dean on the wagon here a bottle lasts a third longer anymore."

"I don't mean the booze, I mean the moon," she says. "It's full. That accounts for at least *some* of the strafing around here."

"No it's not," I say. "It was full a couple nights ago, when Milo and I had us that talk on the riverbank—on the subject of more death and hardship, of course—his beer cans sailing out of nowhere through the dark. *There* was some strafing for you. The moon's merely gibbous now."

"Only what?" she says.

"Gibbous," says Milo. "Gibbous. As in gibbous this day our daily bread."

"Oh bullbutter!" Finally Mom has torn herself away from the window. She comes to the table daubing a tear up on her knuckle, smiling.

"There now, you see?" Milo hands over a white paper napkin for her eyes. "I can crack the hardest nut."

She says, "You haven't changed anything by a long shot."

"I believe I know your problem exactly," he says. "Mother."

Mom, taking care of her thirst and frowning, answers, "What?"

"Hitched up to the past as you are all the time, you're just another sentimental senior. Just a sap and fighting it."

"Every time I see or hear that word senior I want to scream. No, that's not it at all," she says. "My problem, if you want to know it, is guilt. I don't know why I can't get angry and stay angry, but I always get guilty. I think it was heaped upon me as a child."

"There it is. Don't you see what you're doing? *Pummelled* by your past. No one else gives a shit about your past."

"My husband, too. We were not allowed to be selfish and soft like you boys. I don't think you realize."

"Ugh!" goes Milo, struck, "Duty-bound, you mean."

"That's it."

"You and your husband both, I suppose, in that noble capacity."

"You better believe it, my husband. You simply don't realize."

This brings Milo's feet to the floor. "All right, if we're going to haul the dead horse out here and kick it around again, then let's by all means haul him out. Let's *realize* here!"

"Do we have to go through all that again?" I object because, like Milo said, we've practiced taking turns stomping and protecting the old boy's ghost, and all it's ever yielded, as far as I'm concerned, is snarling and discord. To wit:

"I mean, why don't we get somewhere with it for once?" says Milo, "instead of wallowing in it to no good purpose the rest of our lives the way he intended for us to?"

Surprisingly, Mom takes the contest. "Let's."

"All right, I happen to have an angle, a whole new angle on the subject. I've been saving it."

"You've never saved a thing in your life, least of all your opinions," says Mom.

"This is no opinion," he says. "This is a whole new interpretation of this family."

Milo catches me out of my seat. He asks me where do I think I'm going.

"Just stretching," I say.

"Time out, is that it?"

"Go ahead with your story," I say. "I'm listening."

"Then as long as you're up, reach in there and get us some ice. Bring the whole tub over here. See if you can't find us some finger food too. My appetite's beginning to gnaw at me."

Instead of that I go for the hi-fi, maybe get some music playing—something smooth, like Poulenc. But then she wouldn't keep any Poulenc in the house, so I come up with a Sinatra album, *Come Dance with Me*, with the Billy May orchestra.

Milo turns against me before I'm even back in place at the table. "What's *that*! Can't you see I'm trying to talk here! What *is* that!"

"Poulenc," I say. "The slow movement. What does it sound like?"

"Well take it off! I can't talk with that!"

Mom and I know this record by heart. During the intro we look at each other and then both go into the first chorus along with Frank.

"What is going on here!" Milo is out of his seat, flying against the music. "We were about to get someplace here!" He throws back the lid and bends inside the cabinet. "After all these years! After . . ." he yanks Sinatra off the spindle, "lying for him all these years! And all you want," he boots the screen door, "all you want to do," and sends Frank Sinatra spinning out towards the vegetable garden, "is play records!?"

"That record," says Mom, "was irreplaceable. Now

you've ruined it, if you haven't slit one of your daughters' throats open in the process. If you're just going to be mean . . ."

Back in his seat, Milo lifts up his T-shirt to get at the sweat on his face. His breathing is all stepped up after the noise. "I won't be mean," he says. "I won't be mean anymore, Mother. I just want to say something. All right?"

"Well you drink and you can't control yourself. This conversation has lost all semblance of dignity. And I should think you'd be worried," she says, "that if that beeper thing goes off you're going to be too drunk to go fight a fire."

"For god's sake what do I have to do to get an audience around here!"

"Just say whatever it is and stop beating your breast in hysterics."

"I will. I will do that. If everyone's finished. Are you finished now? Does everyone have what they need? Anyone's foot gone to sleep. Does anyone have to vomit or brush their teeth? Do I hear any more complaints of any kind? Good. I would like it then if everyone's comforts were satisfied for the coming five minutes so that I could say something in one straight line here."

"I believe," Mom says to me, "that he doesn't really have anything. He only seems to want to be mean, and that scares me. If he'll throw my good records out the back door then he's liable to start breaking things again. I'd just as soon leave, if that's what he means to do."

"I won't hurt you, Mother." He's almost calm now, looking down his nose to his crotch, where his fists are gathering. "I don't want to hurt this place. You have nothing to be afraid of. Unless it's what I've got to say—"

"You're drunk, aren't you? We never know what you're going to do when you're drunk, Milo. But if you're going to talk about my husband then I hope you'll at least be civilized about it. I just hope you'll do that for me at least."

"I was nine years old," says Milo, moving it along at last, "and sleeping. I remember my nose. It was cold. It was a very cold nose. I could feel my nose freezing while my feet sweated away down by the radiator. I had my chessboard stuck in the crack down there to keep from burning my feet."

"I thought you were sleeping," she says.

"No. I was supposed to be sleeping, but I couldn't. I remember having a lot on my mind for a kid my age. I dropped off for awhile, not very long, and missed him coming in, but then I smelled the whiskey on his breath and the Aqua Velva, and there he was. It's likely he was crying a while, standing over me like that, thinking I was asleep, because I heard this faint sobbing like. But I was faking it. Listening. Waiting to see what he'd do." Milo pauses to recline again, to cross and recross his feet on the table.

"Well what did he do?" I ask.

"He sat down on my bed. I didn't open my eyes for him until he started pulling on my collarbone, and then, let me tell you, I wished I'd been asleep. More than anything I wished it. Anything but face Dad when he was at that morbid stage. It was sickening. But I couldn't. I could smell the tobacco on his fingers. On his *cold* fingers. And I had to listen to it all. The whiskey, the snivelling, the remorse. The whole ball of wax."

"Where was *I*?" Mom says.

"Hold on, I'm going to tell you what he said. He said I wouldn't have to worry anymore. He said there was going to be no more trouble between us. Everything was going to be all right. When he said that this feeling came over me. It was like, I don't know, pity . . . something. No, maybe it was like he was saying good-bye. You

know, like somebody saying good-bye to someone, only
you're not supposed to know they're saying it? Now right
there's where I'd say I got the first inkling he'd be leaving us—sooner or later. But then Dad said, 'As long as
you don't make any more accusations, *then* everything's
going to be all right.' Now how do you like that? He's
sitting on my bed telling me this is more or less good-
bye, and then suddenly he's making ultimatums—making
a chump out of me. Saying he won't do what I hate
anymore if I'll stop doing what he hates, which is making
these accusations. See, the old man knew all along I was
lying awake in the dark just thinking up a whole *string* of
these accusations, and they were winding out like some
nasty smell, winding their way out to wherever he was,
and he followed them right in to where I was waiting.
Know what? He was that ashamed of himself. But he'd
only half admit it. 'I won't do this anymore,' he said, 'but
no more accusations out of you, either. No more accusations about that which you know nothing of' is how he
put it. Now we're all familiar with that line, aren't we?
That should ring bells with everyone around here."

"Yeah," I answer. "That's the rebuke he used on you
every time you sassed him back."

"That's right. You know that because every time the
man talked to me, since the day I could sit up to eat, I
talked back. And that was the signal for not-another-
word-or-there-will-be-the-flat-of-my-hand. But this here
was different. In the first place, he was real respectful. I
could've said anything and it wouldn't have got him up. He
was worried. Ashamed, like I say. Fact is he was scared
shitless and I hadn't accused anyone of squat. Out loud
at least. Yet here he was, bringing this shit in to me—his
sleepy little dewy-faced Milo. But the second thing is, I
couldn't talk. Couldn't make a goddamn peep and I
don't know why. All this time I've been trying to figure
it. I mean, I can hear that whiskey voice of his all right; I

can hear it right now. But damned if I can hear mine. Now that couldn't have been. I mean I had to say *something*. To say nothing is not in me."

"Does it matter?" I say.

"What?"

"Whether you said something or not?"

"It matters to me!"

"Well, it doesn't to me." I start to leave my chair again, but Milo is up too, shoving me back in with both hands.

"Where do you think you're going now?"

"I want some peanuts or something," I say.

"You stay right where you are. I'm not finished yet."

"I'm hungry," I say.

"I just made a meat loaf," says Mom, "and no one ate a bite and it's getting cold in the refrigerator now."

"I figured eating supper might have been in poor taste, seeing as you were on the verge of suicide and all," I say. "But now I'm definitely hungry. No denying it any longer. You two have your whiskey to keep you going. I don't."

"Because you're perfect."

"How about a meat loaf sandwich?" she says.

"Perfect people bother me."

"That would be fine," I say. "Thank you."

"Well you can just get up and fix it yourself for once. I'm not making anything for anyone. My dinner shift is over."

"I can't. He won't allow it. He's demanding our undivided attention if you hadn't noticed. He's making hostages out of us. Besides, I'm rather craving peanuts. Salted peanuts. Redskins, not those dried out things."

"Well I don't have any peanuts of any kind," she says. "You'll just have to do with what there is, and that's meat loaf."

But before she's finished saying it Milo is standing on the table, jumping off the other side. She guards her cup, but other things fly—the salt and pepper, an old Roseville vase full of pencils. Much of her magnetic fruit is severed from the refrigerator door when he brings out the meat loaf. He holds it up, still in its pan, over the table. He upturns the pan and the meat, of course, drops out, bounces once on its very crusty top, and falls to its side. Milo sets before me a butter knife, the mayonnaise, and a heel of lettuce, and I thank him kindly. He carries this all out in such a way that you can see sweat leaving his head. He puts milk in a glass. Milk pours over onto the floor; it sloshes into my lap when he brings it down. After he's finished with that he gives himself a moment's pause, then goes back for something else. The ice. He holds the tub, too, well over center table and meat loaf, and he dumps it. Cubes scatter far and wide. Then he returns to his seat. He takes ice in his two hands. He is breathing like a run dog. He lowers his face to his hands and scrubs. Scrubs the sharp blocks right in, producing a noise from his nose and throat. Could be laughing, could be crying.

Mom waits a decent interval for him to come down, then says, "At least he didn't throw the meat loaf out in the yard. It's making a nice grease spot in my oak table," she says, poking it towards me with her finger, making it slide like a wet sponge. "Well, go on with your talk," she says. "You couldn't remember why you couldn't talk with your father. I'm sorry for the interruption, but where is this leading?" She drops two of the cubes in her cup. "You surely haven't said anything too illuminating yet. I was expecting something horrible from this story. Instead I've got an ice floe in my kitchen."

"Just hold your horses a minute, would you?" Milo says. "I'm not there yet. We made us a deal. That's it. It doesn't matter whether I said anything. It doesn't matter. We had ourselves a little contract is what he had. Dad doesn't do it anymore if I don't. That's the deal."

"What deal? Where was *I* when this deal was being made is what I want to know," says Mom.

"What?"

"When he came into your room and woke you up. Where was *I*?"

"He didn't wake me up! I wasn't asleep! You missed the whole point so far." Milo swallows a lot of drink and lights up another smoke. "Entertaining," he says.

"What?"

"You were right in this kitchen, you two. Entertaining in here. Some of your friends. Some of those people you and Dad used to bring home from church, remember? The Canadian bacon? The poached eggs and biscuits? The letting down of inhibitions? And then later on getting the poor Christian suckers as drunk as they'd ever been in their lives? So that next Sunday we'd all polish up the shoes and go back to church, where their kids would stare over at your kids as if to say, 'What kind of a shit home do you live in anyway?' "

"Would you not be altogether ridiculous, Milo?"

"Anyway, let's say Dad got desperate in here. Probably excused himself for a minute to pee and decided to drop in and be pals with his son. The little nine-year-old me."

Using the bottom halves of her eyes, she looks over the table at Milo: "What was he so ashamed of that he couldn't talk to me?"

"Desperate," he says. "Desperate with you—ashamed with me."

"If that isn't a hell of a note."

"It's true. Dad couldn't talk to you. I watched him. It was pretty clear he made a whole activity out of *not* talking to you."

"He never talked to any of us," she says. "You know that."

"He talked to me, didn't he?"

"He might have. He might have talked, but he didn't really tell you anything."

"Maybe because he relied heavily on a little intuition," Milo says. "Expected the details would add up to something, and somebody around here would put it together, which one of us did."

"Frankly," says Mom, "I've about had it with the mysteries around here. What are you trying to do to him? Why do you have to chase him down the way you do? You're going to make him into a martyred saint before we're done. Details! What details? What did you know? You were nine years old. You were still playing army, for God's sake. He was *my* husband and I was there, wasn't I? For whatever he had to tell me, wasn't I? Since we were kids . . ."

"Maybe. But he still wouldn't tell you."

". . . Since we were teenagers. Since . . . since the war with the Japanese. Here! Here's a *story* for you. Do you know, when he was in the Navy I went all the way to Norfolk to see him? Do you know it was my first time away from home, and every train in this country was full of drunk, sweaty, horny, disgusting soldiers? And I got through that and survived, but do you suppose your father even deigned to show up at the station to meet me? No. No, I had to look for the base all by myself because I was too frightened to even ask. I had to walk. It was blazing hot down there and I had no money and I was hungry, and I had to keep walking no matter what. Looking and looking and getting nowhere, until I was plain stuck. Stuck in the mud, and all I could do was sit down on a bench, right in broad daylight, and bawl. I had these sailors passing right by, too, making remarks, saying the filthiest things, about . . . things I didn't even entertain, but then *I* even started to believe these things. Till finally this nice gentleman, a lieutenant, came along and sat with me, and we started on the bars. When

Jimmy wasn't in this one then he took me to the next one, this lieutenant. By now I was having to sit every so often, I was so empty and tired. I was afraid the lieutenant would leave if I kept stopping, but he didn't. I remember he bought me a sandwich—no, it was a hot dog. Do you know nothing in my life ever tasted as good as that hot dog? I've never forgotten it."

"That's good," says Milo. "That Lieutenant Hot Dog thing, that's *real* good." He passes a belch, with great fulsomeness, across the table and looks upward. "Hey Dad! Dad heard that," he says, looking back down. "Says if you think you're supposed to be so damn guilty then you ain't gonna assuage it that way. Thinks you might be stacking the deck a mite, tattling on him without a witness. Now that kind of stuff might get you points down here, but Dad says you're losing them up there."

"Very funny, Milo. You just ask 'Dad' where he was hiding out all that time then."

"Bet it wasn't the ship's library."

"We were about as far from the ship as you could get. By now it was pitch dark and I was about half-afraid of what I'd find, if I did. But we found him. There he was, all alone in the shadows, at a table under the ceiling fan, sitting there twirling an empty glass around in circles. I was too relieved to find him to even be upset. But I did ask him why, when he knew I was coming, did he have to start drinking? But you know it was the same as always. As if we were right here in our own kitchen: nothing. Just staring off someplace. Stoned. Mumbling weird things. I wouldn't understand, he thought. He thought I wouldn't understand."

Mom and Milo and I, for about thirty seconds, have all been staring off over the table. You can hear the crickets. Milo's kids out in the distance talking. The gray hill behind Mom's and all up the street is baying with dogs. You can hear way out to the highway, the big trucks airbraking, shifting gears. My sandwich is all made, but maybe I'll wait for a better time to bite it.

"I appreciate your predicament, Mother," says Milo. "But you *wouldn't* understand."

"*That is a lie!*" Now it's her turn to beat the table. She chooses a watery cube, just misses Milo's head with it. The ice connects with the aluminum door and Mom puts both hands to her mouth. "Here!" she says, "Shut that door! I won't have the entire neighborhood listening to our dirty laundry!"

Milo replies in the same wry way. "I'm afraid *he* knew better."

"That's enough, Milo," I say. "You can shut up now."

"Hey! Baby of this family! *You* can shut up, or you can go to bed anytime we feel like sending you. Now he came to me, didn't he? He left Mom behind in the kitchen, he came into our room, but he woke *me* up. Or thought he did."

"You're back on that," I say. "That didn't get us anywhere the first time. Nobody gives a shit anymore."

"You, sister," he tells me, "were asleep right beside us. But you weren't in on this. You were not invited. You were *never* invited. Just him and me, buddy. Me because I was the one that knew. The *only* one."

"Knew!" I say. "If you've got the big answer then put it on out here. Tell us what you think you knew, Chosen One. What."

He comes on with the shit-eating face again while his hand breaks a hunk off the meat loaf, a big one, and shoves it all in. He uses half a bare arm to wipe his mouth. Then follows the usual: another cube, another helping of bottle, another lighted smoke. "There," he says, executing a perfect smoke ring, "now you're getting around to the right questions." He whistles in some drink. "Now let's think about this for a minute."

"I thought I wanted to talk about this," Mom says,

"but I've changed my mind. I'm tired of this. In fact I'm tired, period, and I have a choice. I'm not going to think about anything, I'm going to go to bed." But she only makes a nest out of her arms and lays her head down in it.

"Let's see," Milo continues, "where was I? Yeah, he had the hold on my collarbone. Now you might have thought it was the sort of hold a parent puts on their kid to protect it? Shit no. He was afraid I'd fall asleep on him, like she's trying to do to me right now."

"Go on, go on. Then what?" I say. "What did you know?"

"Then what? That was it. We squared our deal. We sealed it with a hug. A big, tight, overall-type hug, buddy. It almost made me puke, but we hugged on it. And after that, for the next year at least, until I was ten, he didn't do it. That was the year I believed him."

Mom's head rises slowly. "You mean he didn't drink for a year?"

"Darn right."

"Come to think of it, that's true," she says. "Actually I remember that now." Slowly, she goes back down.

"I believed him so much I forgot about it. We all forgot about it. Dean here wasn't wetting his pants and having all his phobias; wasn't throwing up all over his desk at school; wasn't trailing you around the house like the helpless maladjusted idiot he's since returned to. And you, Mother, you weren't floating around here just ahead of Dean in your slippers, with your cigarettes and that stupid face—a blob making faces, going: 'Why, oh why, won't he come home and be what he's supposed to be?' No. Now there was definitely something in this house that stunk. We all picked up the same goddamn odor like a bunch of open milk cartons in the icebox. But that one time, the stink was gone. You see? Look at all the stuff we weren't doing because *he* wasn't."

"So you made the way for cleaner air," I say. "You fixed him up for a year. That does a lot for us at the moment, doesn't it?"

"He even talked to us sometimes."

"All right, he talked."

"He took us to the races."

"Piss on the races!" says our sleepy mother into her arms.

"The only trouble we got from him for a year was him stepping into our disputes over Mickey Mouse and Howdy Doody. And even then I'd give it right back, and he'd get close to whacking me. But I never had to accuse him. We still had that. It was nice around here, boy. Until he broke the deal, that is. Because, then, he wasn't just back to the old stuff, but a liar."

Oh boy, he's getting the claws out—here comes some of that snarling I was talking about. "You're going to tell us you were surprised, right?"

For the impertinence he puts on me a glare that could bend steel. But just as fast he goes mirthful again. "You recall where we were at, Dean, when our serenity was shattered?"

"Where?"

"You'll remember this. We were in the bathtub taking a bubble bath when Dad came falling in with his cheeks all bubbled out like red balloons, all ready to bust with whatever swill he did it with? You'll remember how Dad ran up to the toilet that night and drained his guts out right before our eyes."

"How could I forget?"

"You couldn't. Because you turned white as the very suds we were sitting in and had to jump up out of that tub and share the toilet with him."

"I remember. So what's so funny about it?"

"Oh, I'm thinking about how I had to laugh at the time."

"You weren't laughing."

"You and Dad, father and son, bending over together, bowing down to that toilet like it was something holy. You all white and shiny, with the soapsuds sliding down your legs and that look of abject terror on your face."

"Yeah, well, I don't remember you laughing."

"Yeah, well, you were too busy ducking your head with Daddy. But I could laugh at it, buddy, and I did. Mine was the only stomach in the whole place that could take it. That's how I began dealing with things, you see. Even at that tender age something in my head was saying 'Keep it ahead of you, Milo. Keep it ahead of you at all times and you won't trip and let it mow you down from behind.' So I laughed. It was better, let me tell you, than your plain old *verbal* accusation. It pissed him off. Put a little added strain on things that lasted the rest of his life. He dealt me several blows with the steel ruler for it, of course."

This brings Mom's head up again. "Steel ruler?"

"Steel ruler from the newspaper office. What he used to administer my medicine with. Made a clean little paddle; a nice snappy song over my butt. It's probably still in the same hiding place, wherever that is."

"You deserved it," she says, folding again.

"Why don't you go to bed, Mom?" I say. "Why don't we *all* go to bed?"

"She's not sleeping," Milo says. "She's anything but asleep. No, what she's doing, she's sitting there just waiting for the truth to be told, anxious to the point of prayer."

"Why doesn't that stuff ever shut you up?" I say. "It never shuts you up till the very last, when you fall off whatever you're sitting on and can't get up. Why can't you be like Mom here and run down early, like any ordinary drunk?"

"Because she's an old lady. And because whiskey don't

have that effect on me. See, I possess a certain genetic quotient, probably comes from one of our distant grand-parents. It allows for maximum lucidity at all times. It's the germ of our family—the luck of the gene pool, boy. Whiskey brings the truth out to the surface, wakes the little fuckers up. I mean, some of us can really be truth-ful. When we talk, it's horrifying. The rest of you have conversations.''

He gets up, starts pacing down and back beside the counter. "Now this last part," he says, "takes some think-ing, and therefore some listening on your part. Because it's subtle. That's right, all of a sudden I'm going to get subtle on you, so this is just a warning of it.''

He keeps up his pacing, holding onto the countertop and even then going askew. I feel him behind me, think-ing behind my chair. He says, "This is about suicide . . .''

He circles the table, halts directly behind Mom hang-ing his wrists over her chairback. "Now Mom, don't tell us you know any more about suicide than the rest of us in this family. That's stupid, because we all grew up around it. He brought it home with him and spread it around, and then he took it on out of here when he left. But we all got a healthy dose. That's what I've been talking about. And that's why, when he did it, nobody was all that surprised. I mean, the whole process of having him here, wasn't it just a matter of him passing through? Him wearing some new epiphany on his sleeve? Him taking it up to that room of his with all the books to wait on his next binge, when he could come out and bounce his bullshit off all of us again? And again? And again? When you think about it, all he ever did was just keep us waiting for him to do it. Well, this here is about when he did. When I was here with him. And you two weren't.

"I remember everything, every nuance, every god-damn dust mote. It was August, it was a Saturday just like this, and I was thirteen by now. You two had left that morning for Charleston, to visit Uncle Bimbo over there, and I was just coming in from a hard day of playing to get my supper. It was like an oven, this house; you couldn't breathe. I remember a lot more about it. Let's see, I had been over my paper route, I went swimming up at the pool with Scaparotti and we'd been looking at girls, some of the older ones, and we got feeling pretty sexual, what with all that heat and near-nakedness, so we beat it down to Risch's for a cherry Coke. We always had us two or three cherry Cokes on a day like that. After that we went over to Tom's to work on our bikes. I had done everything I could think of to keep myself away from this place. I even hung around Tom's hoping his mother would ask me in for supper. But she didn't.

"Then I had to come home.

"This house, it was like one of those Bergman movies: everything completely still, with the blue shadows, the slanted sun. You could see the dust filter in through the windows and settle on the furniture. You could hear the floorboards complain as you walked in. You could hear the clocks. And coming in from the neighborhood you could smell where the lawn mowers had been, and you could hear the parents calling in their kids. Their suppers were ready and the dark was coming on.

"Dad was right here in this room. Wasn't doing nothing, he was just in here, just exactly like I expected. When I came in he got up and looked at me, put that sort of let's-get-this-over-with look on me. Then he spooned a can of pork and beans into a pan and set it over the burner. He gave me a plate of beans for supper! Then he went away. After I had a couple bites I put the beans away in the garbage and poured me a big glass of milk and went in and switched on the TV.

"About ten minutes later I heard all this commotion

going on upstairs. Sounded like the floor was giving in. I tried to make like it didn't bother me if Dad was up there throwing one of his conniptions, but it was interfering with my television program, so I had to see what all the racket was. He was up there in that baronial book room of his. He was crying and pouring out sweat and he was crazed. He was taking all those books and dumping them out on the floor. He didn't see me. I stood in the doorway watching. Books were flying all over. He was up to his knees in books, crazed. His Harvard Classics, his *Complete Shakespeare*, his Greek mythology, his Dickens and Abraham Lincoln, his medical encyclopedias, his natural sciences, his *Western Civilization*, his *Medieval Witchcraft*, his *World Economics*, his French poets, his *Rise and Fall*, even the goddamn *National Geographics*. The whole shebang laying at his feet, flying out towards every corner. Had him a little dance going, kicking books away from him like they were rats coming up to nibble his toes.

"Then he saw me. You want to know how crazy Dad was? He tried to get *me* with those books. But I ducked them and backed out of there and hid in the hallway. I counted volumes as they passed by. He started hollering something in regards to those beans—my beans were downstairs getting cold and I better clear out and go eat! But after a while he went back to bulldozing his books and I stepped in again. Without thinking about it I began picking up and stacking books. See, I have a very low tolerance for that kind of histrionics. I cleared a path over to the bookcase—the opposite end from Dad—and when I got there I started reshelving as fast as I could. I was a crazed little bastard myself just then, just like he was, only in reverse, because I was *redoing* everything he was trying to *undo*. So we went at it book for book— for every one he shoved off his end I set one up on mine. We rivalled each other in this very way till there was nothing left to do but stand there in the dark, leaning up to that bookcase, and swallow air."

"If you have such a low threshold for histrionics," I note, "then what did I just eat?"

"Finally I walked out. I walked out of that room and back through the house. I walked down to Scaparotti's and asked if I could stay the night. If I had to I was prepared to spend the night in the grass, like I'm doing now.

"Now there's something none of you ever knew about. How the ex-man-of-the-house had himself that little existential blitz. It began to bother me, what *I* did, too. For a long time after that it bothered me, why I couldn't just let him have it, have his way with it. Like maybe that's all he really needed was to take those books out and set them free and start over. Even if it did break the mold. Become something else, make something new out of himself. A builder, a farmer, a milkman, a bachelor. Something. Something that goes diametrically against our degenerate forebears.

"Anyway, the next morning he was still alive. I was feeling pretty fine, actually, when I came back here to pick up my baseball glove. But then I saw the Sunday paper. It was still on the porch and this was ten o'clock. I gathered the old boy wasn't over it yet or he'd have been in there pouring over the paper like he did every Sunday of his life. I went upstairs and washed my face. Don't ask me why, since I was only going out to dirty it again. But that's exactly what I did. And good, I did it good— behind the ears, back of the neck, everything. Maybe I felt like, I don't know, I was in charge here already. Maybe I figured I was my own man now, I'd best be responsible. So I changed into some clean clothes, stuffed some paper-route money in my pocket, grabbed up my glove, and started to leave. But then something pulled me back.

"I came back and found him. He was all closed in, sealed up in his room. He was on his bed, more awake I guess than asleep, and he was still dressed from the day before. I smelled vodka. How did I know the smell of vodka? You want to know? I didn't. I deduced it. It wasn't whiskey or gin or Bacardi, the bottle on the night-stand, it wasn't anything I recognized. And then the smell, it wasn't that strong but it was stronger. It was the only thing in the air besides the heat. And the atmosphere, the combined heat and vodka in that room, it was volatile enough to combust.

"Now I've already told you this part coming up, how his eyes were those two big open red sores looking at me. No emotion, just hanging open, red in color. And how he called me around the bed to where he could take hold of my arm and say, 'Everything's going to be all right.' There it was again, just like the old days, and I waited on the horseshit about accusations, but he never finished it. He never said that part. He let it go at that: 'Everything's going to be all right.' He was dead serious, too. I just stood there, thinking, What's to be so serious about first thing Sunday morning? But then Dad didn't actually make it to morning yet, see. The way he looked, Dad was still in the middle of last night. The way he looked, he didn't know Sunday morning from baseball, and if it wasn't his whiskey then it was something worse, it was vodka, and I was seeing the vapor of it all around his head. Anyway, he told me that, and it's the next-to-last thing he ever said to me. I just told him something short and stupid—Yeah, sure it is, Dad. Something like that. Like a stupe. I just stood there waiting for Dad to leave go of my pitching arm so I could squirm out and play baseball.

"See, because I knew it for sure then. I knew what he was talking about; what he was going to do. He'd lost it all by then. Lost the war. Not just with me. He was alone. That's the way he saw it—it was in his face. The way he saw the world. The world with himself in it. It's like everything he ever knew, everything that ever was, he reduced it to that. He couldn't exist in it. He *didn't* exist in it. *Going* to be all right. See? How could you miss the meaning of that?

"But here's something else. Here's another thing I never told you about. Church bells. That's right, every goddamn church bell in town. It's almost too much, ain't it. I mean, church bells? At a moment like that? Can you feature it? But there they were, right on time. And we didn't have much of anything to say, so we sort of froze there through all that ringing. It was supposed to be meaningful, right? Like having your own private soundtrack. But we wasted it; the moment came and went. We were hopeless. I told him I'd better go, my friends were waiting. And when I said it his hand let go. It had been on me like the vise of a drowning man, and when I felt it go I stepped out from under his hand and got away.

"Except I turned back from the door and laid my eyes on him one more time. He was stretched out there in his old gray pants and that red checkerboard shirt. I counted the buttons. There were five. His glasses off and his teeth out. His feet bare, and there were the long, cracked, yellow toenails, and I told myself, You had better take a good look, Milo, because this is probably going to be it. I actually said that over to myself. Because—and here's the crux of this whole thing—I not only knew it, but I knew I had the way to stop it. Any number of ways. I might've walked back to his bed and said, 'Hey, I love you, big buddy, don't do it.' At least tell him, 'If I was you I wouldn't. I mean, from my perspective I don't know why you'd want to in the first place.' But then, like you say, Mother, what did I know about that kind of trouble? I was just a kid. A kid with his hopeless Episcopal upbringing. I was too—what did you call it? Soft and selfish? So because of that I couldn't . . . It was sort of like . . . a hair itch."

"Hair itch," I say.

"You know, like one of those itches you get in your nose or your butt? Only you can't do anything about it because you happen to be in the middle of carrying some flabby mattress upstairs. Or you're sitting in somebody's dining room and everyone's looking at you? It's like, how are you going to drop your end of the mattress? How are you going to just go probing your butt in public? *Inappropriate* ain't quite it. *Impossible* is what I'm trying to get at.

"What I'm really trying to say is, it was up to me—Dad's future among us—it was in my hands, totally and completely, and there were things I could've done to stop him. I thought of calling Mom down in Carolina: Hey, Mom, you better haul ass back up here, Dad's into the Stolichnaya and I don't think he's gonna be around much longer.

"It was like looking over at half a ghost. It was like having the power over a dude that's half mortal and half into ghosthood. It was terrible. Like he wanted it one way or the other but didn't know which one yet, and I had the power to decide for him."

"You?" I say.

"Me. Me and me alone. I held the strings. You understand I could've done it the other way. None of this bullshit about love. I could've thrown that empty bottle through the window—I mean *through* it, shattered the fucking window with it; and pulled him up out of there and said, 'Come up out of there, motherfucker, we're gonna take a shower and take a walk, and you're going to stick around. You're going to wait this out and get over it.' "

"Isn't that going a little far?" I say, "Even for one of your drunken delusions?"

"I had the power. The *ultimate power*."

"What power?"

"To save him, you stupid fuck! What power do you think! To call him back from the dust and save his unregenerate fucking soul!"

"Then why didn't you?"

"Hold it. Don't say that. Don't say why didn't I. That's not fair. I already told you I couldn't. So don't put me on that fucking wagon."

"No, it sounds to me, if I'm going to swallow what you're saying, all of it together, it sounds like you just plain *didn't*."

"Oh no. That's a little too perfect a setup, ain't it? For a kid to grow up with and try to outlive."

"You set it up. You set it up that way."

"All right. You want to know why? All right, let's get back to where we were. I was standing at the door taking a long last look while all this was going through my head, and he said to me, he said, 'Play pretty.' Plain as day, just like he was hailing me out the door. 'Play pretty,' he said. And I leaned back in and said, 'Huh?' Even though I heard him perfectly. But I wanted to make him say it again. I thought, Now here's a promising little development, after all this morbid shit, him telling me play pretty. And he said something else then."

"What?"

"It seemed to sort of take the edge right off. Seemed to say, he's made it back to our side of the line now, you can ease up, quit worrying, you don't have to do anything or say anything after all. So, with that in mind, you know what I did. Sure, I went up to the diamond and played. I played real hard, almost forgot about the whole thing."

"What was it he said?"

"Till I ran it through my mind, that last thing he said. Now this is just plain stupid. In fact, for once I wouldn't

blame you of accusing me of the unworthiest of fucking
machinations here. What he said was, 'Like no tomorrow.'

"I was out there and it was all the way to the bottom
of the ninth before it struck me. The little stuff, like the
look in his eye, shit like that, I could see; it's the big
obvious thing that went right by me. And before I could
even look around and see Mr. Sinsel's car driving up on
the track and pull up even with me in right field and
honk me over, before I even turned my head around or
took another breath, I said out loud to myself, I said:
'Oh God, he did it.'

"And he did."

For so long Milo doesn't say another thing, and I look
around to see whether he's made himself cry again. But
all this time he's been standing right behind her, back
straight, feet spread, eyes down at what he's doing, which
is delivering a nimble massage, rolling and rubbing from
the temples to the bumps on Mom's upper spine and all
the way out to her freckled arms. If she's still with us she
doesn't show it by the batting of an eye or letting out a
sound, although the look of bewilderment has never left
her face.

He picks up his fingers. "Are you listening to me?"

"Mmmmm . . ."

"Good. Then I've got one last thing to say. I'm going
to tell you what I think." He palms her shoulders and
begins diligently plying them in circles. He says, "There's
people that pull the plug because it's right for them.
They need out and sometimes that's the best way . . ."

You can tell his head's getting too big and heavy, the
way it gives to one side.

Mom still hasn't budged.

"And then," he goes on, "you've got the ones that'll
never do it; that'll put the scare into their loved ones, but
that's about all. They're not the type. They go right on
living."

He quits rubbing again and folds his arms together. "Did you hear what I said?"

Mom sits up. She hunches back her shoulders, causing them to crack. She says, yawning, "I haven't even the remotest idea what you're saying. Books. Church bells."

"Been the same basic thing all along," I say. "Right now we're back to where you commit suicide."

"Suicide," she says and yawns wide. She takes a look behind her at who's standing there. "Why don't you stop worrying? You know, you share that trait with your father, Milo. You worry too much. You read too much too. You worry and read too much both."

"No," Milo says, stepping over to the window. "I *thought* I was talking about suicide, but you know what? I wasn't. I was talking about surviving. I just realized it. I've been talking about remaining—being the remains, the surplus, the balance, the excess."

"You're on the same exact track. A chip off the same block. I've always said so."

"I'm still alive," Milo says. "There's a trait I don't share with him."

"Not that you'll take the same way out," she says, "but you're all his."

"I," says Milo, pulling his words out of some murky, depressed place, "have been on the other side of him . . . forever."

Here's something I hadn't noticed: tears running out of Mom's eye. Another just balled up and slid down her face. She does nothing to wipe them off, just sits there with her lips pressed and fibrillating. I should probably mention it, take her hand or something, but my brother has found a new horse to climb onto:

"My kids are out there playing with the sprinkler," he says. "You hear that giggling? That's them. Their little naked white bodies getting wet under the moon. I'm

going to call them in in a minute, and I'll tuck them in
and read them a story and then kiss them good-night. It's
going to make them giggle like hell. They'll get embarrassed over how much love and coziness they have to put
up with around here."

Things get quiet again—just Mom sucking back her
wet sadness and Milo's wet, squealing children—till he
goes on:

"Their mother should have called by now."

I ask, "Why? Doesn't she trust you with your own
children?"

"Shut up. Pat's supposed to call in with some news.
Some very good news."

I tell him that would sure boost the occasion.

"Good tidings for all of us," he says.

"Yeah? What would those be?"

"I'm not at liberty to discuss them."

"What are you two talking about now?" Mom says.

"It's about money," I answer. "My savings, which
seem to be in somebody else's hands. What about that,
Brother? You were just getting to that when we were
interrupted this afternoon."

"I told you, treat it like it don't exist. And keep your
mouth shut. Didn't I tell you that too?"

"Hey, you brought it up."

"What are you two talking about?"

"Hand me what's left of that, Dean."

I pass it and he pours into his glass. He runs the last
drops into Mom's cup.

I'm glad to see her not take it. "I've got to get this
place cleaned up," she says. "I don't know how this
fiasco ever got started."

"Leave it," I say. "You go up and take your bath and
turn in. We'll clean it."

But she sits on, eyes still batting and filling with water.

Nobody leaves. Milo is back at the window, watching
out the glass the way Mom was earlier.

"Stare long enough," I say, "it'll disappear."

"They're going to want to sleep in my tent," he says. "But they don't want to sleep out there. It's realy seamy in that tent. The dew soaks up in your back so you wake up every morning feeling like you aged a good five years. It's supposed to be sealed off, but worms get in, and silverfish . . ."

"Maybe you just *think* they do," I say. "Let me tell you what that is. At the end of my drinking—"

"Don't get him started again, Dean."

"He's not going to get me started. Dean ain't got the stuff to play with that's going to put *me* in disgrace. Him and his goddamn temperance anyway. What's he doing here? Why did he have to come back in the first place? All he ever does is open his mouth every time it gets quiet and spout something that's supposed to solve everyone's problems. Why doesn't he go back down to New Orleans, to his homos and his vegetarians, and leave us be? Dean's never had a real honest feeling in his life. He's never had a family, either, and never will."

Mom says before I can get to it, "Listen to you!" She sets her face and turns it on him. "Just listen! All this palaver about your father and yet here you are. Your children are just outside that door and here you sit drunk as any Jesuit priest! If you aren't the very voice of reason itself. Mister Wisdom and Salvation. Milo—man of the century!"

"I am the man of *this* family!" says Milo. "I have been the man of this family since I was thirteen!"

She pushes herself to her feet, goes up to the window and takes Milo by the collarbone. An inch from his ear she says: "Why–don't–you–be–the–man–of–your–own–family!?"

She leaves.

Milo's face has gone to pieces. You see the jaw go, the eyes, the color.

There's enough left in him to get him to the door, draw up a breath, and bellow: *"Hey! Shut off that hose and get in here!"*

VIII.

FINALLY GET TO be alone, which ought to give me ease since I haven't been all day. Sleeping arrangements are I get the porch. I made up a mattress from a pile of things in the linen closet, while Daph and Claude took my bed. An hour ago they came in squealing joy, shaking the wet from their hair, clutching their chests with the shivers. They had bruise-colored lips and smelled like the sun after a clean rain shower.

Their dad and uncle were made to laugh once again.

We all helped get the place tidied up, except Mom. And then I went and sat on her bed.

Something funny in what I saw down there, I told her. Besides all that gas and palaver, the unpopular old lamentation, besides the old man and his memory even; it was something else. Come on, I could see it in the hurt in your face and still can, and can't shake it off. Something darker and more misshapen has stolen over you. It wouldn't be what Milo was yapping about—we've been over that eighteen times—unless it's what we brought up in regards to you doing it yourself.

No. She told me she would prefer not doing that.

What did that mean?

Nothing. She said it was something else. Cancer.

It was cancer she was at the doctor's about. Or could be. I got out of her that they don't know yet if it's the benign type or the other, only some alien tissue living off her chest. Suspicions on the mammogram. Some polyp.

So that's why all the low comedy and monkeyshines in the back end of her car today. But why didn't she just say so, instead of letting us think what we thought and keelhaul her over it?

She just didn't want to talk about it. What purpose would that serve other than to keep reminding her she was fizzling out like an Alka-Seltzer? Besides, why should she go and spoil Milo's favorite fun?

She was being hysterical. I told her that as cancers go, if she didn't already know it, the kind she might have was more often curable than not.

But she wouldn't be consoled. In her state she was as good as gone already. I finally said good-night to her doleful mien and snapped off the light.

Okay. Go ahead. Try and sleep on that now.

Right now I need to get away from this thinking. Sometimes the only happiness is when you sleep, but that's a thing they let you have only late at night, and sometimes they make you wait more, until you've delved into everything in your and your neighbor's past, turned out a symphony of Mahler length, arranged a suitable forecast for the next ten or so years.

I dream of my Dad. In real life he was always arrogant but in dreams he is gentle and shy; he will say things as if it's taken a long time to think it through, and when I come to think of how he is supposed to be dead he'll say, "Oh that, that was all a big mistake." In this one he has on the old checkerboard shirt; his bare feet are sucked in filthy-smelling mud to the ankles. On the horizon is the dark brown Mississippi, like you see it on the map, slugging all the way south to where it spreads open like little black fingers and takes the Gulf of Mexico in a handshake. Dad, meanwhile, is slender and smart as in the days when I was toilet trained. I look closer at what he is guarding in his right fist but can't make it out. He says that everyone is healed now—my mother, Sandy Labounty, my brother, himself. With that the other three come swimming up from the bottom of the mucid river and advance applauding, various-colored leeches barnacled to their muddy skins. "Everything is going to be all right now," Dad tells me, "thanks to you." The applause comes stronger. "Now you have to get out there and show them *all* how it's done," says my dad. "So take your bow and back away, modestly, from all this clapping." I do it, bending from the middle and stepping behind. On the upswing I catch a gander at what he was hiding in his hand. "Ugh!" I go, whapping my head on the ceiling: It was my five hundred bucks!

But something real just walked on my head. It brought real pain and broke my sleep. Seeking vengeance my arm swings out and clips the intruder about the ankles; it comes to the floor knees first and rolls in the dark. "That you?" it says.

"Simon?"

"Jesus, Dean!" The shadow of Simon rocks on its tailbone rubbing the more injured knee. "You didn't have to kill me like that!"

"What are you doing here?"

"I came to say good-bye. I'm outa here. I had to get away from that place; that old guy. I think my knees are broke."

Is this a trick of the light or is Simon completely undressed? I reach over and touch him at the furthest-up part of the leg. "Are you out of your mind? Where are your clothes!"

"Left 'em up in your room."

"You've been in my . . . But—"

"I know. They woke up, too. I had to get out in a hurry. Who are they anyway?"

"Never mind. Did they see you? Of course they saw you."

"I was going to be a surprise . . ."

"Oh my God."

"They probably thought I was a dream or something."

"Or something."

"You don't want me here either," Simon says, "do you? Tell me the truth."

"I hadn't exactly been lying here contemplating it. How can I answer that?"

"All right, fuck you too then!"

"Where do you think you're going?" I say. "You're not leaving. You're as bare as the back of my hand."

"I stashed the rest of my stuff around here at the side. Don't fuckin' worry about me," Simon says, "I'll fuckin' be all right. I'll find something!"

"Wait a minute," I say. "Come here. Come over here where I can . . ."

He does.

"Why do you have to talk like such a chintzy little whore?" I say.

Simon's knees are cool, hard. They taste like salt.
He closes them gently over my ears.

PART THREE

PART THREE

I.

"THERE'S BUGS IN this cereal!" goes the kid's voice.
Must be 8 A.M. or some such thing!

The other goes, "Where at?"

Then the two of them revel with a lot of high penetration.

The sun's pounding the porch where I am. Inside my bedding I'm covered with a film of sweat. Next is Mom:

"It's because nobody eats cereal around here, except me sometimes, for my digestion. Those are gnats."

"Can you eat 'em?" I hear.

"Put that down!" cries Mom. "Give those bowls here. I'll have to fix you something else.

I pull my pants on and walk in. There at the table we used last night sit my two nieces in their limbless pj's, up on their knees in the chairs, spooning grapefruit halves. With eyes long on innocent sleep, all of them glance at me but pretend they didn't—the embarrassment we came in here to face. Just Bill walks in the room saying hi to everybody. He hops on a chair and begins slicking his pelt. For a second I consider going upstairs to finish off sleeping but move instead to the sink and swab my face with the dish towel, make myself an ice coffee, wash down a couple Tylenol for the headache. I can get back to sleep later; for now I want to clear the air, in case there's any gossip in it.

On the table are a vase of new flowers, fruit in a

wooden basket, the infested cornflakes box. I shove the cat over and sit.

A freshly plucked daisy decorates the hair of each young niece. "Feels like Easter in Tahiti," I say.

"I saw your butt last night," says Claudette.

"You didn't!"

"You was walking in your sleep and you about squished me and Daph," she says, "getting in bed with us. You don't wear nothing to bed."

"Quit talking like your mother," I say.

"He wasn't wearing a stitch, Mimi," Claudette squeals.

Mom is whisking her fork through some French toast batter. But she is somewhere else. "All right," she says, sounding very tired.

Mom served us and went away. She can't eat. It's not hangover; she's going to the hospital today and they told her to show up with at least a half-day's empty stomach. Because they have to turn her inside-out, she thinks.

About halfway through the French toast with banana Milo shows up lugging a case of Rolling Rock returnables. "You'd be familiar with the blond-headed delinquent I found bivouacked in my truck this morning?" Milo's in wraparound shades, wrinkled, unbuttoned Hawaiian print shirt, the same shiny jeans. His hair's gone to about Brillo consistency and the smell of him comes over you like certain places in the zoo.

"Not very," I say. "He's the ward of Sandy Labounty. I met him the other day."

"That right?" Milo hauls his case over to the refrigerator, starts shoving things aside to make room. "There I was," he says, "all ready to climb in that truck I worked over yesterday, all ready to make myself and the streets of Ambrose look respectable—"

"You oughta take about half as much pride in your personal hygiene," I say.

He's transferring beers four at a time. "I shouldn't *oughta* do anything. When here I open the door on this half-dressed foundling, looking like he surely oughta have himself a mom and dad in some suburb to look after him—"

"Dad," says Claude, "you have to take me and Daph home, you know. We got to feed and water our horses."

"Description pretty much fits," I say. "So what did you do to him?"

"Well now, you know, there's something about a sleeping child—or a sleeping anything, for that matter—that I try never to interfere with. 'Course this here, this wasn't exactly deliberate; had I known, I probably would have let the poor fella sleep, but as it was, I just sort of happened along. We both were a little perplexed by it, you know. The kid says, 'Oh, I didn't know Dean had a brother. I thought this was Dean's.' He says, 'Why, Dean's a friend of mine. Maybe I better go wake Dean up.' Seemed to know right where to go and do it, too. But, see, I protested in your absence. Because, like I say, that's the way I am about sleeping people."

"Daddy!"

"All right. In a minute."

"Thanks," I say. "What little sleep I did get out there was dear enough." I lay my breakfast aside and pick up a smoke. "I wonder what the kid was doing around here. So he just left, right? Back to Labounty's? What?"

"No. He didn't," Milo says. "Matter of fact, I took him out to the Scenic with me. Bought us some eggs. We had a little bacon, a little coffee."

"Oh," I say.

He's finished stocking the fridge but lingers a while in the cool of the open door. "Yeah. Now this beer," he says, "is for Maureen's party today. You know about the party out at Bob and Maureen's. You're invited."

"I know about it."

"Good. Girls," he says, bringing vitamin bottles out of a door compartment, "go get dressed. Your Dad's going to take his vitamins like a good boy, make a short phone call to your mother, and go jump in the shower."

"Thank God!" says one of them. The two hie themselves away quick.

"Yep," says Milo, "quite a little gentleman, that Simon. Know what? He couldn't give me any money for his breakfast, so he repaid the kindness in a different way."

"Yeah?"

"Well, he insisted on giving me *something* in return."

"Well?"

"So he twisted me up a few joints. He didn't have to do that. That was real nice."

I ask, "That's nice. When was all this?"

"Oh, twenty, maybe thirty minutes ago by now." Milo flicks a pecan-shaped vitamin in the air with his thumb, catches it on his tongue. He chases it back with a hit of o.j. from the carton.

"So you delivered him safe and sound back to Labounty."

"Nothin' doin'. I dropped him off on 33. Slipped him a couple bucks and wished him safe passage."

"What? To where? Where's he going?"

"Who knows? He wanted let out on the southbound lane. Florida, maybe, he thought. Mentioned maybe doing some reconnoitring for the good priest down there. Where's Mom?"

"Huh? She's packing a bag."

"Where's she going?"

"Go ask her."

II.

THE PHONE COMES in for Milo while he's in the shower. It's Velda.

"Hello? Where's Milo at?"

"Not here," I say. "Who's this?"

"You tell him he better hurry it up, he's almost out of time." She sounds like a gangster movie.

"For what?"

"For what is none of your damn beeswax, Dean. You just tell him it better be soon in case he's forgot."

"He's liable to forget," I tell her, "the way he's going lately. Why don't you just tell me when and where and I'll make sure he gets the message?"

"You keep out of this!"

But as soon as I get it out of her and we hang up, the phone rings again. This time it's Sandy, calling from his church over on Main. I can hear the church bells coming through the wire. "It's Simon." Sandy sounds lost. "He seems to have disappeared, I'm afraid. I thought that perhaps he might have come to see you, Dean."

No call for carelessness. Church bells or no, there isn't a way to tell the truth here and not have it stir up a lot of suspicion over at the church; or worse, open some can of worms that I and my brother are going to have to do a lot of answering for. "Nope, haven't seen him. But if I do, I'll be sure and call you right away."

III.

HERE'S MOM AND me in the red Fiat getting her to the hospital. Jane, the passenger, sits a little forward, poised, erect, and cleaving to her purse, knuckles pale with fret. Otherwise, you've never looked at a healthier Jane. A tinge heavy on the cosmetics maybe, but she'll make a lovely entrance—white summer suit and hat, a neckpiece of lengthy red, to match her lipstick and car, flouncing in the wind over her largish bosom. We're at the end of our street and haven't said a word yet.

I turn onto Main. There are the Christians letting out from the Presbyterian—congregation of the slow-moving and discomposed, souring off in the hot behind sunglasses and florid hankies. The worshipers and their church have made us both put our minds to Sandy: the man of God I just lied roundly to, doing his own church down the street, his own private, civilian heart at this very minute perverting on him, no doubt, owing to the unaccountable renegade Simon.

Mom is squarely rancorous: "Sandy's having them all pray for me in that Prayers for the Conditions of Men thing." She unlinks her fist from the purse strap and feeds a while on her thumbnail. "Isn't that a fine kettle of fish? Now everybody can think of me as dead for about a minute and then go on and think about something else. That's what you do if somebody gets so bad their name has to be called out, and don't tell me you don't. It's tantamount to Rest In Peace!"

"I don't wonder," I say, "if that's the way you-all work your religion."

"Generally they'll turn out dead, too. I could name you three—"

"That's okay. And getting all puffed up and brassy ain't going to help either, Ma."

"I've never had an operation in my life and don't want one. All I keep thinking is when Jimmy had his gallbladder—"

"The thing's not an operation, it's only a simple little exploratory. A what-do-you-call-it, biopsy."

"Same thing. I've never had that either."

"Hell, you've had babies."

"That's different," says Mom, "everybody's had those."

Ken is there in the parking lot in his blinding new American make that gets nine to the gallon. He chirps his horn as we're walking past. "There's our little fighter!" he booms.

"Talk to me like a grown man or keep your mouth shut!"

Ken stands up out of his car straightening the wrapper on a bunch of cut flowers. He fetches a cribbage board off the comfortable seat and catches up. "Whoa, what's the hurry?"

"I'm not in any hurry," she says. "And take your hands off this bag. I'm not a helpless invalid yet!"

Ken gives me a nod at the door. "I'll take over from here," he tells me.

I give a kiss and a squeeze to Mom.

"And you better take it easy on that car," she says. "It's the last one I'll ever own."

IV.

I WAS GOING to come out anyway, just to see Maureen in her new place. Then I was going to leave. (I don't stand up to a party nowadays, not this kind especially.) I was going to do that if my brother hadn't changed my mind. This was when he was getting ready to drive his kids back to their horse farm, when he turned to me at the door. I thought I knew how to read that look. Thought maybe it had to do with Mom and her misfortune. It didn't. "Look," he said, "I need you out there today, all right? Just make sure." He had taken his sunglasses off his nose. His eyes looked full of worse misery than our mother's. I had to jump back. "Sure," I said. Sometimes I can give him anything when he seems in need and sincere. I never asked what it was. Could be a lot of things. I'm just let in on the worry is all.

You're driving through the high corn and wheat, breaking the dust to a finer sift. You're breathing dust and pure silage, and the air is the valley of yellow haze your own thinking is dingy with. You see a few cattle feverish under the rare shade, flycatchers low in the sky—the loop-diving swallows and larks. You're driving through heat a dog wouldn't be caught in. Yet out there in the ripply weather a man climbs his farm machine, wearing sleeves and moving slow. Stick your arm out, your skin will sear in its own grease. You see the bubbling tar on the road ahead, so you slow up; your tires blot the little sticky gravel that pelts your fenderwells.

A wide, tameless river used to run here.

Then you take an old bridge, drop down to a wood. Everything dapples. The cold dirt and bark. The wet moss and the sour leaves. The rock. Curve through with the brook and when you come out in the light again you hit the highway Simon went thumbing down.

Across it is more of the same.

I pull in at the mailbox of Bob and Maureen. A little ways on is the sightly barn frame Maureen's husband built, elevated on the banks of their own meadow where Bob fenced in the two mares, Lemon and Granny, and a new colt for Ryan. Out front is glutted with vehicles: half a dozen serious motorcycles, a few of those party-on-parade type vans. One van has the sci-fi mural tattooed to its side—a muscular, spear-wielding goddess with air-brushed hair stalking the foreground.

Nowhere in sight though is Milo's truck.

Around back is the hive of people I know. Many of them that I remember as young and handsome are now spreading out, having children, making lots more money that I make. Teams of them, assembled on the brown grass, waiting to slug the volleyball, arms up, faces burnt, cheering for the point.

Everyone is here. Everyone drinking heavy except for me and maybe a few wives. Grubby kids who can barely walk yet are allowed to pick up and drain the backwash in daddy's can.

Wes McLaird, a skinny wimp we called Wesley in high school, is here. When Wes came back from 'Nam in '73 though, he was a miracle of improvement—long and showy like the stuff of *GQ* magazine. He's around thirty now, like the rest of us, but still maintains the hairless face and hard body the greater part of which just blustered into view like the regalia on a peacock.

Recognizing him summoned up a galling backwards

glance for me. This was summers ago, when many of us were headed nowhere yet; we would cruise the same places over and over, doing multiple 'ludes with the wine and Central American smoke to hold off sweating and irritation. Swaying this way and that we often became loud and emotional, passed over sometimes to the black-out stage where you might then have to vomit. Wes had us out to his place when the other McLairds were on vacation. This particular evening I recall losing everything of awareness. When I came to it was dawn. There were three of us on the parents' bed: someone called Nina Stoltz had come undressed, as had I, and Wes himself was in underpants. I grasped that we had been moving towards a game of Seven Minutes in Heaven with the giggling Nina. I started out laying a diffident mouth to her chest; mainly I wanted to watch the rest of Wes while he covered the too-soft inside of Nina's leg with his face. Then he reached the part on her that stayed him. Nina smoothed his hair. She made those almost subaudible noises deep in her throat. Drawing shallow, fainting breaths, she asked if Wes wouldn't like to maybe fuck. A thing like Wes's, when it is let free, will sober a lady. But it will hypnotize a fellow like myself! I was wet with disturbance. I wanted to turn away and cry. It could be said that I fought the urge, but my hand went out where it shouldn't have. It was more, let us say, than a momentary slip of the wrist, my hand; it sort of rested there, costing Nina Stoltz the hosing she had been aching for, for Wes rolled out like a combat professional and lighted on the thin rug. He turned onto his back, his dick gone flaccid as a wet rope, and tried to act amused—but glad as hell, nevertheless, for his survival training.

After that I expected my name was going to be sullied around here for good. Not by Wes so much—a straight boy will generally keep his mouth shut—but the other, who was giving me back the look of stark mortification.

So, walking by, I try to ignore the looks of the curious. But I do notice a few of them stopped right in their volleyball playing. If there was talk of me before, it seems, lately, the thing that sets me apart has turned into public liability, thanks to the papers and evening news spreading iniquitous facts about the AIDS virus, the death-crazy cancer of homosexuality. Provinces like this one have become breeding places of suspicion and ill-will. I am not unafraid of coming away with the germ, but I am warned: I know to keep the fluids of others on the outside. I know to avoid intercourse, to in general practice a flimsier form of sex. Because I read the papers like everybody else.

A redwood patio joins up with Maureen and Bob's second floor, where a pair of amplitudinous speakers is set out to face the guests. The speakers are throwing a fit of metallic clamor by one of these practiced garage bands. Climbing the steps, I have to fight back a wind of busy guitar licks and cymbals. The bass is a large piston in my stomach. Up here is the spread of food, the seven-foot galvanized bathtub of iced refreshment, and Bob, the host, priming his charcoal. For all you know Bob could be naked under his long yellow chef's apron. He signs me a welcome, points me toward the inside, and I pass through the sliding doors almost colliding with Maureen on her way out with a platter of raw food.

Me and Mo seal ourselves off in the air conditioning. I'm mopping my face with a sponge, feeling pretty bitchy from being under the heat. "What *is* this? I thought up here north of the deep Dixie was supposed to be the cooler part of the planet."

Maureen looks addled, too, in a mood over something. She pops open a beer and hands me a Diet Coke. She's wearing a little mint green terry outfit. I don't often see her drink the way she's going at it now. "Listen," she says, throwing a look over her shoulder at where the party would be, "we got trouble."

"How's that?"

"Guess who's here."

"Who?"

"Quayle."

"Holy shit!" If it ain't the lead figure of Mo's exhusband's organization. Another bleeding sore from the old days. It gives me a certain feeling in the knees and stomach reminding myself of Quayle, his portfolio of misdemeanors. He might have taught Kurt Munroe lessons in snake. "You mean Quayle isn't prematurely dead yet?"

"Him and his buddies come in on those Harleys you saw out there. I was afraid Kurt might be with them too, but thank God he's still in Miami. Him and Quayle split up down there and Quayle took off for Texas. Says he's been working offshore rigs down around Corpus Christi. Hell, offshore drugs is more likely, I told him."

"I didn't see any Quayle out there. How could I miss seeing the likes of Quayle?"

"Surprised you didn't catch the stink off them. Like the three of them followed a manure spreader all the way up from Texas. You should've seen it. He comes in here," Mo's getting excited, picking up speed, her eyelids narrowing in, "starts going through my cabinets and stuff, sticks his beer in my refrigerator just as natural as you please, uses the phone, just like he owned the place and was wanting to make the payments on all this stuff. I told him I didn't need him or his beer neither one!"

"A female would be able to use that tone with Quayle, I suppose, and get away with it."

"*Or* the scum cowboys he rode in with."

"Seems like you succeeded. Your backyard looks perfectly cowboy-free to me."

"Like hell. He's out there someplace. Snooping around

where nobody can see is all. Thought he'd do some exploring, he says. He'll come back, soon as those cold ones he took runs out, plus my almost full Daniel's he swiped. God only knows how many downs he's running up his arm besides. Anyone else, it would kill them."

Perhaps true, I think. But then don't I know one dependable exception? We light up smokes, let a little silence fall. "I just got my answer," I say.

"I didn't know there was any question."

"No question. Well, an open question. My brother put in a vital-sounding request for my showing up here to-day, as if I wasn't planning to anyhow. He didn't give me the reason and I just got it. Quayle would be the reason."

"Milo's not even here."

"He will be."

Maureen tastes her beer, leaving an eye on me. "I don't know if that makes me feel better or worse," she says, "knowing that. No offense, Dean, but you know your brother's not exactly the cat's ass of politeness either."

"Hardly."

Maureen adds, "Especially lately."

"Milo's doing some heavy dosing," I say, "but he's keeping up with his Stresstabs. He'll surprise you, the way he can stand up to so much substance abuse. He's like Randy Quayle in certain ways."

"In certain ways like he can make himself a pretty unpleasant personality when he wants to, too."

"But at least he'll tend to keep it pretty much on the good guys' side. You know, liberty and justice for all? That's Milo."

"Stop making it sound funny! I want to know what this is all about, and I don't like them picking my place for whatever it is, either. Not when my kid is involved. I'd like to know why these guys have to go around pounding ass all the time the way they do. Can't do anything else till they have it figured out which one's got the biggest balls. Must be what having balls does for a person."

To my relief the clutter on tape finally ran down. I point to where the glass door is rattling in its track. "Your husband," I say.

"I see him." Maureen has to go across and unlock to answer.

"What the hell!" Bob says. "What the hell's it locked for?"

Maureen says, "I was trying to keep the skunks out is why. What is it?"

"I want you to come get these dogs out of my food. Willie's setter just made off with about a pound of my burger patties."

Mo steps out. Bob steps in. He gives me a smile, flapping the cool into the sweaty bib of his apron, his spatula dripping hot grease. Bob's the kind that smiles like a kid at everything. "How you doing, Dean?"

"Pretty fair. Nice dump," I tell him.

"Thanks. Get Mo to show you around?"

"Like to, but right now she's too highly pissed off over Quayle and his associates."

You can hear Maureen out there bossing the animals. She'll have them off in pretty short order, what with her nature for getting submission out of a dog—a way she has with horses, too. No dog of Mo's will beg, bark, or leave water in the wrong place as long as she's within sniffing range. She prefers them bred for companionship and protection, rather than the hunt. That's why she'll accept the grinding of so many of her Labs under the wheels of a passing vehicle before she'll ever own a hound.

Bob's been talking: "Why hell, I told her to forget about Quayle. Didn't I say if he started any shit I'd just shoot his face off? Didn't I, Mo."

"That's pretty funny too," she says. She's back, bearing plates of potato salad, weenies, beans. "That is just the right kind of humor at the right time," she says.

"Really. I got the old 20-gauge Winchester oiled up and ready to go. All's I need's a target. Besides, he was begging for it, wasn't he, Dean? Isn't a white person here would witness against me on that."

"Go away."

After he does Maureen clips in a new tape, sits and moves the plastic fork around her food. The music this time is in the Nashville strain, the kind she likes but isn't letting it show. "Men," she says, resting her elbows.

"Don't I know it."

"Why couldn't this be happening at somebody else's place so I could just go home and forget about it?"

"The both of us."

"Bob wasn't fooling about that shotgun, you know."

"Why should he be? Sorry, I didn't mean that."

Maureen spears a charred, blistered hot dog and raises it whole. "It's the kid I'm worried about," she says, pointing the meat at me, "or believe me I wouldn't hesitate using it myself. Not that Ryan'll get hit, but he'll see what kind of damage his daddy can make with a gun like that, and then he'll have to grow up crooked in the head like all boys do and I'd just as soon keep him away from that for a while, you understand? A kid don't need that."

We kill a little time trying to eat. Now that Simon's gone I wouldn't mind sounding her about him—the kid everyone likes. I wouldn't have to cover everything, just enough to slide this elephantine rock off my conscience. The only thing half going my way and now it's gone! (What am I saying?) But Simon tried to rescue me from too much of myself. Last night, after we were finished but still clinging, Simon said, "I want this all the time. I don't know why. You want to know what it feels like, Dean? It don't feel wrong anymore. You want it, don't you? I can tell you do." I thought, What would he like to hear just now? then for some reason said the opposite: "This is everywhere in the world—tired people wanting to be clung to." What's the matter with me? What's so hard about just being in the moment, like Simon?

"Why'd you get quiet all of a sudden?" Maureen wants to know.

But how do you talk about it and not come off looking like one of those pervs that hang around public toilets? "I don't have much to say," I say.

"Well why don't you eat then instead of staring at it? I don't see what you've got to be so nervous about. You're just a bystander. Here I am with property and a child to protect."

"I'm not going to sit here arguing over who's got the most to be nervous about, Maureen. I'm just saying I don't like the wait any more than you. Waiting for it to show up when you know it's going to, when you already have the experience of what it's going to be like. You think of Quayle, your desire for things, for food, even picnic food, just fades, flies right out the window. Don't want to make conversation. Can't even eat."

"*I* can eat."

Mo and I turn. Quayle said that. He's over there in the door, his two buddies behind. He says, "What's on the menu?" moving a step in. He's wearing cutoff jeans (recently altered, by the pink of his legs), huaraches, a leather vest.

"I'm not air conditioning the whole goddamn out-doors!" Mo tells him. "Would you please shut that door, preferably with you on the other side of it?"

"Get in here!" Quayle orders the two in back of him, "and shut it. Jeez Christ!" His bottom half is as petal pink as the top is brown; looks like two different bodies sewn together. He turns back around, his expression gone to sugar. It's a chinless sort of face, a gray tooth in the center of the mouth. "I do hope we're not busting in on anything. But it's so terribly hot out there." He takes mincing little baby steps toward the middle of the floor. "Gosh, I was just out there playing and it was making me awful thirsty. Now don't let me bother you any, I just want to fetch me a cold one and I'll leave you alone. You go right ahead with what you was doing."

The two he rode up with—a little wizened wetback with amphetamine eyes and a fat one with a black beard taking mouthfuls out of a hamburger—are staying, so far, just inside the door. The one chewing says, "This the one, Quayle?"

"No," Quayle says. "This here's his nelly homosex brother." He holds up a limp wrist and looks through his eyelashes at me. He says, "This is where the Ladies Club's gathering this afternoon."

I'm feeling that anxiousness in my groin. Here we go, folks. The party. This is it.

Maureen says, "Your beer's out in the cooler with the rest. The party's out there too."

"No!" Indignation takes him over; disbelief. He covers his heart. "Now, damn it, Maureen, I wanted those separate. See, that was not your common beer, you know. No, that there was your real fancy-type imported. I brought that beer up special just to share with you, Maureen. And here you went and mixed it up with them common brands?"

"That's what I said, wasn't it?"

"Well then we'll just have to go out and liberate it, won't we."

The skinny, sick-looking one's accent is sort of Tex-Mex. "You want me to go leeborate it?"

"Who rattled your chain!" says Quayle back at him. "No. I wouldn't. I would like for you two to go grease the bikes or something. I'm sick of your company. Both of you."

"Later, Quayle," says the porcine one with his mouth full of hamburger. "Nobody I ever heard of ever elected you king of this rodeo. Me and the kid's as thirsty as you. We got as much rights as you."

I couldn't say what kind of face Quayle's making him, but the fat one's mouth stopped chewing a while ago, and it got quiet in here over the interval. Then Quayle moves. His Mexican shoes sound like baskets on his feet. In something of a slow waltz he shuffles over between them and out the door.

We're all watching as Quayle pulls up this side of the beer cooler, drops his shorts to the ankles, and dunks his head under the icewater, leaving us a perfect view: like a white orchid dotted with pimples. Which his retinue, Fat and Lean, find amusing enough to kick up their knees and slap them over.

Then's when Quayle reaches a cupped hand around his hip and lets water dribble into his rear cleavage.

My friend comes to her feet. "That's it, Quayle, that's as far as you go," she says. "I'll wipe your ass for you!"

The burly one is all done laughing. He blocks the door. "Randy can't hear, he's underwater."

"Move out of my way, fatso. BOB!" she screams.

I find myself coming towards the action. I'm not, my feet are. When Maureen wheels around and heads the other way I practically slam into her for the second time today. I go to follow her, but then the big one's arm hooks in front of me, hugs my face to his rubbery chest. I smell armpit and gasoline and beer and the venting burger with onion and mustard. I'll want to check myself over for crabs.

Someone hits the button, stops the music. "BOB!" Mo screams again.

I can feel the shimmy of laughter wiggle through my assailant's belly and his free hand rising between my legs. He inquires, "You had your cherry broke yet, Nell?"

"He been under der too long," the Chicano says.

"Bob! Goddamit Bob!!"

My feet leave the ground. The big guy grunts, heaving me by the crotch, throwing me free. I can't tell if there's any pain yet because of the adrenalin.

Once I'm up and can see again I see Quayle's head raise up fast. His hair throws out a mohawk of spray. In his right hand he holds two of his green bottles triumphantly overhead while stooping to hitch up his pants.

But I don't see any Bob and I don't see any brother of mine either. Can't even find Maureen. Probably ran for the front door and around the side, because her yellow Labrador just chased through after her smell, pushing off like a scared bunny rabbit.

Then I hear the shots. Two of them, through the smoothbore tube, like a bazooka. Bzhhhhhh-bzhhhhhhh.

She pretty much had them tricked the same as the dog. A minute ago you heard the rallying cry and our boys were all over the porch—Schmitter, Montgomery, Walker, Chute, McLaird—making like there was going to be some valorous uproar, until she fired off the two shots from below, tore a couple of wide matching gashes in the air but meant to kill nobody, and the boys turned into a freeze-frame for about as many seconds as it took the noise to double back from the hills and decay. Someone shouted for them to look out, she was loading up again! Which emptied the porch out fast.

Except for Quayle.

And then I came to this window so I could watch and not get shot.

Maureen is holding the gun. She is blood-hot all over. I've never seen so many of her teeth. Between her and Quayle is the pregnant air and the raised Winchester gun. Everyone is like an athlete waiting for the pistol to start their relay race, springs wound and nobody chanc-

ing to draw breath. Kids are hiding behind their mothers'
knees, and the squeamish among the adults would like to
turn and run. But you don't want to do anything sudden
like that when there's a live murder weapon, so you look
at something else, your shoes, anything.

To Quayle, with the drugs and alcohol on his side, it
presents no terrible concern. He stands a little too com-
fortably at the railing and stares directly down the weapon's cobalt nostrils.

She was standing cocked and aimed.

Then she was thwarted. "Give me that thing!" Bob
finally appeared out of somewhere and took the thing
away. Here's a place where he's not smiling. He breeches
it, plucks out the shells, and releases the hammers. "Are
you crazy!"

"But you said . . ."

V.

Now that it's safe to go outside, I can get out of Quayle what he intends doing with my brother. Think I'll warm him up by asking how he managed so much tranquility. The way I imagine a good journalist might have to do. "I would've been pissing down my leg back there, and as far as that goes you didn't even blink."

Sounds like I'm talking to a celebrity.

"You would piss yourself if your mother kissed you funny." Water runs off his greasy hair as it would a duck; a bead is glistening at the end of his nose. He is watching over the heads of people for something. "All it did was to fuck up the high I had going. Now if I was ready to get killed out here it might be a different matter, but it ain't time for me to die yet."

Balls of Douglas MacArthur, thinks me. "How did you know?" I say. "What if you were wrong? What if there'd been an accident? I hear when people kill these days they don't exactly think of the mess on their floors or capital punishment, they just kill."

"Look!" He jerks around like I was barging in on his privacy, "I'm not into intellectual conversations. I just think when I have to think. Now if you're so goddamn worried about it, when I'm ready to get my brains blowed out I'll let you know and you can come watch." He returns to his surveying, feeling down his vest pocket with two fingers.

Down on the ground Maureen is crying out loud for him to go away.

His fingers come up empty. "Give me a cigarette," he says.

I shake two out of my pack and give him one. "Your buddies disappeared."

"I believe they'll be able to handle theirselves."

"Who are you looking for then? Milo?"

"Maybe."

"What might you be planning to do with him?" I ask the back of Quayle's head.

"We have us a little corporation, me and your brother."

"Do you," I say. "So do we, my brother and I."

"Ain't that nice and family-like of you two."

"Yes," I say. "Then it must be we're all in the same business. Only thing, I never did catch what our product was."

"Product?"

"Whatever it is our trade is in. What about it? You'd be on the commodities end, I suppose."

"Then I'll just have to respect my partner's decision," says Quayle. "He's a smart, sound-minded businessman."

"But this isn't a partnership, it's a corporation," I argue, "and I'm *in* the corporation—Milo has five hundred of my dollars—"

Hearing something, Quayle cuts his eyes past me, frowns hard for me to shut up, because Maureen and Bob are climbing the steps. The gun barrel is swinging loose now, safe over Bob's elbow. Before they're too close Quayle advises me, "Maybe you better get you some more business lessons; because that five hundred don't get you a seat on our board. What you got isn't worth but a couple of shares. Now you can wait on us to move your money up, or you can sell out any time."

Bob is bringing her over.

"Prick," she says.

"She wants an apology," Bob says. "You've got a pretty butt, I'm sure, but Maureen doesn't much like it."

"My apologies, my apologies . . ." Quayle is facing out the drive for Milo.

"Prick," she says.

"Probably wouldn't be a bad idea if you left," Bob says.

Still not turning, Quayle says, "Probably wouldn't be a bad idea either for you to put that blunderbuss up out of temptation's way."

"That's none of your domain, is it." Bob gives it a short wait, then nudges Quayle in the shoulder. "Is it? Look at me."

Quayle looks at him. "I won't leave yet," he says, rolling back around, continuing to watch for the empty drive to fill up with Milo, "I'm waiting on somebody. Once he gets here I won't have to stay no longer than—"

"Leave, punk!" Maureen isn't fooling in the least. "Leave, pig!"

"If you're staying," says Bob, "then move away from this house and Mo. I'm not gonna babysit the two of you all day long."

"Yes, you are," Maureen says.

Quayle says nothing, keeps looking away.

"You're going to have to baby-sit *me* anyway," she says, "since I'm going to get drunk. Since you're the one that seems to have control over the situation so good, because I haven't been drunk since that baby was born and I'm *gonna* get drunk. I don't even want to touch that cooler after that pig had his . . . Dean, would you get me a beer out of there? Get me up an American beer, too. One of those common brands." She is smearing grimy tears back on her cheek. "I just hope them caps are tight," she says.

Another twenty minutes and Milo still doesn't show.

Meanwhile, the majority and I came out to this pasture fence where we learned Quayle's friends had already opened target practice with a .38 automatic revolver. Seems as if Mo cleared the way for firearms in general, because the others are into it now with a .22 rifle, sitting thirty paces off in a made-up shooting gallery of old lawn chairs at the edge of the watermelon plot, taking turns blowing empties off the fence posts and the roof of the tack shed, observing for the moment the gentle serious- ness of males getting drunker and drunker yet bonding closer all the time in the spirit of sport. But I say it's a good thing nobody has thought up a leisure game involv- ing chain saws yet.

Right. They have.

Here's a guy I was hoping to see, named Featheroff. Neil will be in his third year up at Harvard Law. He looks about as blissful here as me. "Just a moot question for you, Featheroff. What can a husband get for beating his pregnant wife and causing her to miscarry?"

"Let's see . . ." he thinks. Featheroff's old man, Clar- ence, is a state congressman, the one that cut the tracks up through Harvard for Neil to follow in. Neil will be just one more lawyer in the world, but one in the upper salary range, with the Republican billfold. Neil bears the beginnings of that kind of flab and jowls already, and he's working up to a good cocktail glow. "We're talking about *fetus interruptus*," he laughs. "Hey, that's a good one, isn't it? However, I don't believe that has any precedent yet in case law."

"Come on, Featheroff, be serious. Let's see if you learned anything."

"All right, if we're going for criminal charges then we're charging for plain assault. Are we saying there are witnesses?"

"Let's say not."

"Good. Nothing then. She'd have the burden of proof,

of course, and proving it is damn near impossible. It would be on the prosecution to come up with a pretty reliable, impartial witness or two to win something like that, and without it it would be difficult to even sue for bodily damage, I'd say. Of course it's up to the individual state in these matters." Featheroff beams his flabby face. "There," he says, "how's that? Now when do I get my moot fee?"

"Wait a minute. Let's say the prosecuting attorney himself happens to be a pretty strong character witness against the defendant."

"Well then I'd say you just put your ignorance of legal procedure right on the table," Featheroff says. "Don't you know a lawyer can't testify in his own client's trial?"

"Oh," I say.

"What are you doing, writing a book or something?"

"What? No, I've got this friend . . . So you say he wouldn't have to worry, the husband. Wouldn't even have to consider, say, paying her a bribe to keep it out of court."

Featheroff says, "If you're going to take my counsel to a real live person, Dean, then I think there's something in the ethics that says I have to keep my mouth shut, especially if I haven't even passed the bar yet. And even if I had, I could only advise you to advise your friend to come by my office. Not that I anticipate wasting my time in any piddling little criminal and divorce courts, of course. So, in the circumstances, Dean, I can't give you an answer on that."

"Thanks, Featheroff, you already did."

Walking down from the house, off in the distance, a riotous Polynesian shirt stands out, topped off by the unmistakable inkblot, the flexuous antenna on his Plectron waving and wobbling in the air, the whole thing advancing on us like something obscene. Per usual.

I hurry up the bank to meet him. What's this? For a

second I was afraid that strap over his shoulder was a pistol halter, the kind the FBI and thugs wear under their clothes, only because it would stand to reason. But I see now it's only an empty knapsack. "You're not dressed right for such a serious face," I say. "Hope it's not because you've got disappointing news for Qu—"

He stepped right past without saying.

"Hey! Quayle's waiting for you," I say. "I'd have to say he hasn't made himself too popular so far."

"Shut up!" Milo says. "What're they doing with guns down there?" He stopped dead, like someone noticing their house was on fire from a block away.

"Just playing with cans," I tell him, "now. But Quayle just about gave his brains to Maureen's shotgun a while ago. You should've seen it."

"Dean," says he, "I cannot shit, I cannot sleep, and I have myself a headache that would render the strongest American helpless. So just stop bleating in my ears, will you? How many's he got with him?"

"I wasn't aware I was bleating—"

"How many!"

"Two! Two besides Quayle. One's the fat one who just fired the pistol. A regular Gloria Vanderbilt. Then there's another, kind of on the scrawny side but probably no less refined."

Milo whacks up some long grass with a hard kick. "This is just liable to be worse than I expected," he sort of admits to himself.

"Would you mind telling me what's going on?"

"Come on," he says. "We've got to make this fast. Do you remember how to ride?"

"A horse!"

"Go get a bridle on that appaloosa and saddle her up. No, there's no time for a saddle. You or I'll have to ride bareback."

Most likely I. "Don't you think, if we're going to play

cowboys and Indians, don't you think we better ask
Maureen? That appaloosa's hers." ˙

"Maureen ain't going to know the difference. I just
came from there, she's dead drunk. Now listen, I've got
some very important details to talk over with Quayle.
I've got to get him on a horse, somehow, and away from
here. Alone. That's my plan. So you get that horse ready
to ride, and after that you stick around and keep your
mouth shut, because you're coming with us. I'm going to
need you." For the first time since this morning Milo
looks me in the eye. It's that same fearsome look, deso-
late; it's, well, ominous.

He adds: "All right?"

I don't know why I do it when I have the certainty it's
a sheer leap in the dark. As I go about quieting the boys'
guns to get at the tack shed words like sap and sucker
arise out of some diminishing reserve of good judgment
and bleat in my ears.

Lucky for me the humidity is up where it is so I won't
have far to chase Granny. Still, I approach catlike, the
bridle and bit secreted behind my back. If it wasn't for
these grasshoppers, about the size of bullfrogs, snapping
into life in the hundreds under each footfall, she'd never
have heard me.

When Mo taught me to ride, some years back, she
didn't cover much of the riding part. How you did that,
she said, was a matter for the individual. Instead, what
she stressed was gaining ascendancy over the animal before you mounted it. "It's strong and it's dumb," she
said. "But not as dumb as all that." She told me about a
cousin of hers; first time the kid ever mounted a horse it
took off under him and ran him full-tilt straight back to
the barn. The tin roof on that barn was keen-edged as a
butcher knife, slanting down to about the horse's neck;
even the horse had to duck it to run in. Had her cousin

been a little bigger and not watching out he would have been severed in two at the waist. "Now that," Mo maintained, "was a good horse to learn on. If you don't have enough fear and bewilderment the first time you sit on a horse, then the horse is going to try and put it in you and keep it in you. So if you got any," she told me, "you'd better lose it quick and learn to raise your voice and your hand. The horse don't understand a thing that ain't whumped in."

After all the cavil and abuse it takes to rein her, I massage Granny's muzzle and climb on for a test ride. Right off I can tell she's too wide and too warm to run, and ouchy on the ground because her toenails need trimming. Added to that, as we near the fence, she scares each time a bullet rings out. You hear the crackshots over there bluffing their way through tales of wild animals, on the scale of *massive*, they've had to kill between the eyes. But at least they're still friendly towards each other, as sporting individuals, earnest in their stupid pleasure. Holding loose reins I ride Granny gently through, over to where Milo and Randy Quayle are talking very important stuff under a big tree.

"Here you go," I tell him. "Now where are we riding?"

"Just don't get impatient," says Milo, cradling his portable relay device snug into a socket of the tree's webbed foot. "We're all coming."

"The three of us? On this old plug? Don't you think that might get a little crowded."

"I'm expecting another couple horses here any minute. Quayle here's going to have the privilege of mounting a real live champion saddle horse." My brother's had a change of humor. He's become, in an irksome way, convivial again—no, maybe cocky is the word—for Quayle's sake.

"Fuckin' pony ride," says the beer-sucking Quayle. "Try and make a simple fuckin' trade and this guy wants to take a fuckin' pony ride. Listen, I told you, man, I'll just have my boys go out there and get the drugs and we'll do the transaction right on your front seat. Save a bunch of fuckin' pony rides for later."

"What's the problem, Quayle, afraid you'll get on a real horse and it'll throw you?"

"No. No, I'm not afraid of that. Because I'm completely fuckin' sure you ain't gonna come up with the one that's gonna have a chance of doing that. Business, though, man. Transact the shit first and I'll stay up on anything you got longer'n you after we transact."

"And I said no. My conditions call for an absolutely low profile. There's too many reasons for it where I'm concerned. One is, we got a lot of nosy people around here, and I'm trying to keep my nose clean. I have a soiled reputation; I'm trying to upgrade it. Besides, reputation aside, certain people here are not to be trusted around this kind of money and contraband."

"Point to one, asshole."

"You want your money, Quayle, like I said, do this my way. Or I'll take my business elsewhere, and you can do likewise with yours."

"Fuckin' pony ride . . . And what the fuck is that thing, anyways?" Quayle has been further suspicioning my brother's portable with his off-color eyes. "I been wondering about that. Looks like something a cop would use on a stakeout."

"I'm a civil servant," says Milo. "As a civil servant I'm on call twenty-four hours."

"Civil servant."

"I'm an active employee of the Ambrose Fire Department. If you don't believe me, I've got my badge and my official Zippo with our union insignia on it I'll show you."

I put in, "If you two are going to stand here chatting then I've got time to strap a saddle on this—"

"No, you don't," Milo says. "Why don't you just chill out for about a minute, will you? Just—"

"How come you got it out here then? You ain't even on duty?"

I was wondering the same. But naturally he has the plausible, ready answer.

"I thought I just got finished telling you I'm *always* on duty. This time of year a fire can burn out of control on you inside of a minute. That's all it takes. Mostly your barn and brush fires. We'll get calls on several of those a day, sometimes one on top of another. That's why it takes all the manpower we've got, ready to mobilize twenty-four hours; and since we're short-staffed to begin with, well, you can appreciate where I'm expected to respond to all alarms."

"The fuck you talkin' about?"

"And besides that I'm on good behavior, like I said. I'm trying to live down the stigma of a recent disciplinary suspension. If I'm delinquent from work because I'm out here partying, well, the chief'll have his excuse to give my job to some unskilled, inexperienced rooky. Because he doesn't much like me to begin with."

As he was reciting this bilge Milo gave me a quick wink that was meant to say, This is the place for you to keep your mouth shut. Because he is prattling on like a desperate man and he knows I know it.

"All right, enough with the pyrotechnic lecture," says Quayle. "Let's get this turkey in the fuckin' oven. Where's these fucking horses of yours at?" Quayle is cleaning the picnic food from his remaining teeth with the plastic toothpick feature on his Swiss Army knife. I've never know anyone to actually use it before. He adds: "And they best have saddles."

"Nice try on the vocabulary, Quayle," I point out, "but that's something else, what you're talking about. Pyrotechnics happens to be fireworks."

"I'm gonna haul your faggot ass down off there in about a minute, cocksucker!" His face would be igniting with embarrassment if he hadn't made sure it was rage-red first.

"Didn't know you were so fragile," I say.

"What's this sissy turdfuck coming for, anyway!"

"Shut up, you two," Milo cuts in, "here they come."

From way over in the direction Milo's facing come the two identical bays, gleaming majestic stallions bearing down to beat hell. Can't even hear the clopping yet but I recognize the tiny riders at once (though I've never seen them ride), handling their mounts like the best poised jockeys, fannies raised and backs in line with the ground, forearms pumping in stride, both young bodies in perfect pliant agreement with all that power and fury beneath them. Daphne and Claudette! It's so beautiful I have to hold my breath!

There was even a cease-fire until they got up to us.

"Run the piss out of them why don't you!" Milo yells. "Now they're all out of gas. Look at them! And what took you?" He's addressing Daphne, the older one, mainly. "I'm in a hurry here. I could've walked to where I have to go and back by now."

Claudette dismounts first. I didn't realize they were so close-by, but she indicates they live just over that wooded hill. The firstborn, Daphne, dances her horse in place proudly. Her hair is tied back in a tail. "That really makes a lot of sense," she tells her dad. "First you scream at us for running Harper and Ferry too hard, and then you scream at us for not getting here quick enough. Make up your mind which one we're in trouble for, Dad."

Her attitude strikes me as fairly logical. Also, it smacks strongly of an earlier version of her dad.

"You have to show off your horsemanship and your big mouth both, don't you," Dad says. "Look at that," he says, swiping either Harper's or Ferry's rump, "you could fill a bucket with that sweat! You ought to know better. Now get down. I want you two to stay away from these undesirables and their guns till we get back. Now go on up to the house and play."

"We don't play anymore, Dad," says Daphne.

"Then get up there and do whatever your damn sagacity will allow!" Milo says. "Now!"

"Better let 'em drink," she says.

VI.

DAPH OR CLAUDE'S horse with Quayle on it leads us through the gate—head jogging, nickering, in complaint of what's sitting on his back, I would guess—my brother next, with Granny and me bringing up the rear. If it wasn't for Granny's being overweight, short of breath already, and tender in the feet, not to mention the shadowy nature of this whole safari, it might be nice just to give myself over to the ride.

I was right about one thing at least, that Quayle would take Maureen's wisdom about horses and apply it to the extreme, because he already did. Soon as he had room he used a switch he'd selected from among the sturdier scions and Claudette's horse damn near kicked him off for being so rude. That horse of my niece's is a highbred animal with manners, but also a lot feistier than average. For a second all four hooves were in the air. The rider wasn't thrown, but it restores my faith to see Quayle's face scared raw, so I call: "Easy Quayle, take it easy on him. It ain't some old nag, you know!"

Quayle chokes the horse up as you might expect, leans over and catches hold of my brother's undone, gaudy shirt to say, "I've had enough out of this faggot-ass faggot! What the fuck's he got to do with this!"

Milo swats the offending hand away. "He's coming."

"What for?"

"Because I want him. I want someone with me . . ."

153

His voice trails off appreciatively. "In case anything happens."

Asks Quayle, "What's gonna happen?"

Which was my question exactly.

His reply: "I want someone here I can trust."

It took me with pride to hear him say it. But I feel a little like a dope, too, sitting back here on this fat horse being bandied about.

With his face full of overdone pity, so as to suggest you-poor-creature-you, Quayle asks, "Now, did *I* have to bring somebody *I* could trust?"

"Quayle, if the individual don't exist, it's not my fault. Now let's get moving."

"Tell him to keep a fucking lid on it then or he's gonna be without it. And wait a minute, one more thing. That squawk box of yours, you're leaving it, I decided."

"Did you."

"I'm already letting you outnumber me. Fuck if I'm walking into some surprise you got fixed up."

Milo is carrying the squawk thing over his shoulder, with the wobbling antenna sticking conspicuously out the top of the knapsack. "I told you," he says, "there's liable to be a—"

"If that fire-man profession of yours gives you such an almighty hard-on," says Quayle, "then the sooner you put that fucking thing down on the ground somewhere, the sooner you're gonna get back here to play with your little fire-man buddies."

For an exceedingly long and manly interval they stare each other off. In the middle of it Quayle says, "Now that's good advice." Then, at the end, he inquires, "Or would you want me to have Oliver ride up alongside on his bike with his .38? Maybe make things a little more trustworthy?" The brown tooth shows in the center of his grin. Oliver, that must be the one with so much size. The other, the skinny one, I imagine, would have to be called Stanley.

Milo eventually does it, climbs down and conceals his portable under a bush.

Satisfied, Quayle leads out again. And Milo, setting foot in the stirrup and taking the leather in both hands, looks back with that same hapless face he's put on me twice already today.

"Everyone's going to thank me for it."

Each step of the ride has us pitching forward at the hips; the rest just lags like so much semi-upright glutinous cargo. We're for the time being a ways behind Quayle, Milo facing straight ahead without focus. He adds, still confidentially, "Everybody that's involved in this thing."

Seems I have myself in a situation I not only don't have any choice or say over, but don't have the faintest iota what it's about. Sort of in a way shanghaied. Instead of explaining, he'd prefer to slouch over there like a comatose version of Bozo in the saddle and make me guess. What's wrong is, for one thing, he hasn't had a drink today. There's the green puffy gills; probably nightmares swimming in the bloodstream. He's a lot worse off than sober. "Thank you for what?"

". . . Huh?"

"You were saying."

"Now don't you start in on me too! Ain't I got enough to think about without you heaping more on!"

This seems to have excited the forward cowboy. "Who you callin' a moron!"

"No one's talking to you, Quayle!"

"What're you two discussing back there behind my back!"

"Baseball. My brother and I were just talking baseball!"

"The hell's that blow job know about baseball!" Quayle

appears to extract mirth from the very premise. "Anyways I thought you wanted to ride. This here's more like a fuckin' mule train. That all you can get outa them things?"

With that Milo swifted ahead to ride in the company of Quayle. One more rankling oath to hurl in the face of decency!

It's gone dark under the tree canopy, with the late afternoon rays slicing in from a low angle, windless, but a little cooler. We would come out to woods like this a lot, Dad, with Milo and me along. The cold cloudy Februarys. First thing we'd do was separate. Spread out and just hunt for things in the cold, three separate plunderers. I have that picture of Dad in my memory—head down, looking hard at the ground. My brother and I came up with lots of stuff: empty shotgun shells, bones, agates, bird feathers; if we were lucky, fossils and arrowheads. He never came up with anything. It got cold out there, but going home was something he seemed to want to put off. Eventually hunger made him look up. And then the whole house smelled of Mom's potato soup. He would have been sober on those days. Definitely. Sober, but then, sad. I don't think Milo had it altogether exact, complete, the way he was describing it last night, remembering the way he does. Dad came out here to put his head down and be quiet. It was to a place like this he drove the family station wagon the day he parked it for good . . .

We've accelerated to a lope. I can smell the sweet of Quayle's joint hanging in the air. From behind they appear, on such sleek, perfect animals, ludicrous and inconsistent. Overhead a woodpecker nails a dead tree and quits. They always do that; and afterwards, in the quiet, it's still an unbelievable sound! Now Quayle's up there singing something—a noise indistinguishable from

a host of angels. What are we doing fouling up the great
outdoors like this?

While I've got my mind on the past, there's something
else I remember about last night. Simon, when we faced
that peculiar interval, became tearful in our fellowship,
shivering in every seraphic limb. It was too hot to shiver.
I asked him what it meant and he said he guessed it
meant he was remembering. He told me when he was a
younger kid he lived in Hingham, on the south shore of
Boston, on the way to the Cape. Everything there was
about as normal as it gets. His dad was a musician. His
mom was a hair stylist. She called herself that because
she specialized in men. It was like you hear about all the
time: Simon's dad came home unexpectedly, but he was
expecting what he found in the living room, because he
had the gun handy and loaded. Simon and all the brothers and sisters were upstairs. The three shots woke them
up. "See, Dean?" Simon had stopped snivelling but the
agitation was not over. "You want to, but you can't
really trust nobody. You can't believe anything." And
for no good reason I thought it was a safer idea to agree.
I thought, two scared, pathetic sodomites, huddled here
under the dark. Made me want to just sleep, or drink till
it got nice and sappy again. About all I really knew about
mine was he was in the newspaper business. I wanted to
ask Simon, What instrument did yours play?

A stream. And per Daphne's wishes we jump down
and let them have all the drink they want. Quayle too,
what with all the booze to dehydrate him, falls to his
knees, hands cupped in the flux, and sips noisily.

Meanwhile, Milo takes me between Granny and his
horse and before I know it there's something in my hand.
A pocketknife. "What am I doing with this?"

"Just put it away and don't ask."

"Am I going to have to be afraid for my life now?"

He whispers, "There's liable to be a little trouble."

"Suppose you enlarge on that."

He steps into the stream, sneakers and all, splashes his face, removes his shirt, puts it back on dripping, returns.

I announce that I'm leaving.

"What do you mean, you're leaving."

"I mean, whichever way you go, I'll be going in the other direction." I now actually hear myself paraphrase a Quayleism: "See, I don't believe I'm ready to die yet."

Milo was ready for this. "All right," he says, fast, "not that you're even going to need that knife, but what if I was to fatten your share a little?"

"You better do *something*."

"What if I told you you'd get back . . . double your money?"

"I heard that one before, and it somehow got diminished to 10 to 15 percent. So no to that."

"All right then, I didn't want you to think I was just talking, just throwing out offers so generous it sounded like I was desperate or something, but what I'm going to do is pay you two thousand flat. Two thousand won't hurt me in the least."

"Two thousand dollars?"

"I'd offer you more, and, like I said, it wouldn't even dent my own take, but then you'd just figure what little I expected out of you was going to have to be earned. But all I'm asking is for you to stand by me and hand me that thing when and if I need it—which I seriously doubt will eventuate."

"Then why don't you hold it yourself?"

"I'm not going to argue. Two thousand."

"The price of my life!" I submit, pretty melodramatically.

"Don't let's be melodramatic about it. Let's just call it the cost of my getting me a good soldier."

We go on. Now I am not concerned with any more

bird songs and my reflective mood has been snuffed by the all but certain imbroglio ahead. Which doesn't even require thinking, beyond the girding of loins and tallying up some additional dollars.

Love (affinities of the brotherly sort, anyway) is presently at the business end of a Boy Scout implement.

I suppose, to break up the whining in me that wishes to go on unscathed and living, I suppose I could whisper to Milo what I got on good Harvard advice today: that he has nothing to fear from that malingering female he last married; it's the emptiest of threats, what Velda and Miller are getting up against him. But why bring her up? Why press your karma? On that same account I see no reason to tell him of the phone call I took for him this morning.

Under these trees it's like being in a cavernous garage. You hear things in a sort of subaqueous reverb, especially Quayle, because when you hear from Quayle it's loud, everything he says is loud and sticks to your ears. "Horseraces!" he goes, in sour disbelief over something Milo must have said. "What the hell would I do at a horserace!"

"Just thought . . . It can be a real, you know, lucrative venture, if you've got the know-how. I for one have a great fondness for the track. Isn't that so, Dean?"

Rare that you'll hear him mention it anymore though, since Pat lighted out with her gentleman breeder and settled on his fabulous place in back of those hills. After which Milo sort of lost interest in track gambling—though he was expert at it—out of spite. "Guess so," I say.

"Now you go down there to Padre Island," says Quayle, "take in a good dirt bike contest. Get you a case of beer and some good toke. There's where you get your rocks off. Got a . . . aura to it, a real aura, that half-mile race, them screaming little 2-cycles, that sun in your face, dust in your beer. Think I enjoy watching a boy take a spill off one of them suckers just more'n about anything."

Milo only makes Quayle an unseen, uninterested gesture of give-a-shit.

We go on, leaving the trees and coming to a flat place.

We turn right, follow an old railroad track buried in scrub grass, where the two of them pick up speed till they're getting all the pull they can out of Milo's girls' horses, hooting like Comanches, leaving me behind to coax and sweet-talk old Granny. For a while there it seemed like just him and me. But I see me foraging for myself back here on a lame animal while he is having the steeplechase of his life with the enemy! I came close to turning around before I spotted him again, alone and gray as a ghost, coming back for me out of the dust fog. All right, I'm going to keep my mouth shut for Milo, for this showdown, whatever the hell it is, and my hand real close to the bulge in my pocket. For as long as this takes. Then I'm going to redeem my investment at exactly four times the principal and put the greater length of the Mississippi River between us!

It wasn't much further. Didn't take us long and I never asked where Quayle went to, just followed. Milo was very interested in the time. I didn't know it—not that he expected me to; neither of us ever did wear a watch—but when I wouldn't even calm him with an approximation he felt it necessary to say, "Don't get pissy on me."

We arrive at what you'd call a miserable hovel, and almost the ruin of one of those: shingled in wormy rectangles of scrap lumber and tar paper, buckled at the seams, strangled in flora, scabby tin roof, a rusty heap of sheet metal out front—probably home to a snake family or two. A doorway but no door, two front windows without any glass. Every inch the match of those rotted habitations rising out of the Louisiana jungle. Check this interior: two rooms of unrestricted squalor. Quayle has to kick empties out of the way and step in over one of the three unrolled, reeky sleeping bags.

Milo and I stand in the doorway taking it all in, the filth and fugitive belongings: the cobwebby floor messed up further with candle ends, cigarette butts, paper sacks, dead bugs, and squeezed out condiment pouches from the Burger King, along with several of the King's styrofoam burger wallets. The heat and smell are grievous. I'd give anything to wash my skin.

"This place is a fucking dump," Milo finally says.

"Watch it," says Quayle. Stepping over the middle of the floor, he unbuckles the main compartment on his Harley saddlebag and extracts an unbelievably ample parcel of cocaine. "Least I don't have to pitch camp in the middle of Mommy's rose garden."

"How'd you know about that?"

Quayle says, "What's the difference?" He turns, looks up at us both and answers himself. "The difference is, I'll be riding on out of this hick fucking silo-town tomorrow on a brand shiny new fucking Harley-Davidson. Be up in Ontario, Canada, by Tuesday, where the sun won't burn my titties off anymore. And I'm gonna start a whole new batch of half-Canadian citizens with a little dark-haired pussy I know up there. I'll have me exactly seven point five thousand dollars in cash to play with just as I please, too."

He looked perfectly exalted with himself when he said that, especially about the vagina, his eye rolling over here, mocking, to where I went blind for a second and felt my mouth bunch together.

My eyes come to rest on an old advertisement in the corner, a crusty old sign from maybe a century ago. I'm reading slow, for the distraction in it—SETH WYATT ARMSTRONG, it says, EXPERT CORN MASH—thinking how Seth must have hung his notice out by the railroad to catch business off the defunct B & O, when I catch something go slithering by in my upper periphery. How did I know at least one snake was going to pick this crate for a perfect domicile? It's striped and long, twined around the ceiling joist. It was moving in that stealthy, liquid way vipers have, but it stopped at a shadowed place by the wall. No place else to go from there, a blind alley, cul-de-sac.

I am considerably less fond of a snake that isn't on the ground, where it can at least run away. Thought what I was listening to was its tail end tapping the wood. It's my own heart!

Under the circumstances I am about to break silence with Milo when I feel him shuffle past on his way inside. He says something to Quayle I don't exactly hear, but what it does is make Quayle jerk around on his knee with that force of instant havoc he calls up so easily. Quayle snapped such that for a moment I was tempted to take my eyes off the skulking striped thing and give heed. But I don't. My whole body is watching it, daring it to keep still. Both wanting it to and not. Something Milo said had to do with Quayle's amending his plans to leave, say, the day *after* tomorrow. But that's not the part that ruffled Quayle up like that, and seemed to cause the serpent up there to twitch, flick his tongue towards the noise and shrink tighter to the joist; it was this last part. And Milo said it clear enough, but as if it were merely an item on a shopping list:

"I haven't got the money," he said.

Now here I am, standing in a doorway watching two criminal fools and a snake. There's no telephone or light switch or gasoline engine. Not even a toilet or glass of water if you'd like. This could be two centuries ago! And the one in the middle of the floor is profiteering in more cocaine than Hocking County could smell up in a year, while the one a step in front of me hasn't even got the money to pay for it!

My right-hand fingers rather instinctively find their way into my pocket.

Quayle's jaw hangs useless as I've ever seen a jaw do. He looms up slowly—snakelike as a matter of fact—then slowly quotes straight out, without a trace of comprehending: "You–haven't–got–the–money?"

"It's—"

"You was going to let me bring you all the way out here and show you this, and then you was going to tell me you didn't even bring the money? Now that makes me feel like dancing."

Stammers Milo, "I have it, I just . . . can't get to it right now."

Their voices are small, barely audible, eyes glaring into eyes.

"You have it," deduces Quayle, "only you just don't have it." Leaning twelve inches closer, losing that incredulous look now, he swears, "You had better go get it."

You'd think, with voices this bland and still, the snake might settle into slumber; but it's trying to climb the wall, making for an exit through that gap in the ceiling it can't quite reach. Half its body—a good yard's length—is scaling the wall, stiff as a stick, waving over and back like a broom handle clearing cobwebs.

Milo is shaking his head no. "There's no way I can bother that money now . . ." He turns quickly, makes sure I'm still with him, then imparts to Quayle, "See, it's too busy making more money."

Their four arms are slack, but all the fingers are working, limbering up for what the other might do next.

" 'Makin' more . . .' " Quayle carps back to himself. In full voice now: "What did you think this was?" he says. "I have hauled this shit clear the fuck up from the Texas Gulf on a goddamn . . . over every white-trash

country back road in seven states . . ." His arm starts to
swing.

Raising his sunglasses to entreat more earnestly with
the naked eye, Milo says, "Quayle, I need another day.
Just hold the coke for one more day. *Please*. You don't
realize how crucial this is."

Quayle's red is darkening, blossoming. Quayle is getting ready for hostilities.

"Tell you what, Quayle. I'll, I'll give you twice what
we agreed on. Double what that bag is worth."

"You'll give me shit! Okay?"

"I'll have it tomorrow. At this time tomorrow—"

"Buddy, at this time tomorrow I am going to be close
enough to that Canada border I can spit over Niagara
Falls!" He jumped on that one, collaring Milo, bringing
him close enough to kiss. He spits on him instead. "I am
gonna be a free, legal alien," says Quayle, pinching the
nose bridge and flinging Milo's glasses. "Before too long
after this exact time tomorrow!"

"Take your fucking hands—" If Milo hadn't been choked
off at that late syllable and sort of rubbed into the rotting
floorboards, I would've begun losing a whole lot of respect for Quayle's standing in the ranks of the Terrible.

They're going at it wrestling style, down in the horizontal, both clawing for throats, going for the arm- and
leghold—though there's too much sweat and slipperiness
for either. Owing to the more sizable burr in Quayle's
butt, Milo is losing; his ridiculous shirt is all the way
gone.

While being settled with in this way the loser somehow
meets my eye wearing a look of *Are you just going to
stand there and let this happen!?*

Well, tell you the truth, till it gets worse than it is, I
guess, maybe, yes. Let's say if he had you in a serious
stranglehold, or was swinging one of those empties towards
your skull, then maybe I'd jump in. But the way I see it,

Milo, you overreached yourself on this one. I mean, just how much of that lame, utter mendacity did you suppose one such as Quayle could excuse? What I guess I'm saying to you, Milo—even as the place crumbles, is listing on its foundation under the slamming of your own free-falling mass—well, I actually believe Quayle has himself a fairly watertight argument.

That understood, I resume studying overhead. Dust has begun loosening off the rafters, coating our legless friend with irritation. Its response—to slip back across its own belly and hazard in our direction—does not strike me as the smartest use of the survival instinct. Looking at it a different way though, you figure the thing had been up there roosting away placidly—this cold-blooded, elongated creature that sort of missed out on evolution, this put-upon thing after my brother's rendition of the spider, this child of nature merrily making use of its hot and hitherto unmolested matchbox, making the most of what its reptilian brain tells it is happiness—when along come these country gangsters to slug the shit out of each other over the issues of drugs and U.S. currency. Fit it together like that and you accord the snake every right to bite and inject venom into the ass of every human idiot on the order of these two. And in these humane terms you'd as soon side with the snake as any of them.

But then, its front part crooking far below the roof beam, tongue sending out to get the distance, the harassed creature thinks of dropping to freedom. It's not the tack that's wrong, but the timing. For at the time, as if choreographed that way, I hear a toilsome heave-ho and watch my brother get thrown into the exact square foot of floor the snake was interested in. It and Milo actually grazed.

However, at present Milo wouldn't know from raving incoherence; he is on his feet out of habit alone. His naked upper body is mapped with the orangy red splotch of floor burn and early bruise and he is holding a sore, ringing ear.

While the snake is back up there in a snaggled mess.

Using what little residuum of nicotined lung he has to go on, Milo tries to speak. "Get . . . look . . . don't . . ." he blathers.

Quayle is not exactly beaten out of shape but he's wanting oxygen, too.

For the time being they tide over in their separate corners and sweat.

"It's . . . too . . . hot . . . inside here . . . for this," puffs Milo.

The other one is revived enough to blow out his cheeks and raise his eyes. I watch the face squeeze into contortions of skepticism. But once they recognize what they're seeing the two eyes round out. For a split second a wily grin breaks loose across Quayle's face. He spits onto the floor a wad of stuff the controversy brought up, then approaches Milo again by inches, pulling out the blood red, multipurpose Swiss Army handle and drawing the blade, eyes on the reptile.

"You're losing it, Quayle!" Milo can make a full sentence now, but he's completely in the dark as to the other's intentions.

"Dean?" Milo says, eyes never leaving his adversary.

"Right here," I answer.

"Dean?" he speaks again. "If you're going to do anything, you'll do it now."

It's getting awfully damp down in my pocket. The thing he was referring to slips from my fingers and falls to the bottom.

The grin was what I'm taking the hunch on. Quayle's wearing it again.

"Quayle!" Milo says.

Quayle is moving closer, reaching ahead, making a fist around his knife handle and turning it, eyes lifted

skyward—if you didn't know at what, you'd swear, like
Milo, that Quayle had the countenance of someone de-
mented, gone into a homicidal trance.

"Listen to me carefully, Quayle. I'm trackable. That
portable you made me leave behind, well, I radioed in
my whereabouts before I left the party, before I got out
of my truck even. I have a friend at the other end, at the
fire station, who knows enough about the situation that if
I'm not back in two hours there's going to be a manhunt.
Quayle, is any of this getting through to you? If I'm
unable to walk and talk, Quayle, then nobody gets
benefited."

Quayle stalks. You see practically nothing of his eyes
now but the white, veiny part.

"Dean? Careful. You want to just get your head out of
the fucking clouds and get that knife out now and come
over here." His tone is measured, the soft pillow of
caution that one uses in the presence of a madman or
wild animal on the loose.

Eyes on the snake, which by this time has started back
towards me, my fingers go back in for the knife.

I thumb out the blade.

"Quayle," Milo gulps, "if you figure to hurt me, my
brother has the means to even it up."

That wanted some conviction even for a last ditch
maneuver!

"Dean? You here?"

Is this me, leaving my brother feeling, for the next
critical seconds, that a conspiracy is on between Quayle
and myself? That he, Milo, should get ready to part with
some of that neatly pumping blood we all take for granted?
Some pretty great evil in me, I admit, wishes to leave
him in ignorance It would be fair, after all. Because he
was the one that went and raised the floodgates on this
particular setback. Nevertheless I step away from where
the snake is making progress, and end up across the way

from all of them. Here, Milo. Here I am, knife and all, if you care to notice, over here where you can see now.

Instead it's Quayle who turns over his shoulder to place me, takes a short glance, then makes one hoot of a full-bellied horse laugh and says, "I guess your brother's gonna cut me with his fucking bottle opener."

What!?

Then, before the opportunity was lost, he went for it, letting out a scream of apocalyptic magnitude. The blade traveled through the snake in one good hard whack sufficient to splinter the wood; I heard but could not watch it drive home as through soft butter.

My legs buckle. My eyes take in, yes, the wee bluster of my bottle opener. I feel a bit like throwing up.

My brother I hear wail and fall to the floor for dismay.

Letting myself out the door, I make steps for Maureen's doddering old horse.

A minute later I can feel him looking me in the back. I'm forcing it, but I'm trying to resemble someone out on a reflective afternoon, facing the sunset, casting about: "Wonder how our mother's doing in pre-op."

VII.

THE RIDE BACK is about as blithe as busing home with the almost victorious football team. We're single file, grave, Milo and I, a picture of Quixote and what's his name. (The discourteous biker left us behind, in our ignominy, a while ago.) While I consider my brooding, shirtless brother the solitude allows me to construct an update, sort of trace the line of events that brought me to this juncture—seems there's supposed to be a logical method of linking one crisis to the next, the purpose being to make a reasonably intelligent stab at the future. But since the operative word here is logical I have to give up counting at number one: the place where I deplaned.

I am becoming what I see as an overstressed person. Lots of people just ahead of my age, I understand, are checking into Stress Management, the incidence of sudden death to the relatively young being clearly on the rise; for various stress-related reasons, hearts of modern males in their mid- to upper-thirties just stop ticking. Even the disciplined jogger is dropping dead. Drink and smoke less, advise the physicians, take moderate exercise but find time to be still; get at least six hours' sleep, minimize participation in stressful situations (there's the one!), meditate if need be, but in all events save your young ass while you still have the chance! Now all I need do is knock off early tonight and stay away from my brother tomorrow like I promised myself. However, as there's ever bound to be a snag, this is no exception: I couldn't just abandon him outright (for the same reason Quayle couldn't murder him), much as I might wish, since the future, as far as my money goes, still depends.

Sort of underscores the difficulty of being brothers with Milo.

"So. How long you been living off drug money?" I don't ask it to cheer him up, I admit.

"Get back there and ride. You want to ask provocative questions, ask them of your horse. My whole body hurts, thanks to you."

I say, like someone having a fit of know-it-all smugness, "You know, it's going to be really too bad when you can't satisfy your lenders. Who knows whether you'll outlive the scandal that's already attached itself. Hey, I know," I say, "if there's still time, you might get Mom to borrow on her CDs."

"Thanks a lot. How about sparing us both the goddamn recovery options. And don't come on pretending concern for my welfare at this late date, either. A lot you cared back there where it was needed." He has what's left of his bravely printed shirt wrapped around his hand and is using it to sop up the blood still escaping his nose. "If you want to know the truth, I'm a little pissed at your flimsy showing on the brotherly love end of things."

"Hey, I was there, wasn't I? Just as you requested."

"Brandishing your goddamn bottle opener and all. Christ, I was more embarrassed for you than you were for yourself. Confirms my suspicion," he says, "that you should've worn a dress."

This episode is about to close, so what the hell, let him have that one. "Sure would be nice," I say, "if you could practice usury and make your gains without fucking around with people's biochemistry."

"That's neither here nor there. It's business, like any other. If I didn't do it somebody else would."

"Yeah, well it looks to me like either you've been

robbed or you've had your fingers in your own cash drawer."

"Everything's in order. I'm delayed a day is all."

"That the truth? Or is it your patented excuse for everybody today?"

"If I wasn't sincere do you think I'd be sitting on my daughter's horse right now trying to stanch a bloody nose? All right, listen, you remember I mentioned my wife was supposed to call me last night?"

"Which one? Oh, you must mean Pat. That's right, Pat's the one holding all this money, if I correctly recall where we left off with her."

"Right."

" 'Good tidings all around,' ain't that the way you put it? But she never called, did she?"

"I was in touch with her this morning. I found out we've been delayed."

"Okay, I heard that. Go on."

"Nope."

"Tell."

"We've already had this conversation. And I told you before, I can't. You'd just go out and start filling in blanks for people at the least little ruffle. I'm sorry, Dean, but what we're doing just ain't publishable."

"You know, I'm getting pretty fed up with your part in the brotherly love end of things too, if you want to know the truth."

"Listen!" Milo reins back and stops. "What you don't know don't give you any room for doubt. What you're going to find is, I'm doing more for you than your puny fucking imagination could ever conceive!"

"Bullshit! You're doing it for yourself! Let's look that one in the face for once."

"I stand to gain. That's true enough. And what's more, it's damn good incentive for you to quit getting your bowels all pinched up with fret." Heeling his daughter's

horse into life again, he continues. "Like you said, my
lenders here are of the drug class. And the drug class
don't take too keenly to loss, damage, or delay. They
like for their substances to arrive on time and be of
reliable potency. All of which I have provided for. But
circumstances force me to be one day short. Now for the
last time, I am not shamming or swindling or absconding.
The money's safe. The profit's assured. So can we take
leave of this whole tired fucking topic!"

"Well," I say, "when I think about it I don't suppose
you'd put yourself through all this if there wasn't a fairly
good reason."

"Reason! It's a sonofabitch doozy of a reason! You are
just not going to believe it, Dean."

"But I don't know what you're going to do in the
meantime. I mean about your breach in the contract and
all."

"Don't you worry about it. I've got that figured out
too."

"Because I suspect there might be a few of those
lenders waiting for you at the end of this trail. If I were
you, I believe I'd take myself home and zip up in my tent
for about twenty-four hours."

"There's a good idea. Now anything else you need to
say while you got your big bold mouth working? While
you still got that terrible bottle opener in your pocket?"

"Just the same question, the one that's burning on
everybody's lips. Where the hell *is* all that money?"

*"I took it up on a goddamn hill and made paper
airplanes!"*

Back at the starting point, where we dismount, there's
enough left of daylight to tell the color of the sky, but
everything below it is graying off into twilight. Despite it
there's no slacking of the temperature; it's going to be
another bug-ridden, greasy evening.

The loudspeakers are putting out so many thousand watts of metronomic reggae now, and added to the party noise is a spate of giggles, signalling that the girls and wives must have succumbed to a fair dosage of alcohol and dope themselves.

Meanwhile, Milo is taking a lot of time feeling under the bush for his Plectron. He grunts with the stiff labor of getting up off his knees. "Where is it?" he says, sliding a foot in repeated arcs around the base of the bush.

A kid's voice, coming from the party direction, answers, "I have it!"

We lead the horses over to where Daphne's been waiting. She's holding her dad's Plectron out to him at arm's length. "Here," she says, exchanging it for her horse. "There was a fire. It went off about a half hour ago."

Milo, snatching it from her, says, "I know. Where's your sister?"

Daph says, "She got Ferry back and went on home." She takes Harper by the bridle and looks up at his eyes, then works her way back along the side, rubbing her hands in grooming-brush fashion, inspecting the flanks and withers fastidiously, as for the minute dent or nick in the finish of a new automobile.

"Good," says Milo, "and that's just what *you're* going to do."

"What happened?" we hear Daphne ask just before she appears on our side from underneath Harper's belly. "You fall off?" She's cinching up the stirrups to where they'll meet her tiny bare feet.

"Had a little accident," he says, "but nothing of any consequence to you or your horse. We got along just fine. Here, short stuff," he says, "let me give you a boost."

"No. I can do it." Daphne has to leap to get the horn, but once she swings up she's again like something with wings, something that needed adding on to make a horse look and move right.

Milo takes hold of her leg while it's in the air for spurring. "Thanks," he tells her, "for the ride."

Looking down at her dad with the thinnest of smiles, Daphne lowers to him. "You're welcome." They give each other a kiss. Then, just as she had told him earlier that he'd better let them drink, she says, "You better get to your fire," and pulls away from us, just like that.

VIII.

S OME CARRY A morbid affection for things that make
ungodly noise and drive bullet holes. They gain
attention, which floods the assholes with a type of self-
respect. Notice this one again, the fat Oliver who had his
overgrown self too close to me today, still firing off lead
ammo into innocent aluminum beer cans, swelling with
additional stupidity each time he marks a hit, which is
about every time. Take away his motorcycle and .38,
though, and he'd have to compensate by learning how to
shave, diet, and obey Federal law.

Reason I bring this up is, while passing by in the
direction of leaving, something gets our attention in this
very way: poor Featheroff, future congressperson and
Republican Party delegate, gets fired upon. It wasn't
really *him* so much as the can he'd just replaced on the
fence post that Oliver shot (and hit, by the way). But it
was close enough to count as being fucked with.

Drunk as they all are, himself included, Featheroff did
not take the indiscretion lightly but dove into the grass
and rolled, covering his head with both arms—the reflex
of an ace boot camp trainee—and, looking up from that
prone position, is now giving out a host of stingy, Harvard-
laced invective, beginning with, "That is precisely what I
would expect of so insipid, pathologically misshapen a
brain as yours!"

Milo and I defer our leavetaking to stare a moment at
what Featheroff, from his spleen, is referring to as "You

sorry fat-faced redneck fucking mongoloid hillbilly!" Waiting on what we fear Oliver's type might likely do in response.

His finger playing over the trigger, free arm steadying shooting arm, Oliver answers, "Language is about perfect, but where's your manners at?"—to our surprise benignly. But he shoots again, at something in the neighborhood of Featheroff, and this time nothing comes out. His clip ran dry.

While replacing it he is attacked by Featheroff.

Incidents of violence seem to be the order of things these days, an outgrowth you can depend on. Might *be* the moon, as Mom opined, or the heavy weather. But I feel like apologizing to someone, really, for the behavior of my peers.

Featheroff is overwrought. Look at him trying to strike his opponent. Keep your mouth to yourself, Featheroff, this is not the kind of confrontation that's going to get settled with words! Plus, it's sapping your strength.

Then, out of somewhere, Maureen's Lab just materializes. A dog does not like to see humans fight. It will bare its teeth and bark. She bares her teeth and barks.

"Fight!" so-and-so announces from the darkening sideline, though the canine is saying as much already, jaws snapping, dripping saliva. It's all over for you, Featheroff, because (a) Oliver will kill you first with his bare hands, or (b) Oliver will get the pistol loaded and spare himself the inconvenience, or (c) if he doesn't trample or assassinate you the bitch might.

Because of (c) Featheroff has had to stop flailing, which is a good thing because it was a trifle effete and looked bad. But his mouth hectors on: "Shoot why don't you!" he incites the fat man, spread-armed, asking for it. "Go ahead! We can wipe out the entire human species here today! One good shot ought to do it. One hole through here and the only decent human present will have been immolated for the sake of . . ."

As Oliver stands there aiming like a dualist.

Featheroff, I must say, for all his pastiness and blob, has got a lot of balls!

"That dickhead's just liable to get what he's asking for," says Milo to Wes McLaird, who is standing over here with us, his mouth agape, pointing the .22 down where it won't misfire.

"You're with these pigs, aren't you?" Wes McLaird says. "Why don't you go in there and talk him down, get that gun off him?"

"I never laid eyes on this one in my life before today." Milo stands perfectly insulted but lets it drop. "That rifle have bullets in it?"

"Seems to me you and Quayle been pretty close this afternoon. How's that?" says McLaird. "Huh?"

"Because that's what it seems to you. Why don't you pay attention to the proceedings?"

"What do you think I'm trying to do?"

One belligerent, bare-chested man to another.

"That guy shoots, you'd best be ready to bring him down before he turns and plugs the rest of us."

"Don't you worry about it."

"He's just drunk enough, I'd say, that his judgment might be that impaired."

"He's not drunk enough," McLaird says. "Drunk only improves his aim, I've been noticing. He never had any judgment to begin with."

"Just be ready for him, or hand that thing over to me."

"Quayle!" McLaird yells out—Quayle can be seen coming up behind the enormous pistolero, moving awfully fast, for Quayle—"Call off your animal, Quayle—before he hurts somebody!"

Quayle doesn't come between them so much as stand aside, wary, making it a triangle, and tells Oliver none too tenderly, "Lay down your fuckin' plaything! I didn't come out here to fuckin' play jokes. Lay it down!"

Oliver empties one past Featheroff's ear.

Featheroff goes swoony. Has to then pull himself to-gether and brave up. It's to where he can't change his mind if he wants to now, about being brave, if that's what he's being.

More of Quayle's line of persuasion. But Oliver is not buying; Oliver is shut down as to obedience; he is acting on some loco impulse that makes him want to sink round after round into the grass near the feet of both. Pow, Pow, Pow. Like a youngster that never passed the stage of being mean and sadistic.

Quayle knees the ornery Texan mightily to the balls. He takes the plaything away before Oliver even has a chance to double over and fall down.

Featheroff he tells to get out.

Another thing they say about dogs, they can smell malevolence on a person, and sometimes the smell alone is enough to send them into taking punitive steps. Mau-reen's attentive yellow retriever is going through the changes of one now. And now it's Quayle putting out some pretty laughable, not to say precious, footwork!

Good dog, good dog. Pity, in a way, Mo's drunk and can't witness this.

Quayle finds it necessary to kick her in the teeth. He was a fool of course to think that was the way to make an embittered dog desist. But he'll find out for himself, which is, after all, better. He's got himself in actual danger now, is seriously scared for himself (as was the case earlier, when Ferry wished him to get off in a hurry and ride someone else), and we observers are getting the same satisfaction out of it too, for the more he spins, blocks, and kicks, the harder her big teeth come snap-ping back at his pink and brown flesh.

Granted it would take a while, but eventually someone might have stepped in. But by the same token it's useless to expect any other solution might ever have occurred to

Randy Quayle than the one he finally remembers is at
hand:

He shoots her.

Unlike his handling of the snake, there was no hiding
away from this one. One hears the discharge, along with
the rending caterwaul, still sitting in the air; feels one's
own heart pierced, lungs sucked out. One finds it damned
unbearable that such an animal should not be alive any
longer and that Quayle should!

Before dropping it he fires a second round into her. To
make sure. All one sees is a gray heap not much disturbed by a little, fast, manmade lump of lead. And then
Quayle backing away.

I'm glad Maureen isn't up after all.

The one that started it, Oliver, is having a lot of
unrelieved pain yet in his middle, making a fist of himself—
what you call writhing. He's there like a beached whale
beside the carcass as his provisional boss merely deserts
everything he's done, leaving it there to wallow and to
decompose.

There's nobody unstunned enough to do something
about it yet either, stupified we are for the memory of
that mellow pet we watched go out ferocious, ferociously.
It's like the hush after the climax in Cinema One, the
mass conscience wondering what made killing necessary,
as if everyone just remembered there was a rule here:
There's To Be No Killing Today. And yet there is going
to have to be some atonement for why she had to die so
young, that dog. Maybe the wondering is going to produce the *something* nobody has come to yet.

It does. The rifle changes hands and goes bang at the
sky. "I can't but take hard what you just did."

Quayle stops and, eventually, looks. "That dog liked
to kill me and you know it. You seen it."

"I can't but consider that kind of thing unacceptable."

"What are you gonna do about it then?"

"I would never shoot a man, Quayle, who didn't deserve it or know which way it was coming from, and why."

"Wonder why you ain't near so honorable about your business obligations." Quayle gives himself time to look at the ground and back. "You ever shot a man?"

"Nope, never have. But those are the conditions I'd lay myself for doing it." He advances a little, in the almost dark, on his target. "I'm going to shoot you," Milo simply puts.

Since the circle of gunplay has widened, the outer circle of spectators backs up a ways. But nobody issues a dissenting opinion. One brazen individual in fact hollers, "Shoot the cocksucker up, shoot 'im up!"

"Might want to think about that." Quayle is slightly more defensive than he was towards the earlier gun. "I'm unarmed now."

"That's true of many things that get shot," says Milo.

All right then. Looks like you got yourself a pretty good excape-goat then—"

Quayle took one high in the leg. It moved him back a step and he stood up for another one, in the other leg. Then he passed out.

Last thing Milo's going to remember is taking a bottle over his head. It was that little Mexican hombre. I saw him go running off in the dark.

IX.

IT TOOK A couple of us helping him up to his truck, what with his spotty orientation, his legs alternately giving up and coming back. I got in the other side and started her up.

Every buckle in the road has him raising a higher hue against the pain. What the concussion did, he says, was to blind him. "Take a look at me. Tell me if I have my eyes open," he says.

I ask whether his skull might be opened up too, if there's any blood coming out. I know he isn't listening; he's begun beating his head against the doorframe, shaking it out, squeezing the temples between his fists, blinking hard and then doing it all over.

Once we smooth over onto asphalt he starts laughing. Not a healthy sign either, thinks me, but maybe he's past the blindness. "Okay, what have you found to laugh at?" He's rolling with the chuckles, teary with them, hands clasped POW-style on his head. "Milo, bring your hands down and tell me if you've got blood on them."

"Know what?" he says, "I don't think the sombitch'll do much walking for a while!"

"What!?"

"Yeah, he's seen the last use of his legs, I'd say, for a good long while. Don't you think that's pretty amusing, Dean?"

"A piece of fluff. It's a fucking bagatelle."

"Well I think it is."

"And I think you're missing a few teeth off your main sprocket is what I think. Have you got blood on your head? It's important."

"Not even to the toilet!" Milo's jag has risen to maniac proportions. "Tell me how he's going to get to the potty, Dean!"

"Shut up, will you! I don't care! Just shut up and let me drive here!"

"Maybe he'll never walk again. I can't help it, I keep on seeing stumps. Can you see it? Quayle as a double amputee, scooching around the corner on one of them skateboard things? He'll come up to about eye level on your average dog—he'll chase dogs and beat the fuck out of them with his knuckle protectors! I can't help it!"

"I'd be worried about reprisals if I were you, instead of carrying on like something up in a tree."

"Fuck a bunch of reprisals!" he says. Then, turning thoughtful, "Unless . . ."

"Unless what?"

"Maybe you're right, Dean. I mean, what if Harley-Davidson starts turning out a line of 750cc wheelchairs!" And he's off again, wailing like the happy primate in the branches I was mentioning. "Then I can see where I'd be in for some reprisal."

It occurs to me I've been keeping a steady watch on the lane behind us for the encroaching eye of a motorcycle. But there's nothing in the rearview, so far, but black. "Trouble's apt to run you down and smell you out no matter what," I tell him. "You seem to prefer it that way. I think what you're *really* trying to do is becoming clear to me now."

"Little brother speak with cryptic tongue."

"Only I wish you'd just get it over with and stop dragging others, like me, down with you. Can you answer me a question or two now? Think you're *compos mentis* enough for that?"

"Can't tell you if my head's bleeding or not, Dean. I'm numb clear out to the fingertips. Except for this damn head. What it needs is a drink."

"I can't help you with a drink."

"You can. The bar's right under where you're sitting. You'll have to reach it up to me; it hurts too bad to bend over. I did it, didn't I. I shot him."

"Then let it hurt. That's a warning you're supposed to attend to something."

Whining, he brings from under me a half-empty fifth.

"You know," I say, "I actually prayed this afternoon that once I got down off that horse I'd get my dull life back together. Figured it might have been earned by then. Yet here I am looking at you again. When's this going to be over?"

I hear the kiss of the bottle leaving his lips. "You can *use* a little excitement, Grandma. Shake you out of your torpor."

"I can handle torpor," I say. "I'll take a couple *years* of torpor after today, thank you. About all today has going for it is maybe a nice fish story for later in life. Something *you* can repeat for your grandchildren, without a single embellishment." I try picturing Milo with a grandchild on each knee, in front of the fireplace, somewhere off in the next century. "I take that back. I don't believe even the *slowest* kid would buy this one. Nah, you couldn't peddle this shit at the county fair."

When I don't hear anything coming back I take a look to see if he's still conscious, I find him sucking at his bottle, so I move ahead to the next nearest point: "You better get out of here."

"How do you mean?"

"You're too famous."

"That so. You're back on reprisals. Well, how do you foresee such a person getting around such a thing?"

"Perhaps using some of that money—the part that isn't

mine—and renting himself a secluded hacienda on some Mexican hill for about a year."

"Yeah?"

"I'd miss you, Milo, something awful."

"You don't mean that."

"But I'd keep your whereabouts a solemn secret."

"Whereabouts . . ."

"You could count on it. I'd visit you at Christmas—"

"Switzerland," he says. "Maybe northern Italy or Switzerland. Rather be cold, see. I'd want snow. I'd want me an Alp."

"Then if you have any desire left for saving your scalp that's where you'll go."

"Alp, scalp," says Milo, "just take me where I told you." Using his thumb to stopper the bottle he sprinkles whiskey over his probably bleeding scalp as you would hair tonic. The sting makes him *ssssst* in through his teeth.

When we were leaving Maureen's he told me to get him to the fire station. He intends to suit up and go out there. "That's just what I was coming to," I say. "Just how you knew there'd been a fire."

He lets this one fly out the window, then turns himself in the same direction, to play dumb. "You got any smokes?" he asks me.

I slap the bare ball of his shoulder and he turns and takes the cigarette, lights up with his professional union Zippo.

"Well?" I say.

"Well?" he says.

So I'm forced to take up the red-eyed contraption, which has been blinking on the seat between us, to illustrate with. "This thing," I show him. "When Daphne handed it back to you she told you it went off, and you told her you knew it did."

"Intuitive sorta guy, I guess."

"No."

"No?"

"Mind you I know better about this brushfire bullshit you tried putting over on Quayle. I'm way ahead of you on this one, buddy, because, after a while, if one's going to learn to second-guess Milo, one starts with the farthest-fetched, most improbable, farthest outside guess there is. Which is this: I think a fire alarm came over this thing all right. And it just happened to be coincidental with your getting wiped across the floor by Randy Quayle. Didn't it? You tell me if I'm very far off."

"Now they could *use* genius like yours over at the CIA."

"You've had some asinine ideas, Milo, but this one—"

"Whereabouts . . ." Milo enlightens himself again.

"What's this about whereabouts? What do you keep saying that for?"

"Trying to remember . . . I remember now. Yeah. Actually, as it turned out, this little thing served a double purpose. Or would have, if you hadn't let Quayle take it away from me. See, the original purpose was to account for my whereabouts."

"What do you mean?"

"My whereabouts. Between the hours of seven and ten on this particular date on the calendar."

"Why?"

"Well, in a word, Dean, alibi. But, see, it also, I figured, might come in handy if my negotiations with Quayle didn't go very nicely. And they didn't."

"So this was supposed to be the second half of your insurance against Quayle, where I was the first."

"Actually, Dean, *this* was first."

"Thanks. Thanks a lot. You think that's funny? Just let me know when you need help again."

"The way I saw it, Dean, I knew but two things I could count on. Number one: you were liable to chicken out on me; number two: that I'd better have a contingency for when you did. Because I had to go out there and come clean. I'm just not the kind of guy who'll run away from a little setback like that. And then again, there was half-a-dozen other faces out there I wasn't too keen on souring either. I don't know, some days, Dean, some days just seem fraught with peril, obstacles of this sort, and the trick, the challenge, is to overcome them. So of course once the cat was out, about my being thrown off a day and all, well, I saw nothing wrong with a neat little expedient, in the way of a fire alarm, to get me the fuck out of harm's way, if it came to that. And it did. But see, there was another thing in my way. And that's these portables. As far as these portables go, Dean, whatever you say over one, it's heard by all. That means you don't go communicating your private, personal complexities over the airwaves. Not unless they're actual fire-related complexities. Legit. So legit it had to be. See, Dean, the upshot is, well, we set a fire."

"You what!"

"More for the first reason, of course. That being to account for my whereabouts between the hours of—"

"What do you mean, you set a fire! You're saying—"

"Arson. I'm saying, yes, I, a certified firefighter, committed arson. And that is a word we are never going to repeat, are we. Not ever, to anybody."

"Arson . . ."

"Sure. Up that alley on West Second, back of Flossie Lowry's place. Hell, it's nothing but an old gardening shed—a few rakes and a couple thousand years' worth of Christmas ornaments. We checked it out, made sure nothing stands close enough to catch."

"Why! I mean, we're talking arson. Your felonies are stacking up faster than Quayle's."

"And if everything went right, why that sonofabitch is burning to the ground right now. Serves her right, too,

Flossie, the old dyke, for kicking me off the safety patrol in sixth grade. Anyway, motives and shit aside, I have to get there. I have to be on the payroll tonight and accountable."

"You're going to do time, Milo. You know that? You're going away big-time, on multiple charges! I don't what to hear anymore. Just stop there, Milo. This is a nightmare. It's all a portrait-quality fucking nightmare!"

"You're always looking at the downside of things. No, look at the bright side, Dean. I shot the legs off the guy, didn't I? And got away! All in all, it wasn't as bad as I feared." In celebration of it he goes back to his bottle.

We're starting to see the shadows of a few familiar places go by. The landmark Feed & Grain. There went the Scenic. I ask Milo, "You know what you are?"

"Save it," he says. "Pull over—"

"A little townie hood. A little petty hood that pays too much respect to petty little townie trifles. Well, your little townie trifles they got a little too large for you this time, didn't they?"

"Never mind. Pull over, will you? I have to throw up."

"You're so deep in your dumb-ass trifles now you'll never get—"

Milo is out of the cab already, puking, as I crawl to a stop. I coast on a few yards to wait. With each paroxysm jerking his insides around his feet shift gravel. I listen to his guts extrude, then the splattering of his insides all around his shoes. He moans miserably for what it's doing to his head.

When it seems to be all over I throw the truck in reverse and pick him up. The dome light reveals a set of watery pink eyes, dried up tributaries of blood mixed with whiskey streaming his cheeks; his skin has the creepy pallor that sets in after so much has gone out. "Get it all out, did you?"

"Think maybe I'll cork this till it clears up down below." He pokes the bottle in between his legs, fencing it round the neck with his fingers as one might secure his own organ.

"You're pathetic." I put the sight of him back in the dark and drive on. We maintain a respectable silence past the Hocking Sand & Gravel, the G.E., Holl's Dairy Burger. Then the front porches, bug lights, parked cars. Neighborhoods.

A stoplight holds us up. "I'll let you off at the hospital," I tell him. "After you get your head stitched up you can walk down the corridor and pay a visit on the rest of the family. I'll leave this thing in the parking lot and you're on your own after that."

"And you've got yourself an overactive imagination, Dean. I told you where I'm going, didn't I? I've got a job to perform. Smitty is particularly anxious to see me."

"Smitty's in on this with you?"

"And it's absolutely imperative I see him. And you can tell Mom . . . you can tell her I left for Switzerland."

"Look at him," I insist as if to a second passenger, "his head's laid open and he's half-naked and whipped from head to foot and he wants to go perform a job."

"What I said, asshole. You can stop in up here at Bailey's. I'll pick me up one of them tractor hats with the pretty polka dots; that'll hide the blood should the chief be hanging around. And when I come back out with my hat on you're going to give me your shirt, and—"

"That's what you think."

"What I *know*. And while you're at it you can lend me your hankie."

The light changes. I pull ahead fast. This is getting unrelievedly annoying! "I haven't got a hankie."

"What?" says he. "You call yourself a faggot and you don't even carry a hankie!"

That did it. Kicking in all the power this thing gives I jump lanes and shoot in under the breezeway at Bailey's, a sort of conglomerate Sunoco, grocery, manure crusher's boutique, and drive-thru beer. I lay a set of skid marks to rival those I started out with back at the light. "Get out."

"Now wait a minute, Dean. By the tone of that it sounds like, when I come back, you're not gonna be waiting for me."

"OUT!"

"And if that's the case, then I believe I'm fit to drive now."

"*I* have the wheel, and the next stop this thing's making is home."

"You don't know what you're saying. I can't go there either. Now I want you to do what I ask."

"The station's a block away. Walk."

"Don't do this, Dean. This is the most important thing you'll ever do for me. Believe that. Don't do this to me."

"If I keep believing you, like I have up to now, and you keep pushing it back in my face, like you have up to now, well, it doesn't say a whole lot for my savvy, does it."

"Fuck your savvy! Just get me over there. Or slide out, one. My life might just depend on it."

"Your life depended on everything I did today. Yet I can't see I've done anything except follow you into the same quagmire you're waddling through. And guess what? You're still here. You said so yourself. I think I smell the coffee. Now get out!"

"It almost sounds like you mean it—"

"I'm through. I quit. I'm clocking out."

"Dean?"

I have nothing more to say.

"You're going to do it, Dean. You'll give me your shirt and you'll drive me where I'm going. You know why? Because you're my brother and I'm yours, and you will always give me the shirt off your back when I ask for it. Even after I tell you, as shirts go, it's unbecoming and demeans the very notion of masculinity."

Letting myself out on my side I go around to his, yank him forth and deliver him, his pocket knife, and his portable blabbermouth soundly to the pavement.

He was so weak with laughing at me there was nothing to it.

Between sobs of what seem like genuine felicity he is at the same time trying to apologize. Begging me not to leave him.

"You don't realize what you're doing!" It sounds like he's crying. I don't know; by now I'm back at the wheel. This time I will not give myself time to soften. When I throw him my shirt and pull away he is still horizontal, raving.

X.

"TRUCK'S HIS, ID'N it, Dean?"
A minute later I'm being detained by Officer Leo
Plummer, a man my age, with his droopy Baptist face
flickering red, white, and blue in the strobe of his police
cruiser. Peering in through the window of Milo's truck,
it's the identical face in every feature to, believe it or
not, the Leo Plummer of Cub Scout Den 239 which once
upon a time convened in my attic. With Jane paying her
civic dues as den mother. Cub Plummer was long on
everyone's list of ne'er-do-shits and knew it. He was
inept at everything. Plus he indulged in the unsavory
practice of chewing his nose dirt. Finally, Leo was responsible for shortening the careers of all ten of us in the
organization. For our first merit badges we were required
to stitch, tool, and stain leather wallets, from the official
ready-to-assemble kits; but because he was trailing the
rest of us by such a disgraceful margin, Plummer arrived
early one week and sabotaged our nearly completed proj-
ects with fingerpaint. Mine was a sticky revulsion in
Della Robbia blue! After sending Leo home, Mom tried
consoling her scouts: "I know it's a tough break, fellas,
and yes, we're pretty angry with Leo. But there's nothing
to be done about it now. We'll just have to work fast and
maybe we can earn those badges yet, with something a
little bit easier." But I didn't want any merit badge, I
wanted my wallet, with the exquisitely tooled effigy of
U.S. Grant! Next day we converged on Leo, held him

down while Milo hammered his painting fingers with a flatiron. The outcome for all ten of us was a unanimously declared, lifelong moratorium on scouting.

The only difference between the Leo of then and now is he's grown proportionately larger and changed uniforms.

"You know it's his, Plummer. What do you want?"

"Been looking for this little baby all afternoon, Dean." Plummer is checking his notes with a flashlight. "Priest lives up on Flattop come in and filed a Missing Persons today—on a boy name of Donovan, around seventeen, blond hair, good looks, medium to slight—"

"I don't know anything about him."

"—Bud Greenman, he runs the Scenic out there on Saturdays and Sundays you know, he told Deputy Sigler he seen Milo in there this morning, had a boy with him fits the description perfect."

"Then why don't you go ask him. You'll find him making his way towards the fire station. I just dropped him off a minute ago."

"Donovan?"

"Milo!" Stupid pussface lummox!

"You know this Simon Donovan do you, Dean?"

"I just told you I didn't, didn't I?"

"Big troublemaker. Priest says so hisself. Says he fished him outa jail up in Boston, brung him down here, wanted to give the boy a taste of our decent Christian community, maybe save hisself another soul. Know what I told him? I says, 'Father?' I says, 'See what'll happen you turn a monkey loose in your own parlor? A man gets hisself locked up with niggers,' I says, 'specially a boy with a impressionable mind like we got here, why he's no better off than your city nigger don't matter how many Ambroses you brung him out to.' What I says, 'You got to habilitate 'fore you can rehabilitate.' That's where all these priests and social workers is mistaken, Dean."

"That's a fact, Leo. If that ain't just how it is," I say.

"Well," I say, "good luck with your manhunt, Leo. I'm sure you boys are conducting an expert investigation." Slipping into gear, I start creeping away.

"Just a minute there, Dean. Hold on." Leo places his hand over my door. I would like to greet it with a flatiron. "Have to radio in the truck's been found," he says. "You just hold tight, won't take me but a minute."

"Sorry. Can't. Have to go."

"Won't take a minute."

I was afraid of something like this. "Look, you can't hold me here, Plummer. I'm not harboring your fugitive."

"Never said you was. But we might wanna impound the vehicle though."

"What!?"

"Fingerprints." The word must have made some connection, for Leo inserts a dirty digit up his nostril.

"Where did you get your training, Plummer! Fingerprints! I tell you you've got a witness right down the block. That's a live witness, Plummer. Walks, talks everything. Now why don't you go play police science—"

"Settle down there, buddy!" says Leo, directing his flashlight at my face. "If you don't know it already, I am sworn to protect the peace of this city. And if you ain't gonna cooperate, why, I'll have to take you in."

"Knock it off, asshole, before I get out there and check your vehicle over for finger*paints*!"

I just unblocked twenty years of oblivion for Leo. Which he betrayed in the momentary flagging of his beam. Raising it again, he says, "Now there was no cause bringing that up, Dean—"

"You get your goddamn light out of my face!"

He says, "Your face is pretty bad flushed. Looks like you been drinkin'." He pokes the light under my nose, illuminates the seat where, sure enough, Milo's bottle is distinctly laid.

"Listen, Plummer. How bad do you want to pick this kid up?"

"Huh?" Plummer takes time to consult his mental file on this. "This a trick question?"

"Look, I'm not being uncooperative with you, see. Only trying to straighten you out on a few priorities. Do you follow baseball, Leo? Remember when we were kids?"

Leo finally switches off the flashlight. His face brightens up in its place, as if remembering 100 percent sunshine of the mind. " 'At was pretty fun back 'en, wad'n it? When we's kids . . . 'Cept about them billfolds—"

"No, Leo. Listen. I'm talking about baseball. Remember what they told us in Little League? If the ball's hit out to you and there's a man going for first and a man going for third, which man—"

"But you know why I done 'at," Plummer breaks in, "They was pretty. They was prettier, Dean. I thought they was. I thought I was doin' something nice for you-all."

"Forget the wallets, Leo—"

"You-all was s'pose to 'preciate it, 'stead of . . ." Plummer's actually going to start crying here!

"I didn't know that." I try to speak softly, not shift my eyes like a liar.

"Pretty dumb a me, wad'n it?"

"But you're an officer of the law now, Plummer. Let me tell you something. Let me give you a tip. I happen to know my brother has information that will be very useful to your department. It'll for sure sew this case up for you. Give you strokes with your superiors, maybe a commendation from the mayor himself. Kudos beyond belief, Plummer! But you've got to think. Time's running out. And meanwhile Milo's over there stealing third base."

Lord Almighty, let it work. As deceiving goes it's naughty but not without honest intentions, and probably best for the long haul. Besides, I didn't come through today knee-deep in shit just to have to do it all night!

"Dean, if you're lyin' to me . . ."

"If he's not right where I told you then you come get this pickup and dust it all you want for prints. It'll be over at Mom's. I'll leave the keys in it for you."

Plummer steps back, tips me a salute off the bill of his hat. "Check," he says leaving dutifully for his cruiser, caparisoned with so much jangling stuff as to resemble a pack mule in the Rockies.

I put in under Mom's open-air garage and shut down the motor and lights. Bad will trails me in. Then there's the headache that preceded me. I fit the heels of both hands into my eye sockets and push, igniting a panoramic view of the recent past and its people—like so many Armageddons and god-awful zombies on the loose.

And what was I saying about stress and the resolve to combat it?

Look here. I don't give two hoots in hell, I tell myself and light a cigarette, sitting back a while breathing out gustily. You are trying to rise up and be the blot on my conscience, I can feel you trying to do that, I know the signs, Milo, and I can tell you this: Don't waste your time.

I'm having to talk it out with my senior sibling in his absence.

Say you want reasons? How's these. You come along begging help and when I show up to offer it you jump smack in the way of my being any. It's worse than that. I went the gamut, I feel, while you hurled the banana creme in my face at every opportunity, and there's where you made it too difficult to go gentle!

One thing and another. I am reminded of my Cajun buddy down there, Beauraine, who's a jazz musician and a biologist, how he expressed that life among the human species issues from a succession of *fucks* and fuck*backs*. That's in every true sense, verb and noun. So now when they start talking about your Golden Rule, says Beau, why, then you plug in this simple axiom and start paying attention. You'll not only be in the real game then, Beau says, but way ahead of it. You might even survive. Not cynical, really, just the way the real world works. In some small way I'm getting happy and comfortable with it. Like I say, even if I do have to keep reminding myself, I don't give two hoots. I don't give a *single* shit what happens to you, Milo . . .

Turning over my shoulder with the sudden feeling someone is hanging around in the radius of my insight, I make out a shadow puffing on a cigarette, same as I am. When she starts it's like a great big Hoover vacuum was turned on under her: "I could shoot you! If I had me a gun I would and I mean it! Didn't Dean ever tell you I called? I don't s'pose you even considered for a minute you was carrying every last cent I'm worth while you're fucking off all over the place taking your sweet time about it. I've been out at the Isaak Walton since six o'clock. I was out there three and a half hours waiting on my drugs!"

I say to myself, Here's one of the zombies I forgot about. As a matter of fact I was planning on making the rendezvous myself, for no other reason than I was mildly curious and wanted to be sort of sadistic with her. But that was before I found myself leading old Granny through the underbrush, etc.

"I knew you wasn't going to show!" she continues having her say. "Well? And now I s'pose you're too fucked up to stand out here and face me, Milo."

"I'm not who you think, Velda, and you're cutting in on my night philosophy."

"You!!"

"Who?" asks a distant, deep-throated other shadow.

"Who's that?" I ask.

We sound like a bunch of owls.

"Where is he?" Velda insists. "Where is he!"

"Who am I? My brother's keeper?"

"Oh shut your smart-ass mouth!"

"Who's in there, Vel?" questions the gentleman shadow again.

Velda says, "No one. He's harmless, Ottie, just the little brother, home on leave from Cocksuck, Louisiana. Now where—"

I push my cigarette out in her neck. It smarts her good. She shrieks, flapping and moving back as I step out of Milo's truck.

Ottie? thinks me. Otto? Not Mr. Otto Miller of the county prosecution. Of course! This is no gentleman, it's Miller, the slimy spectator of water sports who never learned how to swim, who dresses himself up like a Nazi war criminal.

"Hey, what's going on there!" Ottie Miller wants to know. "Vel? Are you all right?"

Vel is not. Vel is flapping the front of her clothes where cinders dribbled down her tits. She tries coming at me with her cigarette. I catch the orange eye making an arc for me and reach out and take both wrists in one lucky grab—they're thin, moist, cool—and twist till the ember falls at our feet. She covers my face with a spray of spit and tells me I'm as bad as my fucking brother.

I tell her. "Every inch."

Then she repeats, "*Where is he!*"

"Vel?" Miller says stepping closer.

I tighten the clamp on her wrists.

"Let go of me!" Velda says. "Make him let go of my—"

"Don't come any closer," I forefend, "or I'll snap her arm like a toothpick."

It works. She whimpers awfully for Otto to move on me but he doesn't. It appears I'm having some success lately with my threats and deterrents. Feels good for a change. I feel calm and powerful, like a Brando or De Niro when up against almost certain catastrophy.

"Milo's playing in the snow," I say, pushing Velda back against the shutter of Mom's house.

I take my leave, heading towards the back door. Slowly. Attaining this doorknob has been the hardest thing I've ever had to go through and I'm going to make it last. I can hear Velda back there belting out the words "CHIC-KEN-SHIT!" at her chickenshit boyfriend.

XI.

EMPTY IN HERE, like I expected. Upstairs, in the room I and my nieces use, I found the mattress bare, the pillows undressed, clean sheets and pillowcases folded and stacked at the foot where someone began the housework and suddenly lost interest. I found Simon's dirty jeans and T-shirt thrown over a chair with clothes of my own. I stepped out of my clothes and sat on the ticking staring over at his things and getting ashamed. I had to jump up and shut the door.

Later, wandering naked through the downstairs, I asked myself, How about a nice big mess of eggs, bacon, and hash browns? Got the place to myself, don't I? Maybe just a dollop of that leftover potato salad on a bed of lettuce, with a light sprinkling of freshly ground pepper?

Well how about dipping into a good book then?

But I doused the lights, came up and collapsed on Mom's four-poster, on the whole pretty spent.

All right, after feeding the cat, some deep breathing, then the pills with milk (no recreational narcotic or anything, just an old script from her medicine cabinet labeled such-and-such before bed), I'm ready for sleep. But it doesn't come. Got moonshine and a little breeze in through the scalloped voile curtains; got slightly over the recommended dosage in me besides, and the eyes still won't close. Such a thing as too tired to sleep, I guess.

Very well, if I have to lie here this way then there's

only the one thing to do. I'm not saying I make it a habit, or that it's a good one to form. In fact I think of it anymore as a pretty lousy dead-end pursuit, which dulls the memory, dampens enthusiasm, curbs ambition; it can distort our natural appetites and maybe even severely tarnish our self-image. But then I have always had an overzealous endocrine system and find it necessary sometimes, for peace of mind, to fall back on. I can remember, as a youngster, I would stay in Wednesday evenings while Mom and Dad were out playing bridge and watch a show about a trick dolphin and his young pal, a skinny blond who did nine-tenths of the program in his bathing suit. I secretly cared for him and whacked off studying the beads of water on his stomach and shoulders; lost myself in the coves, creases, and crack of his trunks; took unctuous delight in his dialogue and memorized it. The solitary alternative had me and I found myself addicted, doing it in people's garages, showers, closets, basements; in hide-a-beds and swimming pools; sitting, standing, crouching; I've done it in both the Atlantic and Pacific; on a bus once, curtained behind the *Cincinnati Enquirer* (does anyone but me ever get crazy riding a vibrating bus seat?). I even did it once in a motel room in the desert when Mom and I drove out to Los Angeles, and she was right beside me, tossing and turning. Afterwards I felt unclean, but slept like a log.

You have to watch out though; you develop knacks for things and it's not long before you're more interested in what's not there than what is. Like anyone, I have weaknesses, certain devotions to certain details . . . But I like to take my time zooming in, put things in proper order and sequence, prolong the mystery. This calls for a scenario of sorts:

The way a hip slides out of a pair of jeans . . .

The way an underthing hangs from an ankle . . .

The way a knee raises . . .

The way a waist bends . . .
The way a back curves . . .
The way an underarm smells . . .
The way a rib stands out . . .
The way a nipple catches on the side of a thumb . . .
The way a butt gets muscular then gives . . .
The way male baggage has of becoming taut and leath-
ery . . .
The way a tongue wanders . . .
. . . leaving a cool snail track behind on a thigh . . .
The way the whole masculine vortex sends out a pecu-
liar fecund scent . . .
The way a grown man can whimper like a terrified
puppy . . .
The way, when you leave it alone, it twitches, dances
on its own in the air just before going off. Lashing!

And that pretty well did it. Wild and with a kind of
otherworld life of its own there for a minute, and not too
much decorum. And you see? Whatever problem there
might have been, it's out of my hands now, spent into a
jagged reflecting pool around the area of my belly button, growing wider and deeper until, rolling down my
sides are the big, heavy tears of come, down onto my
mother's and late dad's bed.

Sinking back, gazing down to the far end, eyes glazy
but coming back, I realize the family cat has been hunched
like a roosting chicken, eyes in slits and all along wearing
that same wise, Oriental grin.

PART FOUR

PART FOUR

I.

M OM IS AWAKE in 133. Not only that but sitting up reading a *McCall's* through her half glasses; hair brushed and humming, mildly, a tune from *Porgy and Bess*. Cheeriest damn tune there is! No machines to monitor the recovery, no life-support apparatus surrounding her bed, but lots and lots of plants, with note tags, pots done up in colored foil.

"From the look of you I oughta be at death's door," she says. "Well fasten your jaw. I'm benign as that geranium."

"You are?"

"I am."

"Here I was expecting some limp, wasted lady with a face like oatmeal, strung up to the IV, off in a Percodan fuzz—"

"And about ten pounds light in the breast area? Well, sorry to spoil it for you, kiddo, but all they did was take a little wedge out of me here and sew 'er back up. What you call a simple wedge resection."

"Sounds rhapsodic."

"Word from Pathology is she's in the pink. Totally."

"Great news," I say. "I've been worried sick."

"I bet you have." Her lips wrinkle like raisins.

"What's that supposed to mean?"

Pause. I turn my eyes to the TV, where the sound's turned down below a whisper, and watch a few frames of a sunburn unguent commercial.

205

"I wish you'd've brought candy instead of those irises," Mom says. "I mean, I appreciate it and all."

"You've never eaten candy. You don't like candy."

"I like irises even less. But the problem is I'm hungry. I haven't taken a bite of solid food in . . . let's see, it must be since breakfast or lunch Saturday."

"They don't feed you here?"

"No. Some orderly came around a while ago with the food trays and I told him to make mine rare and he says, 'We can't feed you, ma'am, it's too soon yet.' Too soon! I was ready to eat before they wheeled me back from Recovery. 'Who says?' I asked him. He tells me 'I say.' So I told the little pimpleface to go to the devil. I said, 'Who's the doctor around here, you or the doctor!' " She takes up a remote control and starts fussing with the buttons. The backrest of her bed whirrs to a more up-right position, the TV glitches off, then she leaves her thumb over the Nurse Call button for a good quarter-minute.

Releasing it, she asks me, "How's things at home?"

"At home? Fine."

"Oh?"

Pause. She plunks the control box down where it disappears into the sheet between her legs. "Let's try that again," she says, removing her reading glasses, "with you looking me in the eye this time."

"Hey, what's going on here, Ma? You going spooky on me or something?"

"All right then, I'll put it to you a different way. How's things at home?"

What's she getting at? Does she know about yesterday, or just assume as many transgressions as could be perpetrated in the space of her absence, as when we were teens on dope. Must be some sort of trick question for *me*. Designed to milk me for a confession. "Fine, I told you. Fine . . ." Is fraudulent written all over my face or what? "I mean—"

"You mean your brother hasn't committed all-out murder yet?"

"What?"

"You heard me. Hasn't he shot the legs out from under one already?"

"Umm."

"This *is* a hospital, don't forget. And busy as any other, I expect. And it so happens they've given me the busiest mouth in town for a nurse. Does more jabbering than nursing. And it also happens that my family's been the joy and thrill of her nosy existence since word trickled in here last night, along with the blood of Milo's latest victim, that one of my sons was the one pointing the rifle that pumped the lead into that boy's two legs."

Mom rattled that whole thing off in one breath as if it had been something she had to get rid of before it bit her. "Easy does it now, Ma, there's an explanation—"

"So I haven't exactly been in a coma for the past twenty-four hours. A woman in this place will pick up what goes around. Whether she wants to or not. Here and all over town as well. I knew something like this was going to happen."

"There went *your* Georgie Gershwin mood in a jiffy."

"I've always felt a hospital was about as good a place as any for your private matters to get around in, but now, if you think about it, why, they've got the contract. It makes good sense and I've figured out why."

"Think I pretty much get the picture, Ma."

"All this going around shoving flashlights down your gullet, poking around; and these others sponge bathing you, emptying bedpans, rolling you off down the hall to God knows where and putting you under so the surgeon can take his turn. The surgeon asked if I was married, and, if so, was I still active sexually. Now you see the full implications of a question like that, don't you? What else? They asked about alcohol of course, and whether

I'm on any tranquilizers, if I've ever had a venereal disease, if I ever took birth control. On the basis of that I'm probably on file here as a lush widow sex-fiend." Mom gathers in her hospital smock collar, sighs. "An *old* one."

"You're using a chamber pot, are you—?"

"The way they get you into these joints and shake the crumbs off you is degrading. Of course they make you think these are just routine things. But things you can't deny. Oh, they count on that; they'll take it and run with it. And then you watch it get exaggerated. All right, word came in here last night that there was a shindig out at Maureen's and the guns were firing off every which-way and one of my sons shot this Quayle boy once in each leg. I don't have to wonder which son, either. Or whether this one's much of an exaggeration."

" 'Quayle boy' my butt!" I'm short of forbearance at the mention of the name. Period. "He murdered Maureen's dog—"

"There was a lady around here by the name of Quayle," Mom recalls. "She used to keep the books at Stein's roofing shop. She robbed him blind. He sacked her of course but they never got a dime back. She was too clever. One of these people that has a good brain with lousy thoughts."

"Quayle killed one of Maureen's dogs, Mom. Shot and killed it for no good reason, in plain view of everybody. Did you hear that part?"

"It does not surprise me that the children of naught would be naught."

"So Milo was only doing what he thought he had to."

"I know that. But these are people that don't know the meaning of the word compunction. Start trading gunfire with them and there's going to be hell to pay."

"I tried real hard to impress that on him, Mother."

Mother looks me over, bland, unbelieving, and reaches

for the white desk phone without a dial. She says into the mouthpiece, "Hello? No, I just want to see if you're putting them through . . . Well, I'm asking again . . . Don't get contrary with—" and she sends the dead receiver back to its hook so volcanically that a spasm of pain seizes her tender, corrected breast. She stops everything for a moment to wince and take stock of the hurt. 'It wouldn't be for shame Milo's not calling me," she says. "He has none that I'm aware of."

"He told me to tell you he's gone to Switzerland. Thought a good long Alpine vacation might make everyone breathe easier."

This information passes through her like an adjunct to the breast complication. She says, "Not funny."

"Not supposed to be. But then you're not looking at the whole pie either; you don't know the full extent of Milo's knavery of late, do you? Or even the half of it. Nobody has all the pieces of this one like I do." So I fit a few pieces together for her, stretching back a fair ways to where I started getting hip and on up to last night, when I dropped him off on a hot sidewalk and later learned his present wife was not suing but buying and wanted to bully *me* with rancor. "That thing with Quayle's legs, that was only incidental. Milo's made himself enough added enemies lately to sink a battleship. So you'll understand why he might want to move over a couple counties, if not a hemisphere, for a while."

After this her face turns cold, in effect viewing the whole thing sardonically. "Lit a fire? Heavens to Betsy."

"I don't think he did it today though—Switzerland that is. His ship's supposed to be coming *in* today, not going out."

"But why would he go and start a fire? On top of everything else?"

"Why don't you ask me why Milo's still alive. Given the line of goods he's moving. Considering his associates. Anyway, how should I know? He said something about an alibi. But I'll tell you one thing, you best keep it down in here, about that fire. I have a funny feeling," I say, head still, eyes stealthily ranging the room, voice dampened to a thin confidentiality, "they're hiding a surveillance device on you."

Mom says, in like manner only slicing her whole head askance at the four corners, "Where?"

"I don't know. Probably a thing that has to go in and out every so often. Your bedpan, for instance." I had to do it. To sort of pay her back for rusing me the way she was when I came in.

"My mother said it to your father and I'll say it to you!" she goes, obstreperous enough to shake the windows, "Your impudence is singular!"

"Your mother was a Republican. She'd say that to anyone who wasn't."

"And as for your bedpan," she says, "I've never used one in my life! What use would I have for one now if they're not going to feed me!"

On the way out a nurse with anthracitic hair against her paper white costume pushes through the door and stops right there to look at me, holding up my exit. Her name badge spells Dorothy.

"You want to quit staring at him and show a little attention this way?" When the question doesn't take effect Mom hollers, "Do you feed the inmates around here or do they have to get up and forage for themselves!"

"Is this your boy, Jane?" asks Dorothy, stressing the *this* to signify hard to believe.

"He doesn't much look like a killer," says Jane, "but I wouldn't want to stand in his way."

Dot moves out of my way fast.

II.

MOM'S CAR FETCHES up a number of short coughs and finally peters out on me, right in the Main and Walnut intersection. It says EMPTY. This morning Maureen was good enough to hot-wire and drive it in for me, although she was hung over and sorely implacable about the dog she had to bury. That was it for their parties! Everywhere was a mess, she told me—the yard a blight and riot of mustardy paper plates and splintered plastic utensils, a played out heap of char wood and cans from where they had burnt a bonfire.

Dirty weather hangs on. The governor's talking disaster relocation for the elderly and asthmatic that don't get enough air conditioning.

Mo wished it would just quit.

Country people go riding right past as I usher the Fiat, a hand to her door and one on the wheel, over to the curb. The country people are nodding piteously but leaving me nontheless stranded, tortured in the lungs. Wouldn't a few of these nice folks carry an auxiliary can in their pickup beds? Unleaded or whatever? Something about 90-100 degree weather makes them want to go their own vapid way instead of being neighborly.

Boy, it's hot! Feel the sweat run free. Long gritty ribbons of it under your clothes.

My eye squints up and down the storefronts after a can of gas. Storefronts only. Folks talking hogs, corn, coal. A pair of township trustees rolling Mail Pouch around their cheeks. "Where's all the Mobil?" I say, near to hyper-ventilating, "Where's all the Texaco!"

But a few paces on is the fire station, where I was headed in the first place. I pass through the yawning garage doors, between the pumper and the big yellow Sutphen aerial tower, and rap the door of the inner sanctum.

In here smells of petroleum solvents and scorched coffee, but at least Smitty has the AC humming. He allows me in. Following a short introduction, without the handshake (which is an amenity I'm agreeable to dispense with) Smitty steps back to a grimy desk upon which is a fishing reel separated into pieces. He is wearing the matched deep blue department worksuit, black and white sneakers, camouflage Saigon sniper hat. He has the roguish face of a man of outdoor sport enthusiasm, romantic with a light mustache; he is broad shouldered, tall enough, built for a day's grunt work but with the leading edge of affability. In this look I picture all the men of Michigan. Sitting down and taking up reel fragments, he asks, "Know anything about these things, Dean?"

"Afraid not, Smitty." Just want to drink in some of your sweet refrigeration. Large draughts, or sip it in like Grand Marnier. I'm standing over his shoulder, watching, and I forget what I came in here for. "Looks like someone's fixing to do some serious angling though."

"Taking me a long vacation. I've been saving up my time."

"Where to?"

"North. I'll start out in a little place up in Ontario, fish my way south to Bear Lake, Michigan, as the weather cools. Up and do a little fly casting, which happens to be my specialty."

"Going after trout?" I hear myself presume.

"Better believe it," says Smitty brightly going about

cleaning and lubing one of the manifold delicate parts of the reel. After wiping off the excess he snaps the piece in place and works it. "You might go after some pike and rock bass to warm up with, but you go for the trout. Catch the end of Indian summer up there, which is a paradise in surroundings undreamed-of, and then you run after those beauties till the season's over. Find you these little finger lakes and runoffs, an infinite variety, just waiting for a guy to pull up the waders and step in and start casting."

"You make it sound extremely inviting." I think: Icewater, icewater all around you, winter, aurora borealis, Ontario, Switzerland. Land of the Afternoon Moon.

"You a trout man, Dean? Flycaster?"

"In spirit only," I say.

Smitty doesn't turn around but goes on working the little gizmos. I spot his fly rod, a good eight feet long, with a cork handle, lying across the arms of a stuffed moth-eaten chair. He inquires, more out of curiosity than of provocation, "What do you mean by that?"

"My Dad and brother and I, we used to go fishing," I tell him, "up at Buckeye. Off a little rowboat on the lake. We used bamboo sticks and worms. The lake was about two feet deep all around but you couldn't see the bottom once. We might catch a few dirty cats, a bluegill now and then. It was a joke. Trout, I understand, take a lot of . . . flair. A certain intelligence."

"Might say it's not only a fine sport, but a fine art. It takes some imagination, that is a fact." Smitty pinches another moving part in the jaws of his slip-joint pliers and fits it in, adroit as any watchmaker. Everything snug and tight.

Now that I'm decently cooled off, have had enough of the fish lingo, the Trout Mystique, I remember why I came.

But this is Smitty's ardor, his transport. You can see that. And besides, I genuinely like the guy: he's a match for my brother in some respects, which is unprecedented around here—something about him makes me want to know his past. "I've gone after the ones in California," he is saying, "the big ones heading for the sea. You can have all you want without half the pursuit. But then I believe, even if the ecology is somewhat superior out there, too much supply tends to diminish the hunt. Wouldn't you agree?"

"Now that you mention it," I agree.

"Nothing the matter with your brook trout, nothing at all. Sometimes I prefer staying closer to home, anyway. People seem to take the attitude fishing is a slow and rather tedius endeavor. But then those individuals haven't had an instrument like this in their hands; haven't cast for trout. It's a thing of it's own. Trout you've got to think. Like you say, think all the time. You're up against more instinct than ordinary, more tricks than you've got different sizes and shapes of waterholes. You want to figure they've got every likely feeding habit, and some that aren't so likely. See the rises out there on the surface, they all look the same: your fish might be cruising a mayfly or it might be just sitting there listening, free-floating, waiting for nymphs. You never know what's going on underneath. That's why you have to be careful in so many ways: where the light hits, where your shadow falls, where you're wading, which fly to use. When I don't tie my own, I use these Adamses. They're the best.

"Then of course you've got your upstream bait-fishing, if you want it. That'll land you the big ones that take to the bottom when it's too warm up top. But there you're handling worms. I'm not partial to worms. If you're looking for your brother, Dean, he's not here."

"Huh? Oh yeah. Milo. Where is he?"

"Good question. In fact, I was just on the verge of using it on you." Having finished the assembly now, Smitty slips a cap over the exposed unit, snaps it to and inserts a bolt. He turns sideways in his chair, taking me in for the first time since we met eyes at the door. "I've always known the man to be pretty slippery; but now, I mean, well, he's missing. That's what I mean."

"But what about last night?"

"What about it?"

"That fire of yours. He was in some terrible hurry to get to it."

"That fire you mean."

"He was adamant about it, even though—and I don't have to tell *you* this—he was in pretty rough shape. But he was feeling very loyal to the department all of a sudden, for some reason . . ."

"I can see why he'd want to demonstrate some of that *esprit de corps* this time around. The chief was a touch unsettled about giving his badge back. Oh, plenty of faith in Milo as a firefighter, see, but he's never sure which way the man's mouth is going to run. The chief feels that can be a liability. Then too there's that hair Milo's been wearing around."

"You know, Smitty, it was more like he was intrigued with this particular fire itself. Like he had the feeling there were, I don't know, ramifications. Mysterious overtones."

Smitty's eyes betray only a quick stab of recognition.

I add, "Maybe even suspicious origins."

"I wouldn't know about that. Just a routine call, as I saw it. Another old backyard barn. Place was practically burnt to the ground, time we got to it. Personally I suspected oily rags. The old spontaneous combustion. Comes up of its own, you know."

"Like your old Christmas lights," I say. "Can't trust those either, don't forget."

"Christmas lights. Well, if this was the season to be jolly then I might have to agree with you, Dean. But you see, the way it is, I'll have to argue it was rags."

Maybe the two of us will humor each other like this till the bottom falls out. "An old bird like Flossie," I say, "she ought to have known better. I'll vouch for her keenness of forethought when it comes to safety. Pillar of precaution. 'Safe conduct,' she used to call it in the classroom. She was everybody's beloved sixth grade teacher around here, old Floss. She could command respect for home safety, I'll tell you. But she's getting up there in age now, bless her soul, so it may be she's neglecting the rags in her outbuilding. Although I rather hold out for Christmas lights."

Smitty has been patient, hands folded under the knee, leaning back and rocking a little, resigned. Patient. "Do I detect an air of insinuation?"

We all know what they say about boldness: once set in motion, it can be hard to check. Looks like I'm back to being Milo's keeper after all. "It's just that it hurts, Smitty. It hurts me to have to watch a good man sit there and lie unnecessarily."

Could I be any subtler if I used a lead wrench?

Smitty lays aside the sporting good, rises to approach the brass pole (a lapsed expedient nowadays due to the incidence of overweight firefighters with sprained ankles, though nevertheless kept brightly polished at all times). Stopping to look upward through the square in the ceiling, he listens for a noise greater than the air conditioner. Nothing. He turns the radio up to blaring in any case and steps over to my feet. "Who else did he tell?"

"He didn't even tell me." I lie, "I guessed it for myself. He merely supplemented a few details."

"And who did you tell?"

"No one."

"What about the rest of it?"

"You mean all the borrowed money?"

"That."

"I don't know about that part of it and don't want to."

"What are you going to do?"

"Nothing."

Smitty's eyes roll sideways in momentary *extremis*. He confers with himself: "Do I want to believe that?"

"It's entirely up to you. I'd just sort of like to know what became of him afterwards, if he's not here."

"Afterwards?"

"See, I'm afraid there's not a few people out there hunting him, and with less than charity in their hearts, because of a few thousand obligations he seems to have fled. Not the least of which is an ailing old mother laid up in the county hospital. So if he's out there—"

"Afterwards, Dean?"

"After your phony fire."

"Not phony. Devised maybe, not phony. But, unfortunately, Milo was absent from work last night."

"Don't give me that, Smitty; I dropped him off not more than a block from here myself last night."

Smitty takes time closing his eyes in on me. Looks as if his whole locus of intuition were onto something. Evenly, he says, "All right. Then what you know, and what I know, it ought to tell us something."

"I think it does."

Dropping the intensity he reaches for his desk chair, wheels it over and sits. Bouncing the spread fingertips of one hand off the other he proceeds, shall we say, analytically: "Answer me something, Dean."

"What."

"What does it tell you?"

"He's out there."

"Missing."

"Why *is* that, Smitty?"

This comes across as an affront; it produces a light snort; I take it to be amusement. "What did you mean, a while back," he asks, "when you said he was in pretty rough shape?"

"You don't know?"

He doesn't answer.

"We had a little exchange of gunfire yesterday."

"I knew that. From all accounts it wasn't exactly an exchange . . ."

"On account of it," I say, "Milo was hit over the head, and from what I could tell, badly, with a bottle."

"That's rough. What did you do with him?"

"He had the reason knocked out of him. His head was bleeding and needed stitches. He was delirious. He made me drive him over here instead of getting it taken care of."

"But you said a block from here. Not here," says Smitty, "you didn't drop him off here. Why?"

"All right, I know what you're—"

"Why!"

"He gave me shit! He fucked me one too many times and I fucked him back! Anyone would have fucked him back. He asked for it!"

"Sure," says Smitty blandly, uncrossing his legs, straightening them out in front of him. "And now you want to know why I didn't help him."

"You got him into this!"

He hooks one tennis shoe over the other.

"I'm not a fool, Smitty. Didn't I guess your whole stupid intrigue?"

"Not all of it."

"That you devised your little inferno there to deliver him from Quayle—which, if you haven't guessed, didn't work—because you've got something bigger afoot than a saddlebag full of cocaine."

"A lot bigger." As if this jogged something, Smitty checks his watch.

"And I'm starting to get a whiff of what it is, too."

"Are you."

"Yes. Something just snapped in place for me too, Smitty."

"Tell me."

"I was just up visiting the hospital, and on the way out I checked the admissions and discharges. Quayle was on both lists. I happen to know that Quayle was passionate about reaching Canada today. Now it seems to me I'm hearing an awful lot about Canada lately. I think that's the rat I'm smelling in here. It almost feels like we've got us a forced migration on our hands."

"If I were you, Dean," Smitty slides his fingers down his pockets, but not another muscle moves, "I'd probably not commit such a thing to words."

"No, maybe I better correct that. It's not a rat I'm smelling, it's a mole. I think someone might be working both sides of the street. I suspect that wherever Milo is right now, if Quayle's been there, well, I suspect there's a lot of money on its way up to a little place in Ontario right now, safe in Quayle's pocketbook."

Smitty steps over and uses his open hand on my face. I avenge myself in the same way and it becomes a fair fight, lasting about three minutes. There is no winner; we just end it and sit up and dust off.

"You were way out of line on that one, buddy." He hoists himself to his feet, fixes his hair and shirttail, lowers into the aluminum and vinyl desk chair.

"I had to try it. I wasn't getting enough . . . direction here."

"Last night, Dean, I had two men here. They waited for him. After the fire I sent them out looking. His radio was dead. They've been looking ever since. My shift is up here in twenty minutes and then I go looking myself. Dean, I hate to leave it like this, but if he'd made it to that door last night . . . Well, I'm afraid you left Milo in a vulnerable situation. Now that's about all the direction I can give you."

I find it impossible to say anything. Not just because I'm winded.

"I wish it was something else, Dean."

"Yeah. How about a can of gas?"

III.

I DISCOVERED SIMON in the backyard. He was up to his knees in the peony, head declining toward something at his feet. He didn't appear to notice when I slammed the car door and called his name. Seeing him back gave me a moment's reflection: shirtless and shiny as the day I found him. Crossing the yard, momentarily, I had a rest from everything besieging me, save for the heat boring in at the top of my head (bringing back the time, when I was a kid fooling around Dad's basement workshop, I had reached for something on the overhead shelf and instead brought down the coffee can of turpentine, which seared my scalp like this, only for three days). But the look of Simon told me that whatever was out there was going to take pretty good care of my respite. And our welcome home too.

Milo was naked on the ground. Spread-eagled in the place his tent used to be, stretched tight, wrists and ankles manacled to the ground with quarter-inch steel twine, and gagged.

I got down and yelled to him.

"He ain't there," said Simon. "You can't wake him up. I tried."

Simon had a pocket knife. I cut the cord from around his head and removed the rag stuffed in his mouth. It had been soaked in piss. Various places had been razor cut and some of the blood had smeared; along his bare arms

221

and legs were whole handprints in blood, and where the skin was broken the blood had bubbled and scabbed that way. Where there was no tan he was badly blistered. Fingers stiffened into claws. His ribs moved up and down in fast, shallow, irregular quivers. Flies were buzzing everywhere, getting ready to yield eggs in my brother!

He had stopped sweating.

I stood up and looked to Simon. Simon only shrugged. "I just got here," he said. "I didn't know anything, I just got back a minute ago."

The sun was bearing almost straight down, like it does at that time of the afternoon in August. There wasn't a cloud. "All right. Let's move him out of here."

We fell to working on the steel ropes. They were buckled through the stake with a catch and rivet, too close to the skin to even take hold of. Not Milo's stakes either; these were wrought iron, barbed and sunk deep, secure enough to hold up a circus tent.

Somebody wanted him here a while.

Worst of all was his face. The eyes were suppurating, the lids like bacon (you could just about feel what it was doing to the cornea) and you could see bristles of new beard pushing out where his cheeks and chin were scorched to a kind of mottled lunch meat; lips like corduroy, almost salt white, peeling back away from the teeth.

Neither of us thought to cover him up.

We tried digging with our hands, but you couldn't even bring up a good clod; the grass broke when touched and the dirt held together like asphalt. Useless. Simon tried his knife and lost the blade.

I told Simon to go in and phone. I had to stay. Someone did. He had to be moved goddamit. He was dying and we couldn't even flip him over. I had an idea. I ran for the side and grabbed the hose off its saddle and ran back getting it caught in my feet, between the legs, kicking, stumbling. When I got back, the nozzle was too hot to touch and I had to use my shirttail. All right, come out Simon, you've had enough time, he's got to be covered up, I'm ready and I've got to go ahead. But it's not happening, something's wrong, it isn't working. I forgot to turn on the goddamn spiggot!

I dropped it. The stiff rubber tried to recoil. The nozzle-end whipped back on me traveling faster than its own free weight falling and struck Milo on the forehead. It made a smart hollow report like a rim shot. I can still hear it. Then I noticed the caked blood in his hair, remembered the Mexican trailing off in the dark whooping it up like a wild Apache, and the last thing Milo went to do was buy a hat to cover the bleeding with. Now the top of his head was a lusterless dry mud. And added to it now a brand-new knot on the forehead. I heard him cry. I leaned over and looked hard, waited for the eyes to move, made sure his ribs were still breathing—the eyes didn't and the ribs were. Sweat rolled off my nose and ran down his cheek. All the sweat he had. Then I heard it again, and it was only me.

I was losing time. I looked to the house and back. The flies were all over him. The hose kept wriggling its way back home like a live thing—it was so used to being where it came from—dragging the nozzle away in the grass. I think it was doing this to remind me of what I was doing, because it did. I ran to do it, get the water on. Why didn't I tell Simon to do this? Look at the mess I'm making of it. And me do the calling. He won't know the goddamn address anyway, or our last name either, for Christ's sake, once he gets someone. After all, he's the yardworker, isn't he? The one that in all probability would be just excellent with hoses! In fact, Simon was the last one to use . . . no, it would have been Milo, yesterday, no the day before, washed his pickup right here with this very hose, while his kids . . . and then drove it deep in the yard, past those bushes and into the

shade to do his waxing. So where's the sirens, Simon?
Get out of that house and tell me it's done you sonofabitch
little street urchin cunt!

When I reached the side and was twisting the water on
I heard the aluminum front door slam. I looked around,
caught Simon hoofing it up the sidewalk. I hollered. But
he kept on and yelled back *"The phone don't work!"* and
was gone.

The hose was going wild at Milo's end. I caught it and
strangled it off. *You mean to tell me it took that long to
figure out the phone doesn't work?* Water dripped from
my wrist, going from mild to ice cold. I stretched more
hose out than I needed and had to play the excess out
around me like some idiot rock 'n' roll front man trying
to tame his microphone.

His face was different. The flesh was darker, tighter,
bloated; cracking up like shabby plaster. The jaw had
gaped open exposing every dry yellow tooth; purplish
goggles had come up around the eyes. He looked like a
permanent wail, a puffed up skull.

I began with a soft, wide mist which settled on him and
frosted and raised steam. The flies buzzed and scattered.
I found, wherever the spray was guided, a bar of rainbow, and I stepped back to watch the drizzly light, this
sprinkling halo of primary colors. I felt a little soothed
myself just watching. He looked like a blob of glass now.
Laquered. The water licked the parch out of his lips;
they came back to color, although there was a deep slit
now in the middle of his lower lip, and you could see
deep inside, the liverish tissue.

He suddenly twitched all over as if he'd been electro-
cuted. His eyelids parted for less than a second, long
enough for me to notice where the whites were ruby with
blood, and as soon as they caught the light they closed
and his whole face curdled in disgust. I cried MILO! The
muscles of his arms strained and his fingers balled into

fists. I dropped the hose, knelt closer and shaded his eyes. MILO! His lips came together, his jaw fastened. He made a sound but it sounded like gargling. Then he started to choke. Yet another stupid thing I'd done, sprinkled water into his mouth. I had to roll his head to the side while he coughed it out and vomited, convulsing, his whole body convulsing yet unable to double over and do it naturally. Soon as he could catch a breath his Adam's apple rolled up to his chin and swallowed. The jaw began chewing. I cried again and he heard me. He said WHAT. Who did this? I said, and he said WHAT. Who? And then I understood what he was trying to say. It was WATER. So I wrapped my hand around the nozzle and dripped some slowly into his mouth. He chewed, his lips closing over his tongue, his tongue fat, white, and sticky; it was hard for him to swallow because he was on his back and breathing too fast. The crack was there in his lip looking sore and raw; it had split wider. But he took the water down his throat carefully, and it even looked like he was smiling.

By now the rest of him had dried off, so I wet him down again, made the rainbow again, then back to his face, where he was still chewing. Then off, before it made him sick.

He was starting to shiver. Going into the next degree of burn probably, the next layer. His voice was gurgly and weak. "You trying to kill me?" he said.

He was trembling all over. I had to cover him with something. I took off my pants and shirt and laid them over him, then hosed them down until they were saturated. I got on my hands and knees over his head, made myself a canopy for his face. "I've been trying to get you out of this. But I can't."

He coughed. "I can't," he said.

"I can't do anything except stay here and keep putting water over you and wait. They're coming," I said. "Any minute." I bunched the collar of my T-shirt up around his throat like a bib. "How's that? How do you feel?" I said. "God you're ugly!"

"Can't feel," he said.

"You can't?" I raised up and looked around. No one coming. I would hear the sirens first, anyway, wouldn't I?

He was shivering. "I was dreaming," he said.

"You were?"

"Dean?"

"Yeah?"

"Why'd you bother me?"

"What?"

He coughed. "It got nice. Only thing I could feel was me slipping through. I could feel it go. I had my prayers said . . ." He coughed. I was shading his face with mine. An inch between us. They were weak little internal coughs. I couldn't feel his breath. "You brought me back from a long way down, buddy."

"Who did this?"

I waited.

"I was dreaming," he said.

I heard it and raised up and looked, but I couldn't see it. I listened for a siren, way off. Then I looked behind me and saw Just Bill. He had walked onto Milo's belly and sat down. He was back there cutting off Milo's breathing, making him cough like that. He did it again. His squalling goddamn Siamese voice is what I was hearing. I cuffed him good upside the head and sent him crying out of the yard, then turned back around and said, "Dreaming!" I shouldn't have been yelling at Milo but I was.

"Nothing like it used to be," Milo said. His voice was elderly and spotty, every other word in a whisper, but distinct, even though I didn't know what he was trying to tell me. "Not like you remember," he said. "Nothing you have ever imagined."

"No," I said.

I waited. It seemed like a long time, and for some reason I started whistling—not loud and not any real tune.

I touched his face with my tongue.

He said, "You remember way back? When we used to sit up all night and wait for it? Remember how good it was?"

"Yes," I said. I didn't know what.

"This was another thing. This . . ." He coughed again. "This was more than you ever asked for. You wouldn't believe it."

"No," I said.

"You wouldn't believe it."

"All right," I said.

"The old man was there. Wasn't drunk this time. He's the one that told me what it was."

"Was he?"

Then the shivering just let go. And something about the way it happened told me that's what all of him did. He said: "It was. You know. Christmas."

IV.

DR. WING, THE tiny Oriental physician in ER, says it
was heat stroke. He has other names for it. Sun
stroke, thermic fever. Specifically, he says, hyperpyrexia.
Body temperature extremely elevated due to external
heat. Can no longer regulate temperature. If victim is
conscious, can be lethargic or hysterical. Can hallucinate.
Body holds all fluid inside, uses to save vital organs. That
is why sweating discontinued. I did properly to treat Milo
with hose, he says. But couldn't save. Change in blood
pressure in lungs forces fluid out of blood into lung
tissue. Lungs become waterlogged, victim very depleted,
very short of breath. Eventually blood pressure drops to
nothing. Heart stops. Breathing stops. Victim dies of
total circulatory collapse.

Of course coroner will have last look: authorities have
ordered autopsy.

Unfortunately, adds Dr. Wing, lacing his delicate, im-
maculately scrubbed yellow fingers together, with chronic
alcoholic, greatly lessened probability of survival.

I had to get out. It was doing weird things to my
balance in there. I was on my way to getting it over with
in 133; I had been thinking, *It needs a way to be told*,
when I started losing my legs. Before me the corridor
continued on the straight and level, but I felt myself
descending stairs. I fainted and came to in a little exam-
ining room, with ammonia under my nose. I had lost my

shirt somewhere and my jeans were still soaked with hose water and cold; I found they had been undone at the waist. The two young orderlies were trying to hold my head down between my knees. They were giggling and, when I raised my head, exchanging secret eye contact.

I had one cigarette and now I'm having another, sucking too on a big Coke with crushed ice, for the stomach, which is rising. I'm sitting at the parfait counter in the nearby Dairy Kwik. Out the plate glass I watch boys and girls Simon's age drive in from the lake, living out the last of their summer in bathing-suited bliss before college. But no time to be thinking back on happier times. There's this to consider: word's traveling through that hospital, as of an hour ago, better than it ever did yesterday, so you'd best get on back and make sure it doesn't happen again.

First, though, I have to put a call through to the police on this pay phone. Wouldn't you know I'd connect with Leo Plummer. No one else available, so I dictate a pretty accurate capsule description of the prime suspects and tell Leo to contact the Canadian border with it, right away. He raises the argument that he's supposed to take a formal statement before calling in a second agency. Warrants must be processed and served. "Dean, we got here what's known as protocol—"

"Now!" I tell him. "Do it right now, goddamit, or I'll kill you!"

Just in time. The nurse was getting ready to enter Mom's room when, silent on bare feet, I sprinted up from behind and surprised her with my voice. "You!"

Spinning around, chafed, the nurse softens immediately. "Oh," she says. A seasoned pro, she makes the eyes blink mistily and puts on her best forlorn appearance. "I'm awful sorry, sir," she says.

"Why? Did something go wrong?" I tip my head,

indicating the patient behind the door. "Because she was just fine when I left her this morning."

"No, I mean . . . Why, her boy. The other one. The one . . . Why, sure you know. Your brother—"

"I do. Sure. Question is, does she?"

Her look drops to my chest, then navel, then skips down to the feet and back up again. She feels her shelf-like hip, smooths the uniform shift neatly over it. *"No,"* she says, picking up nerve, picking up the vibes.

"You weren't just on your way in there to tell her or anything, were you?"

"Sir, I—"

"Dean. The name is Dean. The single bloodthirsty remainder of that lady's family!"

"I wouldn't never—"

"Because if you were to go and do that again, then I'd have given you a whole 'nother reason to be sorry than the one you already have. I'll just take that." She was carrying my mother's clothes on a hanger. Through the cellophane dry cleaner skin I could recognize Mom's white summer suit and bright red scarf. I had to tug and finally wrench it free from the squealing female.

"Sir! Now just a minute now, sir!"

"Now get out."

Inside, I find Mom sitting at the edge of the bed, makeup and jewelry on, fixing her hair to go home. She ceases fixing as I take a seat beside her, draping the clothes over my knee.

What is it? What is it? What is it?

Searching my vacant mind for a way to do this, I find there isn't one. Only a deep breath and so many hard, unspeakable ejaculations.

Afterwards a deep dam breaks free in back of her eyes. She releases her mirror.

The clothes just fell to the floor, too.

Everything keeps on falling.

V.

IN THE MORNING I wake up hearing Simon whisper in my ear. We're upstairs, sharing my bed, one of his long slim legs lodged between the two of mine. "What?"

"It's really pouring out there."

Simon just reached around, brushing my sunburnt back. "Ouch!" The disturbance brought on a sting, then a prickly chill.

"Sorry," he says, jerking the hand away, taking it down, clapping it over half my butt.

His close breath touches my eyelids.

I was dreaming about something or other, but yesterday just came along and squished it like a big heel. In the second before opening my eyes, my memory hits the start button on a tape-recorded review:

Yesterday, after the worst was over, I dropped Mom at Evie's (she refused to come home) and then drove over to check on the police-end of things. Father Labounty was there, waiting for Simon's release. (The moment Simon had arrived, stammering, carrying on over the exigencies of Milo, the cops had nailed him for the runaway they were after.) They had him in a back room, grilling him through his delinquencies past and present, over the punitive repercussions of breaking probation. For probable cause in the Milo matter yet! And now Sandy was there, waiting, looking ashen, lost, on the whole as rudderless as I. Seeing me, his burden tripled.

"I've just heard. About Milo." Sandy seized and held me tight about the tops of my arms, a deep solemnity in his throat: "I was on my way over, Dean, as soon as we cleared things up here with Simon."

The office was empty, except for the dispatcher, a myopic old guy craning his neck over the countertop from time to time to check us out, eyeballs magnified to the size of his yellowed bottle-glass lenses.

I told Sandy I was all right. But it was hard to say with Jane: on top of everything she was just out of surgery. Still pretty medicated, probably, but plenty grieved. She wouldn't come home—suspecting home was crawling with reminders, news mongers, and the morbidly curious. Which it was.

Did I need anything?

Yeah. I could've used a drink.

Sandy cocked the ear with the hearing aid in it towards me. The word struck alarm in the sober priest. When I reiterated for him he looked terrified. "You just disabuse yourself of that one, Dean! You stay close to her now and don't do that! Best thing you and Janie can do is keep going: keep the mind on the surface and don't look around and start thinking. Don't reflect, either of you, for a time, or you're liable to crack. In any case, even if you feel like cracking, *especially* if you do, you don't want to pick up that drink, Dean."

If this was good advice and heartfelt condolences I was hearing, then I was none too respective. I suppose I was finding the preacher, at this particular time, kind of hard to swallow. Then, too, I was really bent on having that drink. "That's fine to say. You're a preacher," I told Sandy, resonating very close to his ear plug. "Ain't it your province to rope us around and keep us protected? Your bounden duty? But I'd kinda like to get real blitzed out, Father, on lots of drugs and alcohol, like the old days."

"All right. I'm a preacher," the priest went on, un-bowed and clearly right. "I'm said to be hell on a pipe organ, and I'm a pretty fair builder. A homosexual, too, if you like."

This was news to me. We both looked around, at this juncture, just as the dispatcher's head was ducking out of sight. "A lot of things," Sandy concluded.

"Okay. Sorry."

"Such as an ordinary drunk, like yourself. Don't for-get, though, that we surrendered, Dean. Remember?" He waited on me to remember. I didn't. "There was a war and it's over, and the hooch won," he recalled. "Right?" I neither agreed nor disputed it. Labounty said, "All right, if you think there's another drink out there that you forgot to take, then you go find it and drink it. If you want so badly to shake hands with Milo!"

It was possible. I could have taken it all back, as intended, but maybe not wake up; and the fear of those insects and crustaceans recurring was enough to dim the light on the whole idea. I resigned. "Maybe."

Reassured, Sandy put off the absurd notion and smiled down at me and, without actually doing so, patted me on the back. Then, looking towards the private back room, he sighed. "The Lord giveth and taketh—though I don't suppose we can appreciate it yet. Shouldn't we at least try to be grateful for His returning Simon to us?"

"Not right now, Sandy," I told him.

He bent his better ear. "What?"

"Nothing. Only I can't see Him as being very just, is all!"

"Oh, it takes an awful lot of faith and forgiveness, Dean, I'll grant you, to be grateful at a time like this. But Dean," he took in a good breath; here it comes: "there's mercy sometimes in what seems the gravest in-justice. Which means simply that although Milo is gone from here, he is taken care of. He is safe now, free of this world. And yet . . ." He looked again to the back, ponderably, "Simon has returned." He added, "Each man, if only we may accept His will, is where he belongs."

I thought about it. I found the flaw. "Don't shit yourself, Father. I don't believe the two compare, exactly. What you're giving me is a sack of beans for my sack of pearls. Simon doesn't weigh in the balance."

Of course Sandy rejoined: "It's not for us to judge. I'm sure that if any one of us had the power, with our selfishness, our pettiness and pride, well, I expect we'd make a pretty damn mess of it."

"Sometimes," I said, "your Savior there can make a pretty mess of it all by himself!"

"Watch it now, Dean."

"*Me* watch it! No. I did my watching. Watched him cook, thank you. Slow cook! Milo was blistered meat, Sandy. He was already dead once and your merciful friend lets me bring him back so he can die all over again. You didn't watch that, did you. Well, there wasn't an awful lot of mercy in it. So you'll excuse me if I'm on the opposite end of grateful."

"Then only believe this," he said, the original solemnity back in his voice, "that where Milo's gone, all of his suffering will be repaid."

"Yeah. Well I just came by to see if I couldn't facilitate some repayment for the ones that cooked my brother!"

Simon came out looking mean, chafed around the eyes. They took me back to the same room. I looked meaner; I slouched down in the chair and spread my legs at the young investigator, who looked fresh out of tech-school criminology. The air was insupportable, but I lit up and smoked anyway. Asked if I knew of any motive I said sure, and prattled the whole thing off—except for the fire; I would have thrown that in too if I hadn't met Smitty and promised him; it was no skin off my ass now.

The investigator said, "What do you know of this Donovan boy? Would you say he as in any way involved?"

"Is this a trial?" I asked.

"If you don't mind, sir, we'll ask the questions."

"Are you in any way involved with this county prosecutor?" I asked. I had held back the part about Miller, too, for certain reasons.

"I am appointed by the prosecutor's office," he said.

I looked at the secretary, who was getting this all down. I said, "Did you get that all down?"

When they were satisfied Simon wasn't in on it they let him go, with a stiff warning from his social worker and probation officer.

The sheriff's department phoned in that they'd found what appeared to be Milo's truck, out on Big Pine. I hadn't even noticed his truck missing. It had been torched, they said. I thought, There went your fingerprints, Leo.

Out in the backyard someone had spray-painted an outline of Milo, a big white empty X on the spot where he'd been spread out and nailed down. I locked up and went over to Evie's, leaving the news and homocide to photograph things, dig up the yard for clues.

By the time I got there Mom had had enough of the prescribed phenobarb to knock a well-fed athlete over, but she was still pacing the floor, puffing on Camels, her fingers twisting her hankie into damp little knots. We talked:

"I just got it from him straight," she told me. "He said everything was all right, and he promised I'd be next."

"Who did?"

"Your father."

"Can he do that?"

"But you have to be careful, Dean."

"Did he say so?"

"You will, won't you? I couldn't bear anymore of this. I *will* do what Jimmy did before I'll have anymore of this."

"I will," I said. "I'm always careful, Ma."

"Don't be silly!" Evie had been listening. She was bringing soup from the kitchen. "You eat and get to bed. You're stumbling around like an old drunk."

"I'm liable to oop it up," said Mom.

We got half a bowl of chicken rice soup down her, and some whiskey, and helped her upstairs. She fell asleep curled up like a baby that wasn't born yet.

When I got home Simon was waiting on the porch. "Least I left him a note this time," he told me. "Said I was worried about you. Thought someone oughta keep you company."

I hear it on the roof now. Pelting sheets of hard wet. From a mile off a terrible thunder starts up, slashing across the sky to just overhead, and the room bears the electrical field you can taste on your tongue. It's cooler in here by twenty degrees. Simon is breathing on my eyes. I can feel his hard-on pushing in at my navel. Now I am broad awake, wondering where the mercy was yesterday! RAINING!!!

The way I sat up, he almost pissed on me.

VI.

WE REACH THE water together. Daph, Claude, and their uncle. We splash forward and swim hard for the other side of the lake. The weather is improved to where the sun is back with us, but it's light, clean, a glorious warm. Fresh as an afternoon might be. There was every reason for doing this, but we didn't talk about it, just drove out under the laundered clouds and dripping trees and took to the water like it was habitual.

Maybe it's kind of a primeval grief.

Daphne rides the surface propelled by her sleek brown limbs, while Claude keeps her head above-water and kicks too much behind. When she catches up we go on, paddling over the string of buoys, freestyling out into motorboat territory.

Great numbers were arriving at the house. They stood in the corners having drinks, filed through to the kitchen for a word with Jane and a refill. They filled the house, a hundred of the lowest velvety voices. It was a minor chord broken up by the occasional fearful wail of Mom's keening. But nobody wanted to step into the backyard, or even look at it.

The headline read:

**Ambrose Man Succumbs
in Bizarre Execution**

With a kicker that went:

237

Suspects apprehended fleeing country

We'll reach the other side or we'll die trying. What with my lungs partly gone from all the cigs, Daphne has taken the lead. Don't, whatever you do, niece Daphne, go in for tobacco like your uncle did.

But wait a minute. What's all this din behind us? It's the lifeguard waving us in from his tower, blowing himself blue on his chrome-plated whistle.

"Keep going!" yells Daphne. And she obstinately does.

"Better not." I have to hook her by the ankle and hold her back. This isn't far from sounding like a supplication (your uncle's breathing will hardly take it; the thumping in his chest is excruciating!): "Too dangerous!"

"For you it is!"

"All right, but look. Your sister's already going in. Let's start back. Come on."

But for the moment we're hanging still here in the middle of the water, me puffing against the strain of staying up, Daphne in full fettle and stamina. Looking at me, she makes her face into a thing so vivid—with the hair plastered back out of the way—so remarkably, indelibly faithful to her parent, that I forget to move and almost sink. The face seems to be saying, When the fuck are you for Christ's sake going to lighten up!

By way of defending myself, I ask, "What were we going to do on the other side, anyway?"

"Just *get* there!"

"Besides, we're caught now."

I watch her escape under the surface, toes flipping lake water in my face like an impertinent dorsal fin. Meanwhile, the lifeguard hasn't quit waving and sounding off, even though we've faced about and are returning to the sand. When Daphne surfaces beside me I tell her to expect us to catch hell for this. "I'll have to pay a fine, probably," I tell her.

She tells me, "Who cares!"

VII.

I'M DRESSED IN the hundred dollars' worth of new shirt, tie, and cotton-poly slacks Ken picked out and bought me at the Men's Shoppe. A fatalist didn't think to bring his funeral things. And now Mom and I are cruising behind the hearse in Yank Rydell's limousine, en route to St. Paul's Episcopal.

Yank's been custodian now to three of our family dead, so we've been here before, Mom and me. Our third ride in the lead car; the third casket, bank of flowers, hearse, limousine, plot, vault, marker, and whatever they did for Grandma's and Daddy's and Milo's looks, that she's signed the check for. Third corpse we've pickled and hearsed over to Sandy's to bequeath to dust and ashes.

The point of this is not to be comfortable, and nobody is. Yank is not comfortable with us, knowing we regard his livelihood as the lowest reduction of necessary evil. He fills the seconds of disquietude with all-out hand-over-hand driving. But slow, taking us through the curves like a slow-motion of an Andretti brother. Soon as Yank straightens out the wheel I look beyond his pink moon head, into the rearview, and find his fat shifty eyes. And when his connect with mine I light up a cigarette. Next I blow out the match and drop the smoking cardboard on the floor. This, I admit, has been done with deliberate hissing effrontery in mind; and for it the old Swedish mortician would like to stomp the brake and tell me to

239

venerate his car or slide out. But we're paying you for your smooth ride, Yank, not any gall.

Lately I've been smoking a lot. For instance, back at the wake a minute ago, I was smoking standing on line with the callers. Milo was reposed in a beautiful casket of solid mahogany. You took in the fresh flowers mingling with the smell of furniture polish. But the lid was on. Nobody said so but they were damn disgruntled. Everyone knows the young dead are at least twice as moving to look at as the old. This held no interest, because Mom had decided, as with her husband's remains, that Milo would be viewed only by the family. Mourners lined up anyway and made the best of it. You felt stupid though, not knowing if you were viewing his head or feet. You never knew for sure whether there was anything in there at all. May as well wake a coffee table, because, in the end, all you got out of Milo's finely burnished lid was your own reflection. I stood a long time with mine, lining up my image with where I reckoned his face to be. I forgot that I was smoking. When I touched us both on the cheek, softly extemporizing a private last rite, my lengthy ash broke off. It dribbled over the sloping lid into the leaves of funeral flowers. Yank saw this. Drawing a handkerchief from his suit pocket he stepped up and rubbed out the blemish of my fingermark, blowing away the lingering specks of ash. "Thanks, Yank, but that was meant to stay put." I remade the five smudges and gave Yank the challenge of removing them. Because it's his required obligation to, he's perfected the look of involuntary pity. I'd never seen him without it, but for me he changed it to something else. "A memento," I explained. "A token of me. A remembrance. A keepsake I'd like for Milo to take with him. And now I'll have to go through my whole fucking benediction again!" Yank went to fetch me an ashtray.

No, I don't guess I like being his passenger, and I care

even less for his handiwork. In fact, let's just say I've
never seen it. When the place cleared out and we were
left—Mom, me, and Milo's daughters—Mom asked if I
wanted to. My last look at him was bad enough, but at
least he was alive, and I'm content with that. "I don't
care to, no," I said. Because, as Milo put it a few days
ago, it's like peeking in on something private. But Daphne
did, and Mom said, "Good for you, Daphne. Bring your
sister too." Daph took her sister's hand. It was so tender
a moment I've never seen the one to match it. Then
Claude pulled her hand away. "No," she said. "You
better," warned her sister, "you'll never get another
chance." Claudette came over to my hand and seized it.
"No."

We went out front to wait.

Claude looked very sad. She bent over and dug up a
rock and began tossing it over her head, following it with
her eyes, catching it one-handed, no sweat.

"It's all right, Claudie." I said, "You know, when your
grandfather died, before you were born, my dad, I
wouldn't look either."

"Grampa killed himself, didn't he."

"Mimi and your dad looked, but I refused to. I didn't
want to dream about him, see. Not that way. I didn't
want my dreams all messed up with what it might've
done. The result is, I never dream about my Dad but
where he's so full of life it's better than he ever was at
the real thing."

Claudette had pivoted away to face the street. She was
now heaving the rock higher and higher every throw.

"So it's okay, see," I said, "not looking."

"I know it." The sport became more daring, the rock
lofting higher and Claudette spinning herself around in
between catches.

"Good," I told her. "You needn't feel bad, either, just
because you're not doing something you don't want to

do. I know it's hard enough without having to go through
with that."

"No it's not." She was up to two spins.

"It's not?" I wasn't too sure this rock business wasn't
taking precedence over the thing we were trying to dis-
burden here. "Why's that? Stop that for a minute,
Claudie."

" 'Cause I was ascared of him."

"Scared of Milo? Why?"

"I don't know."

"Did he ever hurt you?"

"He never hit me or nothing. I just was. He was
always doing weird stuff. He got drunk all the time and
did all that weird stuff to Mom and us."

"That was just him. He didn't mean to scare you, it
was just him and he couldn't help it."

"How do you know?"

"He loved you, Claudie. He said all the time how
much he loved you and you ought to know that."

She reared back with the rock, got ready to throw it.

"Claudette?"

She stopped. "What."

"Don't start drinking, Claudette. Whatever you do,
just don't even start."

She turned and threw it, in a low arc, across the street,
just over a passing car.

"All right with that!" I said.

"Anyhow," she said, "you know what this is today?"

I thought: I think it's Tuesday, August the . . .

"My birthday, today is."

Riding past Mom's, Mom and I look out, and she tells
me, "I'm selling it."

"Why not? Might as well."

"I've never liked that house. Your father and I only
stayed in it after the war because I inherited it and we

could never afford anything nicer. But I don't need all that now. I'm going to sell it and get something small and nice for myself."

"All right with me."

"I've always had lousy luck in there." She is stretching her neck to watch the last of her property disappear. When it does she settles back and faces straight ahead, the hearse. "Way back to when I was little. I've always expected the worst to happen there, and so it has. I've lost my whole family now in that house. In it or around it."

"Just about," I say.

"I could fill up the yard with all our graves."

At the mention of graves the undertaker sits a little more erect at the wheel, cuts his head an inch or so towards the conversation.

"You still have me," I say, "and the grandkids."

"It was awful," says Mom.

"What was?"

"Milo. What they did to Milo. But you don't care. You wouldn't even see him."

"You're going to tell me he didn't look natural. If that's what you're going to say then maybe you'll understand why I don't look. It's morbid, it's heathen, it's very expensive, it's melodramatic—"

"They combed his hair!" Yank does a little nervous bounce on his seat, but Mom doesn't give a shit who's listening. "It was all combed out and I wish they'd have left it alone. I should have told you to leave it alone, Yank!" She cuts back to me. "The part wasn't even where it should have been. The makeup wasn't his color, either."

The driver, in his boink-boink Swedish-American, interposes a remark here to the effect she didn't have to have no cosmetics. "Jane, nobody did force you to make him show."

Jane goes on: "Do you know what Daphne said?"
"What."
"She looked at him and said, 'Mimi, that ain't him. It ain't ain't him,' she said, and she turned on her heels and marched away. She was right, too."
Putting my mind in a more positive sphere, I think: She'll never sell.

The church is already full. Haven't been inside Sandy's church since one or another Christmas Eve, somewhere back in the distance when I had college breaks; and then it was midnight and Mom and I and Milo had all been stinking on our respective parasites Canadian, Daniel's, and Turkey (it was traditional, along with the Harveys for breakfast). But here we are in the broad light of day, the stained glass iconography in the walls strangely backlit with sober exactitude, candles in the afternoon, the tapers and wicks. Scented wax in your nostrils. I do savor the smell of church—a quiet smell, a serene one. (Why do Catholics think they have to fuck theirs up with incense?) We're ushered to the front row to hear a few melifluous noturnos from the organ pipes and wait on the body.
My ex-sister-in-law Pat, Milo's initial spouse, decided to join us in the pew for this. Mom seems to sidestep in front of her without so much as hi or how-do-you-do—a momentary lapse of conciliation. But I see nothing wrong in Pat's being here. She looks very good in her dress, still slim as a boy, with the prominent Native American nose and cheeks. She leans over to give me a commensurate half-smile and her hair, highlighted by all the summer bleaching, falls forward in a long smooth sweep. The eyes reveal she's done some crying. I've always liked Pat. I do still, and wish Milo might have stayed with her. Or the other way around, as the case may be.
Did Milo request the Fauré *Pavane*, his favorite sad

music? Of course not, he didn't know he was going to be here like this. Must have been Sandy. How did *he* know? Anyway, the piece comes through fine in transcription. It makes you weep every time, regardless of the circumstances . . .

Here then is my entire family, along with Simon who's sitting at the end of our bench on my right. And presently Milo is wheeled by, the thing used to convey him hidden discreetly beneath a black shroud with pleats that whispers as it drags along the floor. They park him (the pallbearers would be, of course, firemen) at the foot of the altar steps flanked by two enormous lily pots; and then Sandy passes, followed up by a single acolyte—no doubt the teenage progeny of someone I used to know; something I saw carried through here long ago in a blanket.

Father Labounty appears disinclined to begin the honors. He glances long at the box, then at our separate faces, before going over some general thoughts from Common Prayer (the stuff I've already heard) on redemption and resurrection—the only solutions to life. He assures those of us who care to know it that the spirit of our beloved here present is now and ever shall be in the hands of God. And then adds, rather unbecomingly, for the benefit of those who don't care to believe it, "Or nothing." He hesitates here, giving a blank space which has its effect on the audience in the form of one or the other: spiritual reflection, or, for the agnostic, a chance to wind his watch. Having no notes prepared for the eulogy, Sandy shuts his eyes and rolls back his head to recall his acquaintance with Milo. One perceives in his smile that Sandy is looking back on some harmless scrap of remembered privacy between them, something that pretty much will capture the essence. He has decided to glean from his earliest recollection of my brother:

Milo, he begins, a learned little boy, had evidently

been reading up on evolution. It was during the customary after-service coffee hour in the undercroft when Sandy looked down to obtain the strange tugging on his robe. Looking up was Milo. He abruptly introduced himself, and added: a Darwinian scholar. (News to us in the front row, where grins begin to crack through.) Their ensuing discussion, Sandy says, touched on some of the finer points of the Creation vs. the New Science, and although Milo was in the end set straight with the redoubtable theology of Paul, and given a mild injunction to get into some New Testament, he returned the following week (he did not have to tug this time, because Sandy found himself continually scanning the floor for the precocious kid) to declaim: "Come on, Father Labounty, do you *really* suppose there's any future for your priesthood and your Church?" For it seemed, that week, Milo had been dipping into his dad's philosophy shelf. He had come across, as he said it, an interesting article concerning Christian anarchism, by some count, name of Tolstoy. Sandy's own philosophical feathers were unruffled. On the contrary, he was stimulated by this formidable youngster. Protective of him. (Worried, for instance, that Milo was drinking far too much coffee at his age.) Once again the teachings of Paul prevailed, trumping over Milo's Tolstoy. But only, Sandy admits, by a mighty thin margin. Over the years Milo's love of rational discourse (splendid euphemism!) has not slackened. As often as they would meet, he would beautifully hold forth. All the way from rodent extermination to the big one: Abortion. "And sometimes," Sandy chuckles, "I would actually have to mark my opponent a certified conservative."

He now lowers into glum thought and caps it off: "Human life is a tragedy; it ends in pain and death. But after death . . . when such an individual is gone—so early and so . . . unnaturally, one might ask, 'Why is it God wishes to snatch away the young and vital souls of his

Milos?' It is a fair question. It is what we as Christians are all about. The comforting news, my friends, as I see it, and surely as God must see it too: They're better off."

That's the way to preach it, Sandy! Now that the culprits are in the hoosegow awaiting trial I can see it that way myself. Almost makes you want to run out and catch the old dark-eyed Angel by the sleeve, see if he wouldn't bargain for a closer expiration date.

We're moving towards the outside when we encounter Velda. She's been sitting all alone in the backmost pew, dressed up to about the somberness of an Aztec rug, affecting a weak spine. As I expected, she stands directly in our way, clogging up the whole works. It goes like this:

Me: What. Don't tell me you want sympathy.

Velda: He was my husband. I got a right to come to his funeral.

Me: All fixed up for it too, aren't we? You would've popped his nuts off two days ago.

Mom: We're trying to get through!

Velda: I have to talk to you—

Me: We're going to bury him.

Mom: I don't doubt for an instant that you were responsible for this.

Me: Good guess.

Velda: Me!

Mom: It wouldn't surprise me.

Me: We're going to bury him now.

Velda: Listen. I have to talk to you.

Me: I don't have to talk to you.

Velda: After they bury him then.

Mom: I didn't even have you put in the obituary.

Yank: (trying to wedge through with Milo) Please, please.

VIII.

SAME KITCHEN. SHOWER and change of clothes. Sun going down.

They just put Milo to bed right beside Dad. He and Dad are rubbing elbows again. I don't doubt they both have something to say about that. Milo's kid's—Claudette's —birthday. She's just getting started at this. Welcome to your teens, Claudette.

Mom and I should probably eat something, we think. In a while, maybe. "Go ahead," I say. "Go ahead and fix yourself one. I know you want to. Probably need to. No, not for me, thanks, I'm not drinking today." I should probably curb this habit of mine of pestering the good and think of a way to save it for the bad. It is getting tiresome. But Mom wasn't annoyed, isn't even listening actually.

"Well . . ." she says. Under the sink are dishwasher soap, S.O.S., a tin of silver polish, box of Friskies, Wheeling galvanized bucket, scrub brush, stiff off-color rag draped over the drain trap; all the usuals except the bottle. "We drank it all," she says, automatically checking the wall for the time, "and the State Store's closed."

Must be through breeding, but I find myself checking the clock to confirm. "Those words would've driven me into despair before," I say. "Back then, if I were in your shoes I would've done something crazy."

"Let's not go into that, shall we?"

We sit. Mom fiddles with the edge of the newspaper.

It's time now for a deep sigh or two. *This is*. This is awful! Finally she says, "I feel like I just got back from being away for so long and don't know what to do with myself."

"Where?"

"How should I know where?" For no reason whatsoever, except to maybe contemplate the possibilities, we both look through the same window. She continues: "You know the feeling though. Now we've got to do things again as we always did them, only I don't feel like it one bit."

"Go away then," I say. "Sell the house. Keep the momentum going."

"Go where?"

"I don't know. A trip or something."

"I can't take a trip."

"Sure you can."

"What do you think, that we just go out and have fun?"

"Who?"

"Besides, I'm in no financial position—"

"Yeah, now that you went and ordered up all that pomp and parade—which you wouldn't even have done for yourself—and now you don't have anything left."

"You just leave that alone, it's none of your business, is it, really. Anyway, if it makes any difference, he would have had plenty of insurance to cover him, wouldn't you think? No," she nullifies the whole subject with a cut of her hand, "let's not think about it. Any of it. It makes me feel like a bloodsucker."

"You're right," I say. A fireman *would* be expected to climb out on any roof and fall through and die, on any job, at any time.

"Well, maybe I should," says Mom.

"Think about it?"

"Get away somewhere. I've wanted to see places. Foreign places." Her eyes fill up momentarily with foreign places.

"Well," I say, "that's that then."

"What are *you* going to do, Dean?"

"Go back to work. If anyone can honestly cry poorhouse right now, it's me." What's that? Footsteps on the porch. It's Pat and the kids. All three divested of their mourning and restored to ranch-style. "Pat."

"Dean. Jane."

Daph and Claude take seats out on the porch and Pat comes in alone, lowers into a chair, crosses one riding boot over the other.

For some reason I can't stop looking. She looks the same, but something's different. Something shows up all around her, in her face, like a printed page. At first I couldn't pin it down exactly, but now I have it. Pat's right arm is, you might say, cut off. She sits in that listlessness, not quite seeing things; inertia coursing through her veins instead of blood. She breathes a troublesome sigh, means it, opens her mouth to say something, doesn't.

Mom sees it. Not only that, knows it. I don't suppose I've thought about this once since back in '64 when it happened to Mom, probably because there wasn't occasion to—how they'll do the way they do, these women. I remember Mom, after Dad went, a month or so after, when the friends came, one by one, to fill in her empty space. I watched, unnoticed, from the staircase (frankly a little disturbed at her lack of what I reckoned should have been hysteria), as she let them in and they sat in the living room together trying to talk. But Mom wouldn't, or just didn't. She had no crying left—the eyes were all dried up—but she opened the door and the friends came in, one at a time (women; men would come later), never feeling quite so much like *guests* before. I would hear the guest ask, Would you want to talk about it, Jane? and Jane would say, simply, No. Nothing bitter to it, or

sulky, but a soft sort of finality, a sort of nothing to her
voice that seemed to mean, It's all right, thank you, I
know what you mean, but it wouldn't help, really. Because her man was gone. Nothing to talk about. She'd
done the crying and now was doing a little thinking.
Lonesomeness wasn't even there yet, hadn't started to
move on her; she seemed to know that too, but still it
wasn't anything to talk about. And wouldn't be, I realize
now, until she started forgetting.

Widowhood, plain and simple.

Which is why Mom isn't asking Pat to go ahead and
talk about it.

Oddly, no one blames her for pulling out on Milo. In
fact it was a mutual idea, a not undesirable arrangement
to either one: they'd just seemed to branch off, rather
than strike out, in different directions. Not much settling
up to do on either side, until it came to the custody bit,
and then it wasn't so much Pat that made the kids un-
touchable to Milo as it was the stepdad, who probably
cussed the real father and husband, the insincere romantic wet-brain philosopher Pat and the kids were well rid
of. Besides, after getting inside this new wealth and
security of his, then eventually used to it, well . . .

They all reckoned wrong. Maybe Milo did turn towards
a wife of the intellect (or, more explicitly, a woman
companion who could tie two sentences together: Juliet),
and Pat for a landed breeder who wouldn't squander
every last vestige of family security on turmoil; but each,
eventually, remorsefully, arrived back at that aching void
for the other which only needed owning up to.

In any event, Pat just got handed a long extension to
her void. You can see it working her mouth, getting
ready to speak itself again, and this time, almost to my
chagrin, it does. She says, "We were gonna buy us a stud
farm," eyes shut tightly, holding back a live hurricane.
Mom says nothing and I say nothing. Pat opens up her

brown eyes and they glisten like—well, I can't really mistake it, like polished mahogany. She says, "Me and Milo." The browns, snapping into motion, cut to Jane, to me, to Jane. "We had it picked." And the damp lids slam shut and squint. Then, as if we'd asked where and she was answering, she tells us, "Over in Barber County."

"With what?" I ask it as gently as possible, but, really, that kind of property doesn't come cheap. And that's when she brings out the knapsack. I didn't see it come in because she was wearing it behind her shoulder. But she just slid the thing off as if it contained the burden of so many millstones and dropped it on the table.

"That."

It's the same knapsack Milo carried with him the other day. I recognize its dusty maroon nylon, its manufacturer's tag.

"What is it?" Mom asks.

"Money. It's yours. It belongs to Milo, but . . ." She's left her hands lolling on the table in front of her. They have a lot of dirty callouses, the nails bit to the quick. They seem useless to her now.

Nobody touches the bag. "How much?" I ask.

She doesn't answer but reaches inside, and Mom says, "Whatever it is, I don't want it."

Pat brings out a stack of bills and lays it on the table. She lets the sack drop at her feet. She lolls her hands out in front of her the same as before.

I take up the money. "They're all thousands," I say.

"They're all thousands," says Pat. "Two hundred of them."

"Two-hundred thousand dollars!" I say. "Where did you get this?"

"That's a third of it. Another third belongs to me. Smitty has the rest. We won it. On a horse . . . On three horses . . . It's yours, Jane."

I put the money in front of Mom.

Mom says, "Why? Why are you giving it to me?"

"Because. It was Milo's. It would've been."

"What do you need with that kind of . . ." Mom doesn't finish. "Since you've got a husband with . . ." She doesn't finish again.

Pat's voice goes on, evenly, almost as if she'd practiced for this. "I left him. We found us this stud farm in Barber County. The two of us together we could've paid cash for it, me and Milo. But I got that much of my own," she says, glancing at the money, "and we can take it over for that, me and the kids, and start working it, and pay it off, I believe."

All eyes are on the money.

"You take it," says Mom to Pat.

More cash than I've ever seen and we're treating it like cold mashed potatoes!

"It's a good place." Pat goes on in that slow, even way. "We looked it over. It's got a big house on it, made out of brick. We always wanted us a brick house. It's got pasture and a lot of more room for raising our own oat and hay; there's some big machinery comes with it; it's got stables with corral closed in, and a barn. There's a quarter-mile jogging track already on it, and we were gonna take it."

"You and Milo," says Mom, "again."

"We been together a lot. In private. I stayed with him out there a couple times." She glances through the screen.

"Yes, but how?" I say, still sizing up the pile. "How did you win that much?" I pick up the money again and feel it. For lots of reasons I can't keep my hands off the money.

"We won it."

"But you knew you were going to win."

My continually coming back to it is getting her up. She throws at me, a little fiercely, "We just won it!"

"You didn't fix it."

"We bet on a race!" she says, "A combination. One–two–three. You know how a horserace works? You want me to spell it out?"

Mom says, "I don't want to know."

"Yes," I say.

"We went the long shot. We won. It was a sure thing. Nobody knew it but us. The three of us, and that's how come it paid. Twin trifecta. That's the first, second, and third places in the eighth and tenth. Odds was something like eight-hundred thousand to one. You want me to write it down? Want me to—"

"Take it out of here," says Jane.

Now she can't *stop* talking about it.

"We studied for it a long time. I had the long-shot horse. Been training him to know how to race, only I slowed him up all along. Kept him back, so he wouldn't look fresh in the forms; so he'd look consistent. Number two, similar, only I didn't own him or train him, just knew the rider. We saved up for when it was time, when number three and the right combination come along."

"I don't want this money," says Mom.

"So if he wasn't honest before, he was goddamn honest that one time," Pat says. "I knew what I was doing."

"And Milo's part was to raise the money," says me. "One way or another. Fair means or foul. Hook or crook." Suddenly I don't feel so much the cause of what happened to Milo as I used to.

"Milo made me leave him alone, as far as that. I came up with the horses and he come up with the bet. That's the conditions he made. I had to keep my nose out of the way of what he was doing. You know that's how he is. Was."

Mom pushes the money across the table, says, "I'm giving it back."

"What the hell's the matter, Mom! It's just money!"

"I won't take it."

"He's right, Jane," Pat puts in. "It's yours. It's just money."

"On the other hand," I persist, "it *is* Milo's money.

That's important, isn't it? That means something, doesn't it?"

Mom only twists up her face, flouts the money as if it stank.

I say, "It's nothing to scoff at. It's . . . it's his legacy. Think of it in those terms."

"Then why don't you go ahead and buy your Milo Memorial Horse Farm with it, Pat? Why don't you? Because I don't want it in this house. I don't like the feeling it's giving me."

"Then give it to me."

I said that. It fell flat on the table. Mom shakes her head as if trying to clear it of my echo.

"Take it," says Pat.

"Don't touch it," says Mom.

"Why not?" I ask, but my hand, inexplicably retracting, obeys. "Five hundred of it's mine anyway, plus the percentage that was agreed to. I had that much invested in this." Tentatively, I strip two thousand off the top. "That much of it's mine anyway."

They're not listening. "Take it, Jane. He would want you to."

"No."

"Two-hundred thousand dollars, Mom! You could rent the better part of heaven for that, for the rest of your life. You'd best think about it."

"I thought about it. I don't want it."

"You better sleep on it then. You're just being sentimental over this now. It's only money, for Christ's sakes!"

"One of you pick it up and get it out of my sight. I don't want to look at it anymore. One of you pick it up, I don't care which."

I do.

IX.

THE ACCUSED REQUESTED a three-judge tribunal rather than submit to a jury of their peers.

Otto Miller confessed on the stand. Weeping miserably, cloaked in degradation, he was led to a seat beside the other defendants. I didn't even get to testify.

The other three entered guilty pleas in hopes of mitigating the sentence.

An acting prosecutor had to be summoned to bring the charges, and the state produced enough conclusive incriminating evidence in a single day to seal the case then and there. In Miller's basement had been found the remaining spool of steel cable, which he had senselessly appropriated from the county garage. Besides the usual prints and paraphernalia, the incongruities from one statement to the next, they had even matched up Milo's blood with the blood all over Quayle's pocket knife.

A subsequent search of Miller's place turned up not only the cocaine (which the defense readily produced in its case for reduction of the charge of first-degree), but revealed also an attic torture chamber fitted out with an unseemly museum of S-M hardware, along with photographic equipment and a catalog of action prints. While Miller covered his face, one judge scolded him as to the flagrant indecency of his behavior, especially as befitting a colleague of their profession, although the diatribe managed to center on Miller's getting caught in the first place; his dismal failure to more efficiently cover his tracks. "As one presumably intimate with the details of investigation and detection," roistered the judge, "you ought to have known better!"

Velda, though handed around liberally in photographic depiction, in the act of chewing lots of tool and doing all the rest, was set loose on society again with nothing more than a modicum of humiliation.

After the verdict was read the TV news from the capital wanted to get a statement from me, the brother. While the camera people moved in and adjusted for my talking head, the woman reporter briefed me on how they wanted it. They started rolling. The lady holding the mike brought out her best journalist voice: "And how does the victim's brother feel now that blah-blah-blah?"

"Well," I said, "I'm so tickled I could fart like a horn."

X.

THE TRAIN BRINGS us through the swamp south of Tuscaloosa, through the rain and the jungle. The Amtrak Crescent.

We're riding the train because there's plenty of time for everything now and plenty of money; besides, I've never had a close look at the geography down here, since I was always in a hurry and soaring over at twenty thousand feet.

I slept the night between Charlotte and Atlanta, dreaming Milo and I stood in the snow, a mountain rising high before us. Milo started climbing. He was naked, wearing skis. I watched his buttocks roll, shift, dent, the dark line between slant left, slant right. He was muscular and beautiful against the white. He fell, plunged down the slope. He was laughing. When he reached the bottom he turned placidly (he was cut, bleeding some from the fall), then started up again, making it higher this time, grabbing hold of a pine bough if he needed to. Each time he spilled, tumbled down to my feet, stood up, said something (he always says something; to say nothing is not in him), and tried again. And each time the blood in the snow got darker. It was true, what he was saying, but I never moved. I kept saying, "One of these times you're going to kill yourself and I don't care to watch." Milo said, "Wrong." He said, "I'm giving *you* another chance."

Above it all is where I've been.

Then it was eight o'clock. We woke up pulling into

259

Atlanta. " 'lanta . . ." the old black conductor was singing, gently, like someone calling for a lost kitten in the
dark. " 'lanta . . ."

We moved on for Alabama.

Simon, wired to his Walkman, beats imaginary drums
with imaginary sticks, a celebrated MTV meditation going
on behind his eyelids. He promised no more drugs or
criminal laxity if I would bring him and I yielded. I'm
chancing it with Simon. Because it has ever been beneath
me to do it, to let it happen, to cheat the snivelling
coward in me, to give out the welling scream inside. I
somehow grew to adulthood never screaming. Like this:
Once Dad, drunk and seized with a sudden temper,
struck Mom and flew out to the Elks to finish drinking. I
think it was the only act of deliberate inhumanity he ever
committed, except against himself. I had the scream ready
then but couldn't handle it. My brother, though, went to
the phone and begged Dad to come home, and when he
did they all three met at the front door and started to cry
and hug. While I stood aside with dry eyes, spying. To
me they were one big three-headed make-believe.

I believe I have always been a little tired of myself. So
I've decided to give Simon a chance. I've read through
all Dad's notes to himself, shaken out every book and
read them all. And I couldn't turn up a single line with
my name on it.

On for home. Can't get out of this rain. We're the
great leviathan parting the waters. Don't want to sleep
either; you never know what kind of nightmare's going to
ambush next—like that movie where to sleep lets all hell
come out. Only thing to do is let the memories roll down
your face till it's over. And that's about it. When I'm
delivered from this one I'm going to come back. Screaming.

EPILOGUE

ON THE BALCONY at Lafete's, one of the nicer boys' clubs up on Royal. I'm back in town more than one, maybe two months now. Me and Beauraine and Marcus Augustus, and not even drinking. Well, Marcus had a scotch, a slow one, and I watched him leave some of that in his glass. A man who's learning to have the First Drink. But we have to get to a lot of AA to stay alive down here, Beauraine and I.

I like to say Beauraine. It sounds like an old Confederate, a Frenchman of rank and substance. But he is a Cajun homosexual, a piano player with lengthy fingers that lay down the tunes. And here is Marcus Augustus, finest, blackest set drummer out of the hottest rhythm tribe of Delta Mississippi. They dress in the kind of wear prominent among the vainglorious of Miami and their two voices are the dark, lugubrious South. Two buddies of mine in the music business. None of this Dixieland you hear pouring out on the pavement. They play the cool, sometimes the hot.

It's midnight. The Quarter's just getting happy. This season there's nothing too unhappy stalking the place, unless it's some crazy white guys over from Texas. We were just talking some assorted idle table-talk when my eye caught the kid down there on the corner across Royal. I haven't been snubbing him, but then again, I haven't exactly been shadowing him either. His shoulders were up against someone's shutters, feet sliding out beneath

261

him, body sinking lower all the time; and now people are having to step over; they don't even look back to think about it.

"Kid's lookin' some misaligned," Beuraine says.

When we first arrived he was doing all right. Then I wouldn't see him for a while.

Marcus Augustus says, "Kid's gotta do what he's gotta do."

A pair of youthful blacks appear to be with him, a boy and a girl. A while ago the boy bent over and tried to rouse him. After he couldn't the two stood over him talking; now they've given up and taken a stoop to talk.

Says Marcus, "Got him for sure some bad shit this time."

Now two guys, older whites, are fleecing him. They've cleaned his front pockets and are rolling him over to check the back ones. He doesn't wake up.

I don't know whether he's going to make it this time.

"Sit back down," says Beuraine. "Best thing to help him is stay where you at."

The two that rifled him are crossing the street now, coming this way, looking quickly all around.

Next Boyd, the bouncer downstairs, goes across to check him out. Boyd has the eyes of a bird and the heart of a saint and doesn't even deny being Christian.

"Where's he at, Boyd!"

Boyd looks up and yells, "Still alive!"

We watch the black youths take him by the hands and feet and drag him over to the dark well between two sets of cement steps and leave.

That's where the cops find him.

Maybe Boyd called, for the kid's own protection; or maybe someone else, just to clean the street. Anyway, the police passed by once and missed. But this time the searchlight catches him in his stairwell and two policemen get out. They raise Simon upright against the wall and hold him there while one officer fits his pencil between two knuckles of Simon's right hand and squeezes the fingers hard; you can hear them gnashing from here. This will always work. The cops talk to him for about a minute and leave.

But before long he's down flat again.

"Gentlemen," I say, covering the tab and tip and getting up. I can tell my two buddies wish I wouldn't.

"Why you keep on doin' it, Dean?" Beauraine wants to know.

For an answer I give him a look at my new clothes— things in the nicest fashionable restraint—from the back.

I walk inside and downstairs and when I come out in front a couple of blacks are each holding up one of Simon's legs by the boot. "Don't take that man's boots!" I yell.

I step off the curb and start running them down. "I said don't take that man's boots!"

They drop the boots and take off running, laughing.

℗ PLUME

Contemporary Fiction for Your Enjoyment

☐ **THE ARISTOS by John Fowles.** A wonderfully fascinating and original novel covering the whole range of human experience: good and evil, pleasure and pain, sex and socialism, Christianity and star-gazing. "A remarkable talent."—*New York Times* (260442—$7.95)

☐ **MANTISSA by John Fowles.** The author of *The French Lieutenant's Woman* plays his most provocative game with art, eros, and the imagination . . . leading the reader through a labyrinth of romantic mystery and stunning revelation. "Tantalizing and entertaining!"—*Time* (254299—$6.95)

☐ **WALTZ IN MARATHON by Charles Dickinson.** Harry Waltz, a widower with grown children, is the richest man in Marathon, Michigan. He lives alone and likes it—until his orderly life begins to shift and alter. Most astonishing of all, Waltz falls in love with an attractive attorney—with consequences that astonish them both. (255937—$6.95)

☐ **UNDER THE VOLCANO by Malcom Lowry, Introduction by Stephen Spender.** Set against the backdrop of a conflicted Europe during the Spanish Civil War, this is a gripping novel of terror and a man's compulsive alienation from the world and those who love him. "A masterpiece!"—*Time* (255953—$6.95)

☐ **THE STORIES OF BERNARD MALAMUD.** Twenty-five stories, including "The First Seven Years," "The Magic Barrel," and "Idiots First," chosen by the author as his best. "Genuinely masterful!"—*Newsweek* (259118—$8.95)

☐ **FAMOUS ALL OVER TOWN by Danny Santiago.** This is the Los Angeles of the Chicano barrio, where everything is stacked against the teenaged hero, Chato Medina, his beleaguered family, his defiant and doomed friends, and the future he may not make it far enough to enjoy. Chato, however, is out to beat all the odds—his own way . . . (259746—$7.95)

Buy them at your local

bookstore or use coupon

on next page for ordering.